THE SMOKING GUN

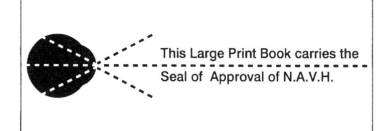

This Large Print Book carries the
Seal of Approval of N.A.V.H.

THE
SMOKING GUN

A NELL MATTHEWS MYSTERY

Eve K. Sandstrom

Thorndike Press • Thorndike, Maine

Published in 2000 by arrangement with NAL Signet, a division of Penguin Putnam Inc.

Thorndike Press Large Print Mystery Series.

The tree indicium is a trademark of Thorndike Press.

The text of this Large Print edition is unabridged. Other aspects of the book may vary from the original edition.

Set in 16 pt. Plantin by PerfecType.

Printed in the United States on permanent paper.

Library of Congress Cataloging-in-Publication Data

Sandstrom, Eve K.
 The smoking gun / a Nell Matthews mystery / Eve K. Sandstrom.
   p. cm.
  ISBN 0-7862-2977-2 (lg. print : hc : alk. paper)
  1. Women journalists — Fiction. 2. Women's shelters — Fiction. 3. Large type books. I. Title.
 PS3569.A51977 S66 2000
 813'.54—dc21   00-064795

To Susan Ivy Clark, administrator of New Directions, Inc., a shelter for battered women and their children, in admiration of the courageous work this and similar shelters do.

and

To Inspector Jim Avance of the Oklahoma State Bureau of Investigation, who is always generous with technical and legal expertise for a fiction writer.

CHAPTER 1

"Michelangelo took four years to paint the ceiling of the Sistine Chapel. If he'd used a roller, he could have done it in a weekend."

Most of us had brought paintbrushes and rollers to the workday at the new Grantham Women's Shelter. Patsy Raymond had come equipped with a batch of painting and repair jokes, which she shoehorned into her usual stand-up routine, belting them out in her raspy voice.

Petite, peppy Patsy — as a bad writer had once described her in a feature story — was the executive director, founder, heart, soul, and dictator of the shelter. She was a cute little thing with a cute little haircut and a cute little figure and a cute little face.

Only her rough and raspy voice wasn't cute. But that was part of Patsy's persona, too. We all knew her ex-husband had gone to jail over the injuries that made Patsy sound like a frog that was getting over a bad cold.

Having a raspy voice didn't keep Patsy quiet. She talked all the time. Since we were all painting and repairing, her jokes fit right in. Which was Patsy's point, of course. Even a professionally cynical newspaper reporter like me could figure that out. A big part of Patsy's job was to keep volunteers happy — and coming back and believing that their efforts were making a difference in the lives of battered women. Jokes were one of her tools.

The stand-up routine was also designed to remind those doubters among us that Patsy Raymond was a wonderful person and that we should continue praising her and giving her money and not listening to those few folks who didn't think Patsy was absolutely perfect.

Patsy was in top form that day.

The most important man in my life, Mike Svenson, was in good form, too. He'd assumed the persona of a volunteer painter and carpenter, putting aside his normal duties as a Grantham police officer. Of course, cops are never really off duty; he'd stashed his pistol in my purse, just in case we should run across a robbery in progress or a kidnapping attempt. Wearing old jeans and a ragged T-shirt, red hair touched here and there with cream-colored paint, he was on his knees inside the office storage closet, installing a stout dead bolt and acting as Patsy's straight man.

"Mike," Patsy said, raspy as ever. "Did you hear about the old lady who called the electric company to complain that the linemen working at her house were using bad language?"

Mike swung the closet door almost shut, and when he answered, his voice was muffled.

"No, Patsy, I hadn't heard about that particular old lady."

"Well, the linemen's supervisor went out to the house and told the two guys about the lady's complaint. 'Boss,' one of them said. 'We haven't been using bad language! All that happened was Joe dropped a monkey wrench from the top of the pole, and it landed on my head. And I said, "Joe! You should be more careful!" ' "

The half dozen of us laughed, and I scratched my nose with the back of my hand — one of my few paint-free body parts. I looked around at the others. I knew I should be taking notes.

As a reporter for the *Grantham Gazette*, the only daily newspaper in our city of 350,000, I was assigned to cover non-profit organizations and other do-gooders. I couldn't pretend that I was thrilled with the beat, which I'd been handed two weeks earlier. I'd always been a cop reporter, writing about robbery, rape, murder and mayhem — topics with a lot of excitement built into them. It was going to be a struggle to make worthy causes interesting to the reader. But it's unprofessional to refuse an assignment, so I was determined to do a good job. I was beginning with a feature about the community-wide effort to move the Grantham Women's Shelter from three ramshackle old houses into a freshly remodeled building that had once housed a nursing home — from a high-crime, rundown neighborhood into a middle-class area. As research, and also to be with Mike, I'd taken part in the workday.

Patsy had spent her day entertaining volunteers, and at five-thirty on a Saturday afternoon, only a few were left. I didn't know much about two of them. Lacy Balke was a tall and elegant blond whom I had picked out as a poster child for the Junior League, and Mary Baker was middle-aged and sweet. The third woman present wasn't exactly a volunteer; Dawn Baumgarner was a meek and excessively neat woman who was on the shelter staff. I guessed her age at late twenties, but she dressed more conservatively than Mary Baker.

I knew more about the two guys still present. Mike was a patrolman and chief hostage negotiator for the Grantham PD and was the guy I planned to marry once I convinced him we could get engaged without a diamond ring exchanging hands. Boone Thompson was the youngest detective in the Grantham PD. They were cochairs of the philanthropic committee of the Amalgamated Police Brotherhood, the local union for Grantham cops. Mike's mom — one of Grantham's biggest real estate operators — was on the board of the shelter and had helped the organization buy its new property. She'd told Mike and Boone the shelter could use a lot of manual labor of the type off-duty cops might be willing to donate, and the union members had okayed the project.

So Mike and Boone had come to be good examples. They'd overseen the herd of cops who'd been there earlier, painting the bedrooms, and they'd stayed on because they were nice guys and there was still stuff to do.

Boone had white, cottony hair and a ruddy complexion that gave him a perpetual blush. He was on a ladder, finishing the paint job on the top shelf of a wall of floor-to-ceiling shelving that would eventually hold office supplies. As I looked at him, he gave a final little touch to a corner. Then he beckoned to me.

"Hey, Nell, help me pack up this paint," he said. "I've got to go home and get a shower before I pick up Martha."

Boone handed me his paint can and brushes, then climbed off his ladder and folded it up.

"Boone, that looks great," Patsy said. "You and Mike have really turned the work out. Believe me, I appreciate it a whole bunch."

"Glad we could help," Boone said. "But I've really got to run now."

"Of course!" Patsy smiled sweetly. "We don't want to cut into an eligible bachelor's social life!"

Boone's face turned slightly redder. He was dating one of my roommates, Martha. They didn't seem too serious just yet, but he'd brought her to a benefit concert for the shelter two weeks earlier, and Patsy had found out she existed.

Now she beamed at Boone. Peppy Patsy apparently hadn't let her own ugly marital experience sour her on romance.

Boone was wiping his hands on a rag. "Before I go," he said, "I've got a question."

"Anything!" Patsy said. "We have no secrets here!"

Except the financial statement, I thought. So far Patsy had cheerily refused to give me a detailed budget.

Boone pointed toward the door where Mike was working. "Patsy, what do you keep in your office that requires a closet with a steel door and a serious dead bolt?"

"Oh, that's our weapons storage," Patsy said airily.

"Are you preparing for an attack?" Boone said. Then he bit his lip and turned an even brighter shade of red.

I tried not to grin. The new shelter was a cheerful-looking place. Once you got by the high-security front door — intercom system, triple locks, bulletproof glass and password — it was easy to forget that the shelter only existed to meet the threat of violence.

Boone was trying to recover from his faux pas. "I mean . . . I mean — what kind of weapons do you keep?"

Patsy ignored Boone's embarrassment. "Oh, lots of our clients pack," she said.

Boone blinked. Then he nodded. "That makes sense. They wouldn't be coming here if they didn't feel threatened. Want to protect themselves."

"Right. So one of our intake questions is about weapons. We can't allow them to have knives or guns on their persons while they're staying here, of course. We'll use that closet to lock them up."

"So that's why it has all those little compartments?"

"Sure. It makes a client feel secure if she knows her pistol or can of Mace is right there, in a compartment with her name on it. And please don't ask us to make sure all the pistols are licensed. That's not our concern."

Patsy moved over to the closet and looked inside. "Is it ready, Mike?"

"You try it," Mike said.

He and Patsy tested the lock, and Mike gave it an extra shot of graphite. Boone left, followed closely by Mary and Lacy. Dawn dithered around until Patsy impatiently told her to go home. I went into the kitchen — equipped to prepare meals for thirty women and thirty children — and put my paintbrush to soak in the sink. I washed the paint off my hands, dug my purse out of a kitchen drawer, and combed my hair. Then I returned the purse to the drawer, took a black garbage bag back into the office and began picking up trash.

Patsy had pulled a plastic tarp off a pile of furniture that had been shoved to the center of the room. She took a key from the pocket of her blue jeans and opened a drawer in a desk she'd uncovered.

"I already moved the weapons over from the old place," she said. "They're stashed in here." She pulled out a cardboard box and began to unload pistols and knives. She laid them on top of the desk. Mike took a couple at a time and carried them into the closet, putting each in a compartment at the back.

"I hope none of these pistols are loaded," he said.

"We keep any ammunition separate," Patsy said. She pulled out a couple of boxes of shells and handed them to Mike.

I went back out to the kitchen, emptied the kitchen trash into the big garbage bag and went out the back door to put the bag in the Dumpster at the back of the parking lot.

I was lifting the Dumpster's heavy lid when a man's voice startled me.

"Are you Patsy Raymond?"

I jumped, almost dropping the lid, and whirled toward his voice. My heart was pounding.

The late-spring sun was almost behind the two-story house next door, and its glare hid his face. All I could make out was a blue shirt.

He didn't look threatening. He wasn't very large, and he was just standing there. He wasn't pointing a knife or holding a club or reaching toward a shoulder holster.

So I tried to react in a calm way. "Patsy Raymond is inside," I said. "Did you want to see her?"

"Yes, I'd like that."

He was polite, too. Another good sign. As I walked back to the kitchen door, he followed — a husky, dark-haired man in his early thirties, non-threatening, wearing khakis and a knit shirt.

I remembered Patsy's safety rules when we reached the porch. "Wait here," I said.

But when I opened the screen door, the man took it out of my hand and followed me in. He was still smiling politely.

"Wait on the porch, please," I said.

"I'd rather come in," he said.

"Sorry!" I deliberately raised my voice. "The shelter rules say you have to wait outside."

He didn't say no, but he kept coming in.

"Please, sir! Wait outside!" I tried to push the inside door between us, but he shoved me aside.

It was time to call for backup. "Mike! Patsy!"

The man and I scuffled, shoving the door back and forth, and I heard running footsteps. They were too light to be Mike's.

Patsy burst into the kitchen.

"Get out!" She ran across the room and began to help me shove at the door.

But the man slipped inside and grabbed at Patsy with his right arm. And, suddenly, as if it had grown there, his left hand held a large hunting knife.

I imagine I screamed. He kicked the door back, and I nearly landed flat on my back. Patsy jumped away and dodged his clutch.

"Mike!" I know I screamed that time. "He's got a knife!"

The man ignored me and headed for Patsy. He didn't run, he just came steadily. She retreated across the kitchen, but she backed into the refrigerator. Before she could dodge sideways, he was on her.

"Stop or I'll shoot!" I didn't know where Mike's voice came from, but it didn't slow the guy down. He grabbed Patsy's wrist. She yanked her arm, keeping as far away from him as she could. The thin guy pulled the knife back. The point was aimed at Patsy's belly.

A loud boom filled the kitchen.

And the guy in the blue shirt fell heavily, pulling Patsy down with him.

Blood seemed to be everywhere.

17

CHAPTER 2

Everything got really silent for a few seconds. We all stopped breathing, I guess. Then Mike materialized beside the man in the blue shirt.

"Call 911," he said. He wasn't speaking to anyone in particular.

Mike rolled the guy over, off of Patsy's legs. The man's eyelids fluttered. The shoulder and chest of the blue shirt were soaked with blood.

"Get me something to apply pressure," Mike said. Again, he didn't seem to be talking to either Patsy or me.

Patsy pulled her feet away from the mess, and she stared at the bleeding man. I scrambled across the kitchen and began to open drawers. On the third try I found a stack of kitchen towels. I tossed them at Mike, then I ran into the office and snatched up the phone. It took me a few seconds to convince the dispatcher we needed an ambulance and police at the *new* shelter — luckily I knew its address — not at the old rattrap it was replacing.

"Tell them to come in off the alley," I said. I ignored the voice telling me to stay on the line, hung up and ran back into the kitchen.

Patsy and Mike were kneeling over the guy in the blue shirt.

"I think the bleeding's easing off," Mike said. His voice still sounded calm.

Patsy whispered, "Mike, I think he's dead."

"No! No, the bleeding's stopped. He's stabilizing."

For once Patsy wasn't peppy. She shook her head slowly. Then she put her hand on Mike's shoulder. "Mike — "

"It's okay," he said. "He's better. If that ambulance will just get here."

He looked at me. "He'll be all right." His voice almost sounded confident. "He'll be okay, Nell."

And I knew I'd never loved Mike as much before as I did at that moment. Mike is big and tough and strong. But he's not violent. He's clever and persuasive. He's the kind of cop who talks the bad guy into surrendering. He may even wrestle him down. But he was proud of the fact that in ten years as a

policeman, he'd never fired his pistol anywhere but the firing range.

And now he'd shot someone.

He hadn't had any choice — that's for
sure. If he hadn't fired, we'd be applying
kitchen towels to a major wound in Patsy
Raymond's stomach. But Mike did not want
the man to die.

I went over and knelt beside Mike. I
wanted to reassure him. But the guy in the
blue shirt was looking terribly smooth. He
looked just the way my grandmother looked
five minutes after she died. Waxy. Artificial.
Dead. I couldn't think of anything reassuring to say.

Mike was still holding blood-soaked
towels on the collar of the blue shirt, pressing firmly against the wound in the man's
neck, when we heard sirens. Patsy went to
the back door. I could hear her yelling at the
ambulance crew and the patrol car. Then a
woman and a man rushed in. They wore
white coats and were draped with medical
equipment.

I stood up, and I tried to pull Mike away,
but he wouldn't move.

"Put your hand on this pressure point," he
told the male EMT. "If I let go, it may spurt
again."

The woman had dropped to her knees

and had her stethoscope in place and was listening. "Don't worry, buddy," she said. "He's not going to bleed anymore." She sat back. "DOA," she said.

Mike didn't move until the male EMT nudged him, and until I pulled at his arm. Then he stood up stiffly. I led him across the room, and he leaned against the cabinet. The EMTs talked on their radio. They ignored us, and we ignored them.

"He can't be dead," Mike said. "There's no way I could have hit anything important firing from that angle."

His voice was frighteningly rational. "He just can't be dead," he said again.

I put my arms around him, tightly. Patsy came over, and the three of us stood there until two uniformed policemen came in and talked to the EMTs. One of the patrolmen was tall, and one was short. I didn't know either of them, and neither of them seemed to know Mike.

The tall one turned to us. His voice sounded harsh. "Which one of you shot the guy?"

Mike's voice still sounded wooden. "I did."

He reached for his ID, in his back pocket, but the cop's voice got even harsher.

"Hold it, buddy! Where's the pistol?"

And I realized Mike was in a heap of trouble.

Maybe not trouble in the sense that he might go to jail. He had Patsy and me as witnesses. And the knife the guy in the blue shirt had carried was lying there on the floor, covered with his fingerprints. But Mike was facing trouble in the sense that this was not going to be an easy situation to get through.

I stood aside while Mike pointed to the pistol, which he'd laid on the end of the kitchen counter. He identified himself — verbally, then with his badge — and the two patrolmen seemed to relax a bit.

"Sure, I know you," the short one said. "Sorry I didn't recognize you right away."

The two of them exchanged a glance, and I could see the message flash. The old chief's son, they told each other wordlessly. Knows lots of top brass. Just about to make the move from patrolman to detective — way ahead of schedule. Long before either of them would make such a move. It was the kind of message Mike hates, but the kind he has had to live with since his dad died and he decided to leave the Chicago Police Department and return to his hometown force.

"I'll have to keep your pistol," the tall one said.

"That pistol's not mine." Mike said.

"What do you mean? It's a nine-millimeter Glock. Looks like department issue."

"But it's not mine."

"Didn't you have your pistol?"

"I was working in a T-shirt and jeans. I hated to wear a holster. So I stuck the pistol in my girlfriend's purse."

The cop frowned. What Mike had done wasn't strictly according to regulations, though cops do it all the time. They're supposed to have their pistols on them. But what if you're swimming? What if you're in church? There are lots of other situations in which having a pistol on your hip could be a problem. So putting the pistol in a gym bag — or in a companion's purse — is not that unusual.

"So where is your pistol?" The tall guy asked.

Mike looked at me. "It's in a drawer in here in the kitchen," I said. I pointed, and the patrolman opened the drawer and took the purse out. "There were a lot of people in and out," I said lamely. "I thought it would be safer there. It was too safe, I guess. When Mike needed it, he didn't know where it was."

The tall guy pointed at the pistol on the cabinet top. "So where did you get this pistol?"

"It was in the closet," Mike said. He explained about the shelter's weapons closet and that he'd been in it when I began to yell. "I had a clip in my pocket, but — like Nell says — I didn't know what she'd done with her purse. I saw that pistol and knew it would take that clip, so I grabbed it up and ran. As for where that pistol came from — you'll have to ask Patsy."

Patsy muttered something about records at the old shelter. The two patrolmen didn't look very happy.

The tall patrolman cleared his throat. "So who was the guy?"

"I don't know," Mike said.

"I've never seen him before," I said. "He forced his way in the back door — with that knife. He said he wanted to see Patsy."

We both looked at her.

Patsy shook her head. "I never saw him before, either," she said. "We see so many people — I speak to a lot of groups — I suppose he's some boyfriend or husband — we get a lot of threats . . ." Her voice trailed off. Then she turned to Mike, and her croak became so rough, I could hardly understand her. "Oh, God, Mike! You saved my life, and I haven't even thanked you!" She began to cry.

One of the patrolmen went into the office

24

and spread some of the paint-covered plastic sheeting over chairs. The three of us were ordered in there and told to wait for the detectives. I was very happy to get away from the vicinity of the dead man in the blue shirt.

Mike continued to get special attention. When the lab guys showed up with their cameras, a detective came with them, and it wasn't just any detective. It was Captain Jim Hammond, the most senior detective at the Grantham PD. Jim had been a protégé of Mike's dad, and he kept trying to take Mike under his own wing. His efforts were responsible for the opportunity Mike had to move to the detective squad.

Jim took preliminary statements, and the lab guys took pictures of all of us.

That's when I realized that Mike, Patsy and I were all covered with blood. Patsy was in the worst shape. The guy in the blue shirt had fallen right across her knees, and her jeans were soaked from the middle of the thighs to the ankles. Mike wasn't much better. He had knelt in a puddle, besides handling the man who had been shot. Mike's hands and his clothes were a mess. I had only a few splatters of blood on my clothes, but I had left bloody tracks across the kitchen floor. I remember thinking that at least these were old shoes. I could throw them away without a qualm.

The shelter was getting crowded. Mike's supervisor, Sergeant Beznosky, arrived about that time. At least Beznosky seemed interested in Mike, rather than in what he'd done.

He sat down facing Mike. "How're you feeling?"

"I'm not sure," Mike said. "Numb?"

The sergeant nodded. "Go on home as soon as Jim's through with you. Okay? The shrink will be over to talk to you."

Like most police departments, Grantham puts an officer involved in a death on automatic suspension. He's off duty until the detectives have finished their investigation into the incident, and until the police psychologist says the officer is good to go.

I think Patsy and I were as numb as Mike, in our own ways. If Mike didn't say a word, Patsy kept the conversation from dragging. She croaked like a whole pond full of frogs. She told us about every disgruntled husband who'd ever threatened her — it seemed to be two or three a week — until she had me so nervous, I could hardly keep from screaming at her. The words "Shut up!" quivered on my lips, but I didn't say them. In between her chatter, she sniffled and wiped her eyes.

I'm not sure what I did. I was terribly worried about Mike. I sat beside him and put my hand through his arm, but he didn't seem to know I was there.

It was nearly dark by the time they said we could go. I had driven to the shelter with Mike, so we left together. We went out to the kitchen, headed for the back door. Jim Hammond was standing there, with the door ajar, and he stopped us.

"Wait a minute," he said.

He shut the door quickly, but I'd gotten a look. The gurney with the body on it was stuck on the back porch, and the people who take care of such things were having trouble getting it down the steps. I took Mike's hand, and we stood in the kitchen until Jim took another peek and told us we could go out.

When we stepped onto the porch, there were two patrol cars and an ambulance in the parking lot, all with lights flashing, plus some other cars. Between the flashing lights and the lighting for the parking lot, the scene was bright. I tried not to look at the ambulance being loaded, but Mike stopped and stared. I tugged at his arm, but he didn't respond.

Then a woman shrieked.

"Mike! Nell! What's happened?"

We both swung toward the sound, and Dawn Baumgarner came running across the parking lot. A patrolman was thudding along behind her.

"What's happened? Is somebody dead?"

Jim Hammond spoke behind me. "Who let her in?"

Nobody answered him, and Dawn kept running toward us, chased by the uniform. "I'll have to call Mrs. Doubletree! I'll have to get the board together! We'll have to have an emergency meeting!"

If Patsy had been nervous, Dawn was hysterical.

But I couldn't understand what she was yelling about, and at that moment I didn't have any patience with hysterics from people who were not blood-splattered.

I know my voice sounded cold when I spoke to Dawn. "I think Patsy already called people."

"Patsy! Patsy's dead!"

"No, she's not!"

But my denial hadn't gotten through to Dawn. She continued to yell, "Patsy's dead! What will we do without her! The shelter could fold! We'll have to get busy, mobilize the board — "

"Dawn!" My voice was swallowed up, and

her voice ran right on.

"She was irreplaceable! She was — "

And Dawn screamed again. She pointed behind us and shrieked.

Patsy had just walked out the kitchen door.

Dawn's scream died away. Then she whispered, "Patsy. You're alive."

Patsy came down the steps and reached out as if she was going to hug Dawn. Then she looked down at her bloody clothes and backed off.

"I know I look half dead," she said, "but, Dawn, honey, I am all right."

Dawn had turned as white as a sheet. She whispered again, "When I heard — I was afraid — "

"I understand, sweetie, but I'm not hurt at all. All this blood came from that man they're taking away."

Dawn collapsed on the edge of the porch, head drooping, hugging herself silently.

Mike still hadn't reacted, even to Dawn's screams. I felt desperate to get him away. I took his arm and tugged, but he didn't move until Jim Hammond took his other arm. Between the two of us, we moved him off the porch.

"It's all an act," Mike said.

"What is?" I said.

"It doesn't matter," Mike said. He walked on, moving as if he were sedated.

"We parked in front," I told Jim. "We'll have to go around."

A crowd of neighbors and reporters had congregated outside the high metal gate to the parking lot. The creep from Channel 4, Grantham's trash TV station, poked a microphone at us and said something, but Jim moved him out of the way.

A strobe popped, and after the red spots left my eyes, I saw Bear Bennington, a *Gazette* photographer, behind it. The *Gazette*'s police reporter, Judy Connors, walked alongside me. "Hey, Nell, can you tell me what happened?"

I shook my head.

She reached out and patted my shoulder. "I'll be at the office. Call me when you can talk."

That time I nodded. I knew Judy needed all the information she could get for her story. I just didn't feel that I could take my attention away from Mike long enough to help her.

Nobody stopped us as we headed around the corner. The sidewalk in front of the shelter building was deserted and, because the branches of tall trees hung between the streetlights and the sidewalk, it was also dark. So I jumped when a figure moved beside Mike's pickup.

"Nell?" The baritone voice was questioning.

It was my dad. "Oh, Alan!" I said.

He caught me in a big bear hug. "You okay?"

That's when I began to cry. "It was awful," I said. "But it's worse for Mike."

I didn't ask how Alan had known where we were and what had happened. He worked for the *Gazette*, too, on the copy desk, and everybody there knew the improbable story of how the two of us had found each other after twenty years of separation. He wasn't working that day, but somebody from the office had obviously called him. He hugged me again.

That's when Mike spoke. "Alan, I'm glad you're here. You can take Nell home."

"Mike! I'm not going home — " I looked down at myself. "Well, maybe I'd better change clothes. But I want to come with you."

Mike shook his head. "No, you'll have to leave when the shrink comes anyway. Better go on now."

He walked around to the driver's side of his truck, unlocked the door and got in.

I ran over to the door. "Mike! I don't

think it's a good thing for you to be alone."

He slammed the door, more or less in my face, then rolled the window halfway down. "I'll call you tomorrow," he said.

I looked around for reinforcements. "Jim?"

Jim Hammond pulled me away gently. "I'll follow him, Nell."

Mike drove off without a second look at me.

I felt like tearing my hair out. This was the man I loved. Only a month earlier, we'd agreed that we'd get married. All that kept our engagement from being official was that hassle over the ring. We didn't share a mailing address, but we shared everything else — thoughts, plans, goals. Also showers and beds.

I could tell from Mike's reaction — maybe from his lack of reaction — that this was a terrible time for him. I'd like to think he would need me at a moment like that, that I could comfort him. Instead, he was pushing me away.

He'll have nightmares tonight, I thought. I won't be there to hold him when he shakes all over. Or maybe he won't even go to bed. Maybe he'll sit up all night watching video-tapes of old movies. And he doesn't want me to be there to watch with him.

Alan handed me a handkerchief and led me to his car. Jim Hammond came along.

"Nell, don't worry about Mike. He's awful shocked right now."

"God, Jim! It happened so fast. And if Mike hadn't fired when he did — well, Patsy would probably be dead. Maybe me, too. That guy just shoved his way in — "

Belatedly, I realized I was missing an important fact. I whirled toward Jim.

"Jim, who was that guy?"

CHAPTER 3

Jim's eyes dodged away from mine.

"We haven't informed the next of kin," he said.

Just as quick as quick, Jim had switched me from friend to enemy.

I laughed. When Jim had walked me out to the car, I'd been his protégé's girlfriend, but I had asked one question and in his eyes I had metamorphosed into a dreaded representative of the press.

I'm not sure just why this struck me as funny. Maybe it wouldn't have in any other circumstances. But I stood there and giggled. My dad put his arm around my shoulder. "Come on, Nell. You're doing fine," he said soothingly.

"I'm not hysterical," I said. "Not yet. But, Jim, that guy in the blue shirt turned my life upside down. I'd just like to know who the hell he was."

Jim had enough shame to drop his head. "I'll tell you when I can, Nell. We don't have a firm ID on him yet."

"Can I assume he's a disgruntled husband or boyfriend?"

But Alan kept me from going into full reporter mode. He tugged me toward his car. "You can assume he wasn't very gruntled," he said. "Come on, Nell. Let's get you home and cleaned up."

I laughed again, and I patted Jim on the arm. "Okay, Jim. This is the reason it's not smart for a reporter to hang around with cops — a rule only Mike Svenson could have made me break. Since I'm not covering the story, I'll let you off the hook. But I bet Judy Connor's got his name already."

"Maybe," Jim said. "But she's not as pushy as you are."

He reached around me to open the door of Alan's car just as a midsize sedan turned the corner and cruised slowly down the street toward us. It stopped opposite us.

"Nell!"

The voice was familiar, but I couldn't place it. I looked over the top of Alan's Toyota and squinted in the dim light. "Yes?"

"Nell, it's Mary Baker. I have Cherilyn with me. We need to go in the front door, so she won't have to go through that commotion in the parking lot. Can you run around and get somebody to open up? It would be better if we didn't have to pound on the door."

Before I could answer, Jim's voice barked out. "I'll go! Park along here, and I'll be at the main door to let you in in a few minutes."

He walked away swiftly, headed around the corner, toward the knot of reporters and spectators near the alley entrance.

Cherilyn? It was an unusual name, and it seemed familiar, though I wasn't quite sure why. But I knew Mary Baker, of course. She was the grandmotherly volunteer who'd been my painting partner all afternoon.

I waited while Mary Baker flipped a turn in a driveway and parked behind Alan. Then I went around the car, to Mary's window.

"You heard what happened?" I said.

"Horrible!" Mary's grandmotherly brow was wrinkled. "When I heard, I went over to the shelter, just to be on hand if they needed an extra volunteer. And, sure enough, the police wanted Cherilyn over here, and she said she'd rather go with me than in a patrol car."

She turned to the woman seated beside her. She patted her hand. "She's being brave as brave," she said.

I ducked my head and looked in the window. It took me a minute, but then I realized why the name Cherilyn had been familiar.

The Cherilyn in Mary Baker's car was usually known as Cherilyn Carnahan Howard. Around five years earlier she'd entered the state's most prestigious beauty pageant as Miss Grantham. She'd won the state title and gone on to win fourth runner-up in the Miss America competition. She'd taken a go at Hollywood, then had come back to Grantham, where she had her own television interview show — a fairly intelligent one — and did supermarket openings and other events calling for a local celebrity. And two years earlier she'd married Paul Howard, scion of Grantham's richest family.

Beauty, charm, intelligence and money. Cherilyn had them all. Yet she'd apparently been staying at the Grantham Shelter for Battered Women.

If I'd had trouble recognizing Cherilyn, it was partly because she didn't look like a beauty queen right at that moment. Her eyes were puffy and her blond hair was disheveled. She didn't look rich, either. She was wearing an old T-shirt and slacks that looked as if they'd come from a rummage sale.

Mary got out of the car, and went around

and opened Cherilyn's door. She almost had to help Cherilyn out.

"It's okay, honey," she said. "You're going to make it. I'll stay right with you."

"I can't believe Paul cracked like this," Cherilyn said.

"You had no way of knowing," Mary said.

"Mrs. Howard's going to blame me," Cherilyn said. "She'll say I should have reported his complaints, taken them seriously."

"Don't be silly! Remember, it's not your fault if your husband gets violent. It's his problem."

"It won't matter," Cherilyn said. Her voice was dull. "Paul's mom will still make it my fault."

Mary linked arms with her, and Cherilyn shrank against the older woman as they went up the walk of the new shelter.

I could feel my heart thump as the full implications of Cherilyn's presence soaked in. I went back to my dad's car, and my knees felt so weak, I almost fell into the front seat.

I whispered, "Mike killed Paul Howard."

I stared straight ahead, and tears began to roll down my cheeks. "I didn't know this situation could get worse."

Alan kissed my cheek. "Fasten your seat

belt," he said. "I'm taking you home, no matter how bad the situation is."

He drove the two miles to my house, while I snuffled into his handkerchief. He escorted me to the kitchen door — my roommates and I always park in the back — took my key from my trembling hand and let me into the house.

I sank into a chair at the kitchen table, still sniffling.

"I'm sorry," I said. "It's just that Enid Philpott Howard — well, that's just the final straw. She has the clout to really make this a mess."

Alan sat down opposite me and patted my hand. "Enid Philpott Howard? Are you talking about the Howard Foundation chairman?"

"Yeah. And about the bank chairman, the political power, the cultural guru, the public policy dictator, the social lion, the hereditary ruler, the community spin-meister and the lord high pooh-bah of this part of the world."

"And you think the man Mike shot was her son?"

"I'm sure of it. That woman in the car that pulled up was Paul P. Howard's wife, Cherilyn Carnahan Howard."

"The one with the TV show?"

"Right. Apparently she's been staying at the shelter."

Alan gave a low whistle. "Wife beating among the high muckety-mucks?"

"The shelter wouldn't take her in for any other reason."

"That can't be right, Nell. Even if she was in trouble, a woman like that wouldn't go to a shelter. She'd have friends or family to turn to."

I blew my nose. "From what Patsy Raymond tells me, lots of times going to a friend or a family member can be the most dangerous thing a battered woman can do. The batterer is likely to kill both the wife and the person who's helping her."

"I guess I've read that. But I can't believe that Cherilyn Carnahan Howard wouldn't have the money for a hotel."

"She obviously did have money. She must have been afraid to go to a hotel. So you've identified the first problem for Enid Philpott Howard. Scandal."

"What would a person like that care about scandal? If she's as powerful as you say — "

"Oh, she's that powerful!"

"Scandal won't cost her any money."

"It's not her money that makes Enid Howard powerful. It's her — well, I guess you'd call it her moral leadership."

"Nell, that's silly. I've been in Grantham six months, and I've been working that copy desk for half that time. The name Enid Philpott Howard doesn't come up that often. I'd remember a moniker like that!"

"Enid Philpott Howard isn't a person who needs to be out in the front ranks of the newsmakers. She stays in the background. But what she says goes."

Alan looked skeptical.

I leaned toward him. "Remember the sales tax proposal? How that died all of a sudden?"

"Sure. But it wasn't such a hot idea to begin with."

"It wasn't a good idea, but a majority of the city council was wedded to it — right up until the day before they were supposed to vote on the final ordinance calling the election. Then — and I got this from one of the secretaries at the PD, who got it from the mayor's secretary — Enid Howard called the mayor. Nobody knows what she said, but that afternoon the mayor called all the members of the council, and that evening the sales tax ordinance was tabled. And the next week it was voted down, and everybody's water bill went up two bucks a month."

"It's hard to believe one person has that much influence."

"Enid Philpott Howard does. She could cause a major stink about her son's death."

"It's more likely that she'll try to sweep it under the rug."

"I hope you're right. I just hope Mike doesn't wind up remembered forever as 'the cop who shot Paul Howard.'"

I dropped my head into my hands, fighting the desire to pull my hair out by the handfuls. "How could this happen to Mike? It could ruin his whole future."

Alan slid his chair closer to me and put his arm around my shoulders. "Now, come on, Nell. It can't be that bad. From what the cops outside the shelter were saying, Mike didn't have any choice. He had to shoot or let Patsy Raymond be stabbed."

"That's right! But that won't make any difference in the outcome. First, Mike was terribly shocked when Paul Howard died. He's — well, I think he's in a state of denial right now. But he's level-headed. I think he'll work that out with the police psychologist.

"But if the man he killed was Paul Howard, he's got a whole new set of problems."

Alan stood up. "Go upstairs and take a shower," he said. "I'll make you something to eat." He leaned over and kissed me on the top of the head. "Mind your father. Go."

I went. The shower did make me feel better physically, though I still felt helpless, like a pawn on a chessboard controlled by Enid Philpott Howard. As I dressed and went back to the kitchen, I was still worrying about Mike.

That was the reason I snatched the phone up when it rang. I wanted Mike to be on the other end of the line.

"Mike?"

"Sorry, it's Judy Connors. I know you'd rather not talk to me."

A pang of guilt hit me. "Oh, Judy, I know I said I'd call."

"That's okay, Nell. You've had an awful experience."

"Yes, but you've got a deadline. What can I do for you?"

"Anything! The cops have clamped down completely on the shooting. They won't say a word."

I didn't say a word either, and Judy went on. "I can't find Jim Hammond anywhere. And the PIO guy won't answer his phone. They've gone completely incommunicado."

I could imagine the excitement at the police department. Jim Hammond and the department public information officer were probably closeted with Chief Jameson and the other top brass someplace between a rock — Enid Philpott Howard — and a hard place — their loyalty to Mike as a fellow law officer and the son of an old friend.

"And Patsy Raymond can't be found, either." Judy took a deep breath. "So, Nell, you're my only hope — unless there was somebody there I don't know about."

"Tell me what you do know," I said.

"Practically nothing. Nine-one-one dispatched an ambulance and a patrol unit at five-forty-seven. I know that, because I heard it on the scanner, and I checked the time. The dispatcher said 'shots fired.' The patrol unit called for backup the minute they arrived at the new shelter. They called for detectives. All this was pretty routine. Bear and I got there and stood in the street outside the *back gate* with the other reporters. The ambulance crew took something that looked like a body — at least the head was covered — out the back door. But the ambulance didn't leave. It just sat there. That odd woman pushed her way in, and there was a lot of screaming. Then you and Mike came out the gate with Jim Hammond. Then Patsy Raymond. We all thought Jim Hammond would give us a statement. But, no! He went back inside, and as far as I know, he's never come out.

"Nell, we can't even get anybody to confirm that there's a deader! What's going on?"

Judy had a real problem. In most shootings, information from the police is the basis of the news story. The cops usually button up the witnesses — sometimes taking them into custody. Eyewitness accounts are often either unavailable or so unreliable that we don't want to print them. The newspaper has to be very careful about what is printed. If an eyewitness puts the gun in the wrong man's hand — either by mistake or on purpose — that wrong man could sue the paper for libel. So the spot news story often boils down to a brief account. Somebody got shot and police are investigating just what happened. A day later, when the police are closer to filing charges, we can print more details.

But in this case, the Grantham PD was keeping its fanny covered. They were preparing to face an irate mother who just happened to be able to hire the best lawyers in the country and who had clout up the kazoo. They weren't going to say anything for days.

In the meantime, Judy and the rest of the *Gazette* staff didn't even know who the victim was.

I opened my mouth to tell her. Then I snapped my jaw closed again.

It had just occurred to me that I didn't know who the victim was, either.

Sure, I might have deduced his identity, but nobody knew I had except Alan. And surely my own father wouldn't rat on me.

Maybe I could get my version of the shooting out before Enid Philpott Howard could act. And my version would make it clear that Mike had no choice but to fire that pistol. And that he had been profoundly disturbed at Paul Howard's death.

I'd been so upset, I'd forgotten that I was a reporter and that my first responsibility was to get the facts before the reader.

"Judy," I said, "how would you like an eyewitness account?"

CHAPTER 4

Alan made me eat a bowl of soup and a grilled cheese sandwich before I started writing. Then I went upstairs to my computer and whacked out an eyewitness account of what had happened. I kept an eye on the clock; deadline for the state edition was approaching.

I tried to keep the story strictly factual. Nine months earlier, when I'd been briefly held hostage by a gunman, I'd written a first-person account that emphasized my own emotions. This time I left my feelings out. I told about the way Paul Howard — I called him "the man in the blue shirt" — had shoved me out of the way to force his way through the kitchen door. I told about how Mike had kept pressure on the gunshot wound and that he had said, "He can't be dead. I couldn't have hit anything important from that angle." And about how Patsy

Raymond had burst into tears and said, "Mike, you saved my life, and I haven't even thanked you."

Alan was checking the story over for me — he's a copy editor, after all — when the phone rang.

My heart leaped again, and I snatched up the receiver. "Mike?"

But it was a woman's voice. "This is Lacy Balke. May I speak to Nell?"

Lacy Balke? It took me a minute to put a face with the name. Then I remembered. Lacy was the tall, svelte blond who'd been on the painting crew that afternoon. She was a member of the shelter board.

"This is Nell."

"I'm sorry to bother you, Nell. I got your number from Wilda Svenson."

"That's okay, Lacy. What can I do for you?"

"Is it true there was a shooting at the new shelter after I left?"

"Yes, I'm afraid so."

"That's awful! What happened?"

"I took the trash out the back, and some man pushed his way past me as I came back in. He had a huge knife. He tried to stab Patsy. Mike had to stop him." That was the quick version. I said it almost automatically, while my brain went into overdrive. Lacy

48

Balke? Why was she calling? What was her place in Grantham? How did she fit into the community? Was she just a conscientious board member? She was a young executive's wife —

I almost choked as it came to me. Lacy had mentioned that her husband was with Grantham National Bank. And Grantham National Bank was owned by GNB Holding. And the major stockholder in GNB Holding was the Howard Foundation. And Enid Philpott Howard chaired both the holding company and the foundation.

Lacy was speaking. "Who was the man who was shot?"

I turned and looked through the bedroom door, at Alan editing my story. And I knew that I had to cut Lacy off. Her husband had probably already heard that Paul Howard, the son of his boss's boss, had been shot. I couldn't let her tell me that. I could not let anybody tell me that Paul Howard had been shot. The story I had written had to come from an innocent bystander's viewpoint. Nobody could know that I knew who the victim was. Nobody could know that I was trying to protect Mike when I wrote that story.

I guess I was silent a long time, because Lacy spoke again. Her voice was low and filled with a combination of dread and excitement. "Do you know who the man was, Nell? My husband heard it was a man he works with."

One more question and Lacy was going to blab the name Paul Howard. I had to shut her up, fast.

"No, Lacy, I don't know who he was. And I really can't talk about it right now. I've got to go to the office. Sorry." And I hung up.

Alan looked at me in surprise.

"I can take this down to Judy," he said. "You don't have to go. Or you can E-mail it."

He stood up, and I slid into the chair in front of the computer. I dug through a box of disks, found a blank one and popped it into the B drive. "I think I'd better go on down," I said. "Judy may have some more questions."

I commanded the computer to copy the story onto the disk, then I looked up at my dad. "Listen, I may be completely wrong about the dead guy being Enid Howard's son," I said. "In fact, the more I think about it, the more I think that's simply impossible."

Alan looked at me, expressionless. "Gotcha," he said.

Then he leaned over and kissed me on the

forehead. "You've been hanging around with the tricky Mike Svenson too much," he said. "Do you want me to go to the office with you?"

I went down alone, and on the way, I thought about what Alan had said. Was it true? Was I getting as tricky as Mike?

When Mike and I had first started dating, we'd bumped heads several times on that issue. I regarded myself as thoroughly honest and open. Mike, on the other hand, had made his mark as a negotiator, a hostage negotiator. He was trained to keep his thoughts to himself, if the situation warranted it. He would sympathize with a hostage taker that he actually held in contempt, for example, if his sympathy would gain the release of the hostage. He would hide his own emotions — or display emotions he didn't really feel — if it gained his point.

Not that he lied. One of the main things about hostage negotiation is that the negotiator must never lie. But the negotiator can certainly slant the truth or conceal the real situation.

Let's call this skill by its right name. Manipulation. Mike was an expert professional manipulator. He'd saved my life at least once by using that skill, and I admired his professional expertise.

But sometimes his professional training seemed to squiggle over to his personal life. For example, I had once stood by while he accused his mother of committing adultery, so that he could goad her into telling him the truth about a quarrel she'd had with his father. He and I had nearly broken up over that one.

During that fight, he'd told me I was as tricky as he was — in a different way. I'd denied it hotly.

Now my father had said the same thing. Was my sneakiness justified in this case? I thought about it, and I answered the question to my own satisfaction.

Yeah.

It was definitely justified, I decided. The Enid Philpott Howards of the world hold all the cards. Even if they're honest, virtuous people themselves — and I had no reason to think Enid Howard was any more crooked or mean than anybody else is — they simply have so much clout that us peons can't hold out against them in open battle. We have to use subterfuge.

With my behavior justified in my own mind, I pulled into the *Gazette* parking lot full of resolution and ready to con my editor. I used my magic electronic card to open the employees' entrance, ran up the three flights of stairs and dashed into the news-room, brandishing my computer disk like a sword.

I headed to the pod of desks used by the three police reporters. That's when the first letdown hit. Judy Connors wasn't there.

I guess I had thought she'd be sitting in her chair, wringing her hands, waiting to snatch that disk out of my hands. But, no, she wasn't there. I looked around, then went over to the city editor, Ruth Borah. Ruth is a tall, slender woman, 40-ish, who tucks her dark hair into a chignon, then ruins the ef-fect by poking pencils into her sophisticated "do."

She was consulting with a page builder on the Page 1 layout, and she didn't see me coming.

"Where's Judy?" I said.

Ruth jumped. "Oh! Nell. You're here."

"I told Judy I'd write a first-person ac-count of the shooting this afternoon." I waved the disk. "I brought it down."

Ruth frowned. "That may not have been a good idea," she said.

"Why not?"

"We've got a little trouble in hand." She cocked her head slightly toward the office of Jake Edwards, our managing editor. "And all this *would* come up when the publisher is in China."

"What's going on?"

"It seems that Enid Philpott Howard herself is interested in how the story about the shelter shooting is handled."

I ground my teeth. My efforts had been useless. Mrs. Howard had struck even faster than I had.

Ruth raised her eyebrows. "I had to call Jake in to talk to her — she wanted the top person, of course. Wouldn't say a word until he got here."

I still didn't speak.

Ruth's eyebrows went up another quarter of an inch. "You wouldn't have any idea about just why Mrs. Howard is interested in this particular story, would you?"

Ruth and I are friends. I didn't want to lie to her. So I evaded. "I guess I could speculate," I said.

"Never mind." Ruth started to speak again, but her phone rang. She rolled her chair backward three feet, to her own desk, and answered it. "City desk."

She listened, then spoke. "Yes, Jake. She just got here."

The phone made sounds again. "Certainly. I'll send her right in."

She hung up and gestured toward the

glass wall of Jake Edwards' office. "You're wanted," she said.

I looked around, and I saw that Jake, Judy Connors and a gray-haired woman were looking at me through the wall. Judy's eyes were bigger than ever behind her thick glasses. Jake's black hair was slicked back smoothly, but his face looked rumpled, and Mrs. Howard — yes, I was sure it was her — looked as if Jake's visitors' chair were a throne.

Jake beckoned, and I nodded. Then I handed the disk to Ruth. "This is the eye-witness account of what happened this afternoon," I said. "Hang on to it, please."

As I crossed to Jake's office, I wished that the newsroom was twice as wide as it really is. I've had to face situations I didn't like before, but talking to the bereaved mother of a man my boyfriend had killed — for whatever reason — made me wish I was out at Mike's house feeding him chicken soup.

But I didn't know that Paul Howard was the victim, I reminded myself. Or did I? I was confused, and the walk across the newsroom simply wasn't long enough for me to work things out in my mind. I was already going in the door.

"Yes, Jake?" I said. I kept my eyes away from the gray-haired woman.

But Jake spoke to her. "Mrs. Howard, this is Nell Matthews. Nell is one of the best reporters we've ever had at the *Gazette*, and she was on the scene this afternoon."

Close up, Enid Philpott Howard looked like old money. It was hard to say just why. She wasn't stylishly dressed, certainly. She wore a pair of gray slacks, a white turtleneck and black loafers. They were ordinary, but those particular garments hadn't come off the rack at Kmart. There was nothing trendy about her smooth haircut. It would have been in fashion at any moment from 1925 until the present. She wore one piece of jewelry, a gold ring that was embellished with some simple engraving, but held no precious stones. The total effect was top drawer.

Mrs. Howard nodded with dignity, and Jake continued. "Nell, just two hours ago, Mrs. Howard received the tragic news that her son was the man shot at the shelter."

I decided I wasn't a good enough actress to act surprised. "I was afraid of that," I said.

"Why?" Mrs. Howard's voice was a deep contralto, low and resonant.

"As we were leaving, a woman arrived — apparently to identify the body. I couldn't tell for sure, but she looked a lot like Cherilyn Carnahan Howard." I looked at Mrs. Howard, and I spoke sincerely. I might not be sorry about Paul Howard's death for the same reason his mother was, but I definitely shared her grief. "I'm terribly sorry, Mrs. Howard."

"Thank you." She inclined her head regally. "Miss Connors tells us that you proposed to write a first-person account of the events of this afternoon."

"Yes. I've done that."

Jake whirled his pica pole around, and I knew he was nervous. A pica pole is a metal ruler marked off in picas, a printing measurement. It's an editor's tool for drawing layouts and measuring type, but for Jake it's also the equivalent of a string of worry beads. His face doesn't reveal his thoughts, but when things are tense, he twirls his pica pole like a baton.

"I left the story with Ruth," I said.

Jake nodded at Judy. "Please go and ask Ruth to make a printout," he said. Judy scurried out, eyes still enormous.

"Mrs. Howard is concerned about our coverage of the incident at the shelter," Jake said.

"I'm sure we wouldn't be doing anything sensational," I said. "That's not *Gazette* policy."

Mrs. Howard's voice echoed again. "I would never dream of interfering with the

57

Gazette's coverage," she said. "I simply want to be sure it's complete."

"That's our goal, of course," Jake said. "And just what facet did you think might be neglected?"

"Perhaps I could read Miss Matthews' story before I comment?"

Her question was actually a command. I wondered how Jake would take it. People outside the newspaper usually aren't allowed to read stories before they're printed. But I didn't see how Jake could refuse.

His pica pole twirled. "Of course, I haven't read the story myself."

"I understand."

Jake seemed to square his shoulders. Was he getting ready for a fight? "And I can't promise that we will change any of the story, Mrs. Howard."

"I'm sure Miss Matthews has done a fine job, Mr. Edwards. There are simply a few facts which she may not have had."

Judy came back then with a sheaf of green-and-white striped computer printout paper. "Ruth sent two copies," she said.

She gave them both to Jake, and he gave one to Mrs. Howard. The two of them read, and I sat down there miserably. It's horrible to watch people read your stuff. I don't even like to see other reporters read a straight news story I've written. Watching a woman read an account of how her son was killed was agony.

If it was agony for Mrs. Howard, she didn't show it. She read the entire printout calmly, without bursting into tears or having hysterics. When she had turned the final page of the printout over, she looked at me.

"A very straightforward account, Miss Matthews."

I nodded.

"This police officer — " She frowned. "I'm sorry. I didn't note the name of the officer."

"He's my fiancé." I said it a little loudly. But I wanted her to understand that I was lugging some emotional baggage, too.

Mrs. Howard nodded. "Yes. I understand your relationship to him. But what is your relationship to Mrs. Raymond?"

"Relationship?" The question caught me by surprise. I'd been concentrating on protecting Mike from the possible wrath of one of Grantham's most influential people. I'd barely remembered that Patsy Raymond was mentioned in the story.

"Mrs. Raymond? She's just a news source," I said. "We don't have any other relationship."

"You're not friends?"

"We're not enemies. I met her only two weeks ago. She's been very helpful in explaining the shelter's operations."

"Do you subscribe to the opinion of her commonly held in the community?"

"The opinion commonly held? Just what do you mean?"

Mrs. Howard held up the printout, and I saw that she had gripped it so tightly, one corner was crumpled. Her chin was trembling, and her voice broke as she spoke again.

"Do you think she's a candidate for sainthood?"

I was so fascinated by the cracks appearing in Enid Philpott Howard's facade that I didn't answer for a moment, and she spoke again.

"Do you think she's the patron saint of victims? Do you think she's worthy of the adulation of the entire community?"

I leaned forward. "Mrs. Howard, I'm a reporter. I'm supposed to keep a healthy cynicism about the motives of the people I deal with. On the other hand, my job is not to debunk everybody, either. It's just to report what they do, what they say, and what they accomplish. Not to judge them."

She gave a gulp that may have been more

than half sob. "Then you have no opinion on St. Patsy — the patroness of the battered woman?"

"I'm a human being, too. Of course I have an opinion."

"And what is it?"

I leaned back in my chair. "I don't think I should share it with you."

Jake made a sound in the back of his throat then, but Mrs. Howard ignored him.

"Then you believe her image?"

"I don't buy anyone's image without looking at the motives and methods that were used to create that image. In Patsy Raymond's case, I'll say this much. I think there's a complicated personality behind her public image. On two weeks acquaintanceship, I don't think I understand that personality. Outwardly, she seems perfectly sincere. Also extremely single-minded. She sees the entire world according to how it will affect the shelter. I don't think I'm qualified to judge further than that."

I sat back and watched as Enid Philpott Howard's facade developed another crack. A tear ran down from the corner of her eye, and she gave a long, sobbing breath.

"Then it wouldn't surprise you to learn that Patsy Raymond deliberately goaded my son into that attack on the shelter?"

61

CHAPTER 5

Enid Philpott Howard must be nuttier than her son had been.

That was my first reaction to her wild accusation of Patsy Raymond. Patsy was far from perfect, I felt sure, although I hadn't yet identified exactly what her faults were. A reporter has to keep emotional distance from sources, not buy their images uncritically. But no human being is perfect, and Patsy was a human being.

However, Patsy had devoted her life to nonviolence. She would never goad anyone into an attack. Enid Philpott Howard had to be crazy to accuse her of doing that. I bit my tongue to keep from saying so out loud.

Mrs. Howard's stony facade had definitely broken now. She was weeping openly. She turned away from Jake, Judy and me, shutting us out of her sorrow with a thrust of her shoulder and a cockamamie idea about Patsy Raymond.

If it had been any other woman, I would have gone to her, put a friendly arm around her shoulder, patted her hand, told her I sympathized with her grief. But Enid Philpott Howard was no ordinary woman. She was an institution. I couldn't comfort an institution. I stayed where I was and kept my mouth shut.

Jake looked panicky, as most men do when faced with strong emotion. Judy was goggling at the scene, and she hovered in the door, moving uneasily from foot to foot. Neither of them was going to do anything.

Mrs. Howard gave a deep sob, and I saw that her handkerchief was completely sodden.

Honestly! Jake, Judy and I were a bunch of wimps. The poor woman had lost her son, and she needed — something.

Maybe it was a Kleenex. At least I could handle that.

I stood up. "Jake, don't you have a box of Kleenex in your drawer?"

Jake nodded, opened a drawer and handed me a flat box of man-sized tissues. I pulled my chair over closer to Mrs. Howard and nudged her arm with the box.

"Mrs. Howard, we're all terribly sorry

about your son. This is a real tragedy."

"It's that woman. She pushed Paul into this."

I didn't answer. I didn't want to argue with her. And while I didn't believe the tale about Patsy Raymond, I couldn't really deny it until I had checked it out, beginning with Patsy herself.

Mrs. Howard turned toward me. "You don't believe me."

"Mrs. Howard — "

She brushed me aside. "I didn't believe it, either. I've never bought into all this battered women fad, but I was willing for Patsy Raymond to operate her shelter. It never hurt me in any way. When Paul told me about her phone calls, I simply didn't think it was possible."

She turned to include Jake in her audience. "Paul — Paul did have a wild streak — like his father. And he drank too much sometimes. But his father turned out to be a brilliant businessman. I thought Paul was settling down." Her face became anguished. "He was only thirty-two!"

I tried to speak soothingly. "I know, Mrs. Howard. He was just a young man."

"I thought he was overdramatizing the situation. I couldn't believe that Mrs. Raymond had made those phone calls."

"Phone calls?"

"Paul said she called him every day, and sometimes at night. Ever since Cherilyn went to that shelter. No wonder he was upset!"

Obviously Paul had been lying to his mother. I felt sure that Patsy hadn't made harassing phone calls to a client's husband.

My disbelief must have shown in my face, because Mrs. Howard pounded the Kleenex box on her knee emphatically. "It's true! I tell you, it's true! I couldn't believe it, so I checked the numbers on Paul's caller ID. One number had called a half-dozen times. And when I called it back, someone answered the phone 'Grantham Women's Shelter.'"

Jake was looking as unbelieving as I felt. He beckoned to Judy, and when she approached his desk, he said quietly, "Call the shelter. Tell them it's an emergency. Get Patsy Raymond to comment on this."

Mrs. Howard wiped at her eyes again. "I just don't want you to print a story about what a monster Paul was — and what a saint Patsy Raymond is!"

She clutched my hand in a death grip. "She's morally responsible for Paul's death. Without her goading phone calls, Paul would never have hurt anyone."

"But, Mrs. Howard, Cherilyn was in the shelter," I said.

"What do you mean?"

"I mean that the shelter will only take in women who have been threatened or injured by their spouses or boyfriends. So Paul must have hurt her, or at least frightened her severely."

"Oh, no. Paul never struck Cherilyn."

"But — "

"Cherilyn was good for him. She had the poise and intelligence to make him a good wife, and the beauty to make him happy. He would have had no reason to hit her."

"That may be true, but the classic battering spouse doesn't really need a reason."

Mrs. Howard leaned forward and spoke earnestly. "But you see, Cherilyn wasn't a true client of the shelter."

"She wasn't?"

"Oh, no! She simply pretended to be a battered wife so she could check into the shelter and research a story for her television show."

Talk about amazement. That statement left Jake gaping so wide, I could count his gold teeth. And I imagine he could count mine. My chin hung so low that my jaw was almost dislocated.

"But that's — " I started to speak, then I shut up.

"That's unethical!" That's what I had started to say. Or, "That's incredible!" I might have said that, too. Or, "That's ridiculous!" That also might fit the situation.

But I really couldn't say, "That's impossible!"

Maybe Cherilyn Carnahan Howard really had wanted to do a story on the shelter from the viewpoint of a client. Maybe she had claimed to be a battered wife so they'd treat her the way they treated everyone else.

Jake would never have approved of a *Gazette* reporter pulling a stunt like that one, but maybe Cherilyn's bosses would have.

There's an old story about a reporter back in the 1920s, when tabloid journalism was earning the reputation it still enjoys today. He supposedly was trying to find out a cause of death, and his normal sources weren't working. So he called the morgue and said, "This is the Cook County coroner." And the voice on the other end of the phone line said, "That's funny. So's this."

Misleading a news source is not only dishonest, it's risky. A responsible newspaper like the *Gazette* would need a vital reason before its editors would approve an undercover operation such as pretending to be a battered spouse. That could lead to charges that might be the journalistic equivalent of entrapment. It's simply not the way to handle things.

Besides, Cherilyn Carnahan Howard was a local celeb. I'd recognized her, even with puffy eyes, messy hair and old clothes. The shelter people would have recognized her, too. And they would all have known who her husband was and who his mother was, the minute she showed up. She wouldn't have been treated like an ordinary client, and she must have known that.

Plus, if a reporter gathered information by going into a shelter undercover, she wouldn't be able to print a word about the other women in the shelter. Unless the news agency was prepared for an invasion of privacy suit.

I couldn't see how the station manager would have allowed Cherilyn to go undercover and subject her husband — a member of a prominent family — to the embarrassment of being branded a wife beater.

Mrs. Howard might believe Cherilyn was in the shelter to research a story, but I didn't. No, it had to be a tale told by Paul Howard to explain why Cherilyn had moved to the shelter.

Mrs. Howard was beginning to regain control by then, and Jake suggested that he help her prepare a brief formal statement of her accusations against Patsy Raymond.

"Nell," he said, "you help Judy get hold of Mrs. Raymond. Or somebody."

Judy and I got on the phone, but all we could get at the shelter that time of night was the hotline. If neither of us was being abused, they couldn't help us. I called the home number I had for Patsy, but it was answered by a machine. I tried the president of the shelter board. No answer. Mike's mom was vice president, so I called her. All I got at her house was an answering machine. Nobody in authority seemed to be around.

"Do we have to give up?" Judy asked. "We simply can't print Mrs. Howard's charges without giving Patsy Raymond — or somebody — a chance to refute them. They're too crazy. We'll look like idiots tomorrow when the cops prove that was just some story Paul Howard was using to fool his mother."

I was glad she saw the whole problem so clearly. But we weren't getting anywhere.

"How about Channel Nine?" I said. "Try the manager — or the news director. At least they could confirm or deny Mrs. Howard's claim that Cherilyn entered the shelter as part of an investigation."

Judy nodded and pulled the phone book over. I continued to wrack my brain. Who? Who could find Patsy Raymond? Who would know what was going on at the shelter?

A universal news source popped into my mind. I even said it out loud. "The secretary!"

In any organization or office, there's always one person who makes sure everything gets done. In our newsroom, it's the assistant city editor. In our publisher's office, it's Beth Malic, the administrative assistant. Grantham's police chief, Wolfe Jameson, has his office manager, Joan Bartlett, or he'd never know where he was supposed to be or when he was supposed to be there. The GPD bureau of detectives has a secretary named Peaches Atkinson, who doesn't need to wear a uniform or carry a pistol to cow the toughest gang member in Grantham, and Jim Hammond himself says "Yes, ma'am" when she speaks.

For a beat reporter, it's important to find out who knows all the details in any office the reporter's covering. And it's rarely the boss. It's usually the secretary or her equivalent.

Patsy Raymond's assistant director-bookkeeper-aide was Dawn Baumgarner. She was the one who had nearly had hysterics as we were leaving the shelter because she had thought Patsy had been killed. I yanked my own phone book out of its rack. Maybe Dawn had calmed down by now. I was sure she wasn't the real power over there — not with an egotistical boss like Patsy — but she might know where Patsy was.

No phone was listed for Dawn Baumgarner, and no one by that name had the initial D. So I started at the top of the list, praying that Dawn's phone wasn't un-listed. I called five numbers before a whiny voice answered, "Baumgarner's Treasures" and said I'd reached Dawn's home.

"She's not here now," the voice said. "This is her mother."

"This is Nell Matthews with the *Grantham Gazette*," I said. "Can I reach Dawn at another number?"

"Well, she's gone to that social club."

"Social club?"

"The Christian Singles. They stay out awful late for Christians, if you ask me. And in my day, Christians didn't dance."

"Where do they meet?"

"The Downtown YMCA."

Finally, a piece of luck. The Downtown Y was just two blocks from the *Gazette*.

"Thank you, Mrs. Baumgarner!"

I grabbed a notebook from my drawer, told Judy where I was going and ran to the elevator that serves as a night entrance to the *Gazette* Building. I walked the two blocks. Grantham's downtown isn't all that dangerous after dark, and walking was quicker than trying to move my car.

The Downtown Y is busy all hours. They have an evening basketball league, and some kind of swimming sessions also were getting out, judging by the wet hair on the people who were coming out as I went in.

But the athletic young man at the desk looked blank when I asked for the Christian Singles meeting. "We don't have such a group," he said.

I thought back. Yes, I was sure that was the name Dawn's mother had given me for the meeting her daughter was attending. But maybe the older woman had misunderstood. The "C" in YMCA did stand for Christian, of course.

"Do you have a singles group by another name?" I said.

The jock shook his head. "Well, we have single parents, but they meet on Tuesdays. The only adult group meeting tonight is the line dancing class."

"Dancing!" Dawn's mother had complained about Christians dancing. "That must be it."

The athlete sent me to a first floor room — after I convinced him I didn't have to pay admission.

"I promise not to dance!" I called back as I ran toward the back of the building.

Line dancing, which doesn't require a partner, is perfect for a group that is lop-sidedly female, and this class was. The men — Christian, single or whatever — were out-numbered two to one. The guys definitely had their pick of the women present.

And one had picked Dawn Baumgarner.

At the back of the dim room, I saw her dancing with a tall string bean of a man. He looked to be around forty, and he was losing a bit of his pale hair, but he was quite pre-sentable. He was wearing jeans and a plaid shirt, with western boots — the proper out-fit for line dancing. Some of the women wore tight jeans, but Dawn was wearing a denim skirt, white blouse and flat shoes. Her partner held her hand tightly as they crossed the floor in rhythm with the country-western tape. Dawn's lips moved as if she were counting.

I had to wait until the music stopped to catch Dawn's eye. She blanched when she saw me, then looked around. I wondered if she was looking for a place to hide. But I was between her and the door. She couldn't get away unless she crawled under the refreshment table.

The thirty or forty line dancers present were milling around, and it took some maneuvering to get close to Dawn. Her admirer followed her closely as she worked her way through the crowd. She looked as timid as she usually did, but she seemed calm. The hysterical woman who'd been screaming on the back porch of the shelter had disappeared, and the obsessively neat Dawn Baumgarner had reappeared, white blouse buttoned up to the chin.

But Dawn's face looked stricken as she came up to me. "Oh, Miss Matthews, you must think I'm terrible," she said. "Dancing after all that terrible business this afternoon. But Joe Bob had already paid for the lessons, and . . ." Her voice trailed off.

"I can hardly criticize you. I'm not exactly in an emotional heap myself. I was even there when it happened, and now I'm trying to work on the story."

"Oh, I don't think I can help you with that!"

"Can you help me find Patsy Raymond?"

"The police told her she could go home."

"If she's home, she's not answering the

phone. And I don't know where she lives. All I have is a phone number."

Dawn looked troubled. "Well, I don't think I could tell you where she lives. She wouldn't like that."

"It's pretty important, Dawn. Someone is making some serious charges about — about her. If we can't get hold of her, we'll have to print them without a denial."

"A denial?" Dawn's eyes grew big. "A denial?"

"They're charges from a source we can't ignore," I said.

"Charges? What sort of charges?"

"Charges of unprofessional conduct."

Dawn's boyfriend, or whatever he was, joined the conversation at that point. "That's what you've been saying, Dawn."

What did that mean? I switched my attention to him and stuck out my hand. "Nell Matthews, *Grantham Gazette*."

His handshake was firm. "Joe Bob Zimmerman. I had the contract for the renovations for the new shelter." He smiled at Dawn.

I smiled, but I decided to be blunt. "What's this about unprofessional conduct?"

Joe Bob Zimmerman opened his mouth, but Dawn cut him off neatly. "Joe Bob, would you do me a favor?"

"Sure."

"I forgot all about getting that brochure on senior citizens' programs for Mama. Would you mind running to the front desk and seeing if they have one? I'm afraid he'll be closed up by the time the lessons are over."

Joe Bob went away meekly. The dancing teacher was lining everyone up again, so Dawn and I stepped out into the hall.

"What's this about unprofessional behavior?" I repeated.

Dawn's eyes danced away from mine. "Nothing important," she said. "I have a masters in social work, you know. Sometimes Patsy doesn't do things by the book. But she's the director, not me. I said too much."

"Well, if there's anything funny going on at the shelter, Dawn, the *Gazette* pays me to find out about it. And I can protect my sources."

She smiled timidly and shook her head. "No, I don't know about any big scandal. I'm just nobody over there, anyway. If I don't understand something, it doesn't necessarily mean there's anything wrong."

"The accusations against Patsy are serious."

Dawn's eyes widened. I thought her lips twitched into a Mona Lisa-ish smile, just briefly. She spoke briskly. "You could try Patsy's daughter's house. Sometimes Patsy goes over there, and Delia sort of hides her out. It's Delia Waters. I don't remember her husband's name, but it's on Ash Street. Near downtown."

I wrote that down in my notebook. When I looked up, Joe Bob was coming down the hall, and Dawn was moving toward the door to the dancing room.

"Dawn, there's bound to be a lot of trouble over this shooting," I said. "And it's my responsibility to cover it. If you can point me in the right direction — "

She shook her head vigorously. "Oh, no! Patsy talks to the media. Only Patsy. Or the board chairman. I've probably told you too much."

"You haven't told me anything!"

"I told you Dawn's daughter's name. That's all I can say."

She grabbed Joe Bob's arm and almost fled into the dance class.

I stared in at the door, listening to "Cotton-Eyed Joe" and trying to figure out what I'd learned.

First, it seemed plain that Dawn believed something funny was going on at the shelter.

She'd confided in Joe Bob, her boyfriend, but she wasn't about to tell me.

Well, that wasn't an unusual situation. Reporters meet two kinds of people — people who insist on telling us things and people who are afraid to tell us things. We've got to learn to deal with both of them.

"I'll be back," I told Dawn silently. And, leaving "Cotton-Eyed Joe" behind me, I headed back to the office.

As I went up in the elevator that served the newsroom at night, I devoutly hoped that Enid Philpott Howard was gone. My kid gloves were getting thin, and I didn't want to deal with any more emotional mothers.

I should have known. When the elevator door opened, two women were standing face-to-face in the reception area.

One was Enid Philpott Howard, whose son had been shot and killed that afternoon. The other was Wilda Svenson, whose son had fired the fatal bullet.

CHAPTER 6

They weren't doing battle. In fact, they seemed to be chatting in a friendly fashion.

Wilda's briefcase was beside the uncomfortable couch provided for visitors, and her purse was on it. Her stance made me feel that she had just stood up. Jake hovered behind Mrs. Howard, but he looked lost and horrified and wasn't taking part in the interaction.

My impulse was to yank Wilda into the elevator and hit the down button. But Jake gestured, and I realized that it was Mrs. Howard who had been leaving. I stepped into the reception area, moved to the side and held my notebook in front of the electric eye that held the elevator door open. I hoped I looked as if I were inviting Mrs. Howard to enter.

Mrs. Howard ignored me, but my movement caught Wilda's eye, and she turned.

"Oh, Nell! I've been calling you for hours. Mike won't talk to me, and I've got to know what's going on."

Jake touched Mrs. Howard's elbow. "Here's the elevator," he said.

But Mrs. Howard didn't budge. "Mike?" she said. "Is that your son?"

"Yes." Wilda answered her question, but she kept her attention directed toward me. "What happened, Nell? Jim Hammond said you were there."

"It's a long story, Wilda."

I gestured toward the elevator, and Jake nudged Mrs. Howard. She still didn't move, but she spoke again. "I guess this is an evening for trouble with sons," she said. "I hope your son hasn't been injured."

And the true situation hit me like a bolt of lightning. Number one: When she read my story about the shooting of her son, Enid Philpott Howard had missed the name of the shooter. She didn't know who fired the fatal shot. Number two: Wilda Svenson knew Mike had shot and killed someone, but she didn't know who it was.

Could Jake and I separate them before they figured it out?

Wilda was answering Mrs. Howard's question. "No, no! He hasn't been hurt physically. At least, I don't think so." She

80

looked at me. "He's okay, isn't he?"

I nodded and waved Mrs. Howard toward the elevator again. She ignored me again.

Wilda turned back to me. "Jim Hammond is growling about how Mike deserves a medal, but Wolfe Jameson is looking really grim and wouldn't talk to me. And they were at Mike's house, and Dr. Benson was there, but they wouldn't let me in."

She moved her hand, and I thought she was going to pull out a handful of hair, but she simply clutched her forehead for a moment.

"Oh, God, Nell! He only got involved with that shelter because I suggested it. I'll never forgive myself if he winds up in some mess — just because he happened to be there when some madman attacked Patsy Raymond."

That tore it. Unless Mrs. Howard's brain was completely numb, she couldn't miss knowing that the woman beside her was the mother of the man who had killed her son.

I heard her gasp. Then Jake asserted himself.

"Mrs. Howard, I'm going to insist on escorting you home," he said. "Our security guard can follow us and bring me back to the office." This time his nudge was pretty close to a shove, and Mrs. Howard stepped into the elevator. I removed my notebook from in front of the electric eye, and the door began to close.

But Enid Philpott Howard hadn't completely capitulated. She reached out and touched the door. It popped open obediently, and Mrs. Howard spoke.

"Mrs. Svenson, are you saying that your son was the off-duty policeman who shot and killed a man at the Grantham Women's Shelter this evening?"

Wilda's chin quivered. "Yes," she said. "Apparently he's so upset that the police psychologist won't let me see him."

Enid Philpott Howard's chin quivered, too.

"Then both our sons are victims of that woman," she said. "Patsy Raymond has killed one of them and has done deep harm to the other."

She moved her hand, and the elevator door slid smoothly shut. And I stood there with Wilda Svenson.

"What was she talking about?" Wilda said.

"Wait a minute," I said. "Let me make a phone call. Then I'll explain everything. Everything I can."

I put Wilda and her briefcase in an interview room, then I went to my desk and looked through the phone book for the phone number for Patsy Raymond's daughter. There was a J. W. Waters on Ash Street. I dialed the number and Delia Waters answered.

Of course she wouldn't tell me anything, such as a number where her mother could be reached.

"But it's vital!" I said. "Some serious charges have been made against your mother — by a source we can't ignore. We've got to print them, and we don't want to do that without giving her a chance to confirm or deny."

"Charges? What sort of charges?"

"I think you could call it unprofessional conduct. But I'd rather tell her directly."

Delia Waters didn't sound convinced, but she said she'd try to find her mother and would ask her to call me.

I hung up, told the switchboard where I'd be and went to the room where I'd stashed Wilda to give my potential mother-in-law a précis of the day's events and to try to explain how Enid Philpott Howard fit in.

As one of Grantham's more active and successful real estate operators — her agency is the third largest in the city and she built it from scratch — Wilda doesn't move in the rarified circles Enid Philpott Howard inhabits, but she had obviously met the woman before that evening. She's a great deal more aware of the ins and outs of Grantham society than I am. I didn't have to draw her a diagram.

She frowned and thought the story over before she spoke.

"Well, all this makes Enid Howard's last words to me quite interesting," she said.

"You mean, saying that both Paul Howard and Mike are victims?"

"Yes. According to what you and Jim Hammond have said, Mike didn't have any choice when he shot Paul. So at least Enid Howard isn't blaming Mike for what happened."

"But her accusations against Patsy seem ridiculous."

"I agree. Patsy's far from perfect — don't quote me on that — and she might lose her temper and pop off when talking to a client's husband. But she wouldn't call him repeatedly, daring him to attack. And that's apparently what Enid Howard is claiming happened. No, I'm more concerned about what Jim Hammond told me."

"About Mike?"

"No, about the gun. About the pistol Mike used."

I stared and blinked for a minute. Mike and Patsy had been stowing pistols, knives and cans of Mace in the secure closet when I went outside to dump the trash. When I'd come back in, and trouble erupted, Mike had been armed. He'd told the first officers on the scene that he simply grabbed up one of the pistols from the storage area and used it.

"What about the pistol?" I asked.

"Jim said it looks like a Grantham PD issue."

"It wasn't Mike's!"

"No, Mike told Jim he took it from the closet, the closet where — "

I nodded to indicate that I knew which closet, and Wilda stopped, then went on. "And Mike's pistol was in your purse, Jim says." Wilda shook her head. "I spent thirty years of my life lugging his dad's pistol to the lake and to church. I see you're now in for the same treatment. Jim has people trying to track the pistol down. Somebody may be in a lot of trouble."

I nodded, too. Yes, if a pistol issued to a member of the Grantham Police Department had wound up in the Grantham Women's Shelter, it probably meant somebody's wife had brought it there. Which meant some cop likely had beaten or threatened his wife or girlfriend. And that some cop was missing his pistol. And that some cop — and/or his wife or girlfriend — was going to face disciplinary action.

A couple of possible culprits flashed through my mind. Any group of a thousand people — the population of the Grantham Police Department — is going to include about a hundred real jerks. I was ready to pin this particular problem on several Grantham cops I'd run into.

But I reminded myself that you can't tell who's a spouse abuser by looking. In fact, Patsy had told me abusers are often charming and seductive — they have to be, or they can't attract the women they abuse.

At that point I realized I'd told Wilda all I knew, and she'd told me all she knew. She apparently came to the same conclusion, because she stood up and said she was going home.

"Try not to worry," I said. "As you say, the psychologist and Jim Hammond are with Mike."

"I know. And Mike is thirty-two years old. I know a mother is not really necessary at this point. But if you see Mike — "

"He told me to butt out, too."

"I know, but if you see him, tell him I'm concerned. If he doesn't want to talk to me, that's okay. But I'm here if he wants me."

She was blinking rapidly as the elevator door closed.

Wilda wasn't the only one who was worried about Mike. So far, Enid Philpott Howard wasn't blaming Mike for the death of her son. But she could change her mind — once the family's lawyers got hold of her. True, I'd been rushing around trying to tell Mike's side, but what good could I do against the kind of legal talent Enid Howard could muster?

And what about how Mike was feeling? He prided himself on being able to talk his way out of difficult situations. I'd seen how upset he was when he realized Paul Howard was dead. How was he dealing with this? Had the police doctor given him sedatives? I was terribly concerned about Mike.

Someone called my name, and I turned toward the sound. Judy Connors was holding the telephone receiver in her left hand and pointing to it with her right. I walked toward her, and she covered the speaking end with her hand. "It's Patsy Raymond," she said. "She's asking for you."

I snatched the receiver away from her. "Patsy, it's Nell."

"Yes, Nell." Patsy's raspy voice sounded as if she were lost in a fog.

"Patsy, some serious charges have been

made about . . ." I paused and thought about how to phrase the question. I decided to waffle. "Some serious charges have been made about the operation of the shelter."

"Oh?" Patsy didn't sound upset. She didn't sound as if she'd heard me. That wasn't like Patsy. A hint at trouble for the shelter would ordinarily shake her cage from top to bottom. The shelter was Patsy's whole life, and nobody dared criticize it or its operations to her.

"Patsy? Are you okay?"

"Yes." She made a noise I interpreted as a yawn. "I'm awfully sleepy. Delia got me up. She said you had to talk to me."

"Did you take a sleeping pill, Patsy?"

"I don't know. Delia, what was that pill you gave me?"

"Just a minute, Patsy." I put my hand over the receiver and turned to Judy. "She's taken a tranquilizer or a sleeping pill or something. Do I dare ask her if she called Paul Howard?"

"You could see if you get a sensible answer."

"How would I know if it was sensible or not?"

"Good question."

I took my hand away and spoke into the receiver. "Patsy, let me talk to your daughter."

"Humf," Patsy said. And in a moment I heard the voice of the younger woman I'd talked to a half-hour earlier.

"I didn't think about your mom taking a sleeping pill," I said.

"I didn't know she had," Delia answered. "I gave her one the doctor prescribed for me when I had minor surgery, but she won't usually take other people's medicine. I'm sorry. I can try to get her to drink some coffee or something. She's really groggy."

"No," I said. "I'll call back in the morning. Sorry we put you to this trouble."

"If it will help the shelter, I'll try to get her awake. You know how important that is to Mom."

"Yes, I know. But it's not fair to ask her to talk for publication when she's not clearheaded."

We both apologized again, then hung up.

I looked at Judy. "Well, that was a washout. What now?"

Judy picked up her notebook. "I managed to get hold of Margaret Doubletree at her mother's house in California. I guess we can go with the quote I got from her."

"What did she have to say?"

"Oh, the usual crap. The board has the utmost confidence in Patsy Raymond's professional behavior, but they'll investigate any charges thoroughly."

Judy flipped through her notebook. She didn't act angry, but her action made me remember that the story I'd been working on wasn't mine.

"Good," I said. "That will take care of it for tonight. You didn't need me horning in anyway."

"If you'd been able to get a quote from Patsy, it would have been better. And I didn't have time to go chasing around town looking for her number and to write the story, too. Do you want to read the story before I send it on to Ruth?"

I declined. I'd been too pushy already. Judy was being nice, but I'd almost committed a serious breach of newsroom etiquette.

The medieval fiefdom is not dead. It lives on in the newsrooms of America, where beat reporters fight daily to protect their turf.

The rudest thing a reporter can do is cover a story on someone else's beat. It's an unwritten law. School reporters don't suddenly take a notion to write about county government. City hall reporters don't, just for fun, write business stories. Sporties don't normally write about medicine, and lifestyles reporters would be out of line if they wrote obituaries.

90

And the city editor or assignment editor has to be careful not to send the wrong reporter out on a story. The angriest reporters you ever heard are the ones saying, "Why is *he* covering that? It's *my* beat!"

Of course, beats do overlap, and there are ways to handle it. If the education reporter wants to do a story about crime in the high schools, she first approaches the city editor and explains the idea and why it's an education beat story, not a violence beat story. Then the city editor goes to the crime reporter and explains why the education reporter is doing this story and how it differs from a regular crime story. Then the education beat reporter, who may already have the story written, talks to the crime reporter directly and asks for suggestions on how to handle it. The crime reporter suggests police or court sources that could help.

It works out, as long as we all follow protocol. But you don't just jump into the middle of someone else's story, the way I'd been about to do with Judy. My years of crime reporting were haunting me. I'd gotten right into the story and forgotten I was just a helper, not the main reporter. The sidebar, not the lead story.

No, my responsibilities were over. I made a final check with Ruth Borah, then left.

I didn't even have to tell my car were to go. It drove straight to Mike's house and pulled into the driveway.

Then I sat there. Should I go in? Mike had been pretty definite when he told me to go home. He might not want to see me.

But Jim Hammond's car was sitting at the front curb. He could run interference for Mike, I thought. He'd probably been doing it all evening. I knew he'd kept Wilda out. I decided to give it a try, but I also decided to act like a casual caller. I left my garage door opener in my purse, went to the front door and rapped softly.

Jim Hammond opened it. To my surprise, he looked glad to see me.

"Nell," he said. "Good. Come on in."

I looked around the living room. Jim was the only one in it. "How's Mike?"

"Doing fine, considering."

"Benson left?" Dr. Bernard Benson is the psychologist under contract to the Grantham PD.

"Yeah. He'll be back tomorrow."

I nodded. "You heard Mike tell me to stay away this afternoon. Is there anything I can do now to help out? Make coffee? Bring a casserole? Lend a shoulder?"

"Actually, Mike went to bed." Jim looked a bit puzzled. "He said something about 'getting it over.' I didn't really understand what he was talking about."

I stared at the floor and blinked. I understood, but I wasn't sure Mike would want me to explain it to Jim.

Mike has an extremely logical mind. He applies this logic to any personal problems he has, working them out rationally. But his emotions don't always keep pace with his intellect. As a result, his subconscious has to deal with emotional problems on its own.

At least, that's my theory. All I know for sure is that after something frightening or exciting or threatening or just plain bad has happened to Mike, he has nightmares.

And as a hostage negotiator he has to face frightening, exciting, threatening and just plain bad experiences a lot more frequently than the rest of us. That's his job. Then he has to go over the whole thing in his sleep, night after night, until he assimilates it. It's not a lot of fun.

So I knew that sometime during the night — if not tonight, then tomorrow night or another night soon — Mike would be up, sitting in front of the television set, shaking like a hardware store's paint mixer.

He keeps a supply of videotaped movies, all silly comedies, which he watches until the shaking goes away. If I'm handy, sometimes he lets me put my arms around him. And in an hour or two, he falls asleep again.

Is the excitement, or the sense of accomplishment, or the satisfaction he gets from handling a frightening situation worth the bad times he knows are going to follow?

When I asked him that, Mike looked at me as if I were crazy.

"Yes," he said.

As long he feels that way, he's just going to have to get up in the night and shake. But did he want Jim Hammond to be around when he did it?

Jim was looked at his watch, then spoke. "Were you planning to stay?"

"Would it be all right?"

"I think so. Mike's pretty sensible, you know."

"Yeah. He's sensible, but he's not simple. There's always a lot going on beneath the surface."

"If you say so." Jim looked as if he doubted my assessment. "Anyway, I thought if you were going to stick around — "

"You could go home."

"Well, my wife's been out of town and — But I could get Boone to come over."

"No, I'll stay. If you think if wouldn't upset Mike to have me here."

"I think he'd rather have you than Boone

or me." Jim grinned. "You can offer — "

I thought Jim was going to make some crack about the fact that Mike and I sleep together. I didn't like that, and I guess my face showed it, because Jim didn't finish his sentence. It's none of his business.

He left, and I got a blanket and a pillow from the back bedroom. I took a chapter of Mike's master's thesis, "Community Policing in a New Century," and made myself a nest on the couch. I read two pages of statistics before I was asleep.

And a couple of hours later, I was the one who had a nightmare.

I was back at the Grantham Women's Shelter, but it wasn't either the new one or the old one. Actually, it had a strong resemblance to the *Gazette* newsroom. Patsy Raymond was running back and forth, yawning and croaking, "Catch me if you can." Then Enid Philpott Howard appeared from behind the city desk — which had turned into a restaurant-sized range like the one in the shelter's kitchen. She was waving a large pistol. She said, "This is a grant from the Philpott Foundation," and she pointed the pistol at Patsy. Then Mike came down off a ladder, and he said, "It's all an act," and Mrs. Howard swung the pistol toward him. And I was standing between Mike and Mrs.

Howard, and the pistol was pointed straight at me. I said, "I'm only a bystander, a fly on the wall," but Mrs. Howard became a skinny guy with stringy hair and he/she pulled the trigger, and I could see a bullet coming toward me, and I yelled, "No! No!"

I became aware that someone was shaking me, and I woke up on Mike's couch, with Mike leaning over me. He was wearing boxers and a white T-shirt.

"Wake up, kid," he said. "You're having a bad dream."

I sat up. "Golly," I said. "Thanks for waking me up. I was back with Bo Jenkins, I guess."

"That's old stuff." Mike sat down, but he didn't touch me. "I'm way beyond that."

Mike and I first got together — as a couple, I mean — during a hostage situation nine months earlier when we were both held at gunpoint by a stringy-haired guy named Bo Jenkins. Oh, we'd known each other for a year or more before that, but we'd never dated before Bo went over the edge. Poor old Bo tried to do the right thing, but his mental balance wasn't good, and he came to a sad end.

"I don't know why Bo reappeared out of my subconscious," I said. "And what are you doing waking me up from a nightmare? I'm supposed to be doing that for you."

"I guess I'm not to the nightmare stage yet," Mike said. "I haven't really been asleep. I'm too curious."

"Curious?"

"Yeah. What is it that Jim and Chief Jameson won't tell me?"

CHAPTER 7

I told him.

Or at least, I told him what I knew. First I told him whose son was killed in the shelter's kitchen.

Mike whistled softly.

"I figured it out when Cherilyn Carnahan Howard showed up right after you left," I said. "The detectives called her over to ID the body. I guess she'd been in and out of the shelter for some time. She seemed more worried about what her mother-in-law would think than about Paul getting killed. She kept muttering about 'She'll say it was my fault' and 'She'll say I should have told somebody about his complaints.' Stuff like that."

"I sure didn't recognize Paul Howard," Mike said.

"Did you know him?"

"Not very well. We played YMCA baseball

on the same team a couple of years. When we were junior-high kids. I think his mother wanted him to have an opportunity to meet common folks."

"Did you go to high school with him?"

"Nope. Paul went to Grantham Country Prep. Where the rich kids go. I went to Grantham Central." He grinned. "Which offered a different set of advantages in preparing its students. But Paul got around. I'd heard a lot about him."

"Do you think he could be a wife-beater?"

"It would be in line with the stationhouse gossip. He — "

He shut up suddenly.

"Yes?" I said. "You were saying?"

"Never mind. How's Enid Philpott Howard taking all this?"

"She's blaming the victim — intended victim," I said. I described the events of the past few hours and Mrs. Howard's accusations against Patsy Raymond.

I tried to be reassuring as I finished up. "So she's not blaming you, Mike. She understands that you didn't have any choice. You had to shoot Paul Howard."

"I guess that's right," Mike said.

"It is right! If you hadn't acted fast, Patsy would be dead. Maybe me, too. Paul Howard was completely out of control. He might even have killed you as well. And maybe himself."

"Suicide by cop?"

"Suicide by cop" is a policeman's nightmare. Most law officers have a horror of running into someone who wants to die, but who doesn't want to take care of the matter himself. Instead, he creates some sort of situation which he believes will cause the police to kill him.

Mike's voice had become bitter, and his face was bleak. But I was the one who suddenly began to cry. I put my arms around Mike tightly and buried my face in his chest. "I'm so sorry, Mike," I said. "I'm so sorry."

For a moment I thought he wasn't going to respond. Then his arms tightened around me. He didn't speak, but we sat there on the couch, huddled in the nest of blankets, and held each other. And in a little while Mike kissed my forehead. "We might as well get more comfortable," he said. "Maybe I can sleep now. I'm sure somebody's keeping an eye on Cherilyn Howard."

We climbed into the king-sized bed in the next room, and I fell asleep almost immediately.

Emotional trauma rarely keeps me awake. I deal with it at the computer. I sit down and write it out, and then I can move on. Mike, on the other hand, has to let his sub-conscious chew everything over.

But as I was dropping off to sleep I wondered what the heck he had meant about Cherilyn Howard. Why should somebody be keeping an eye on her?

Later I decided Mike never went to sleep that night.

He went through the motions. He lay there breathing quietly. But if I roused up enough to check on him, his eyes were either open or just closing.

The last time I woke up — just before seven — he finally seemed to be sleeping. When I got up to go to the bathroom, he opened one eye, but I kissed it shut, and he didn't move. With my immediate physical problem taken care of, I decided I couldn't sleep anymore. Mike was lying on his side, breathing easily, as I tiptoed through the bedroom and out to the kitchen. I made a pot of coffee and got the *Gazette* from the porch.

I had read Judy's story on the death of Paul Howard and moved on to the comics before the phone rang. I grabbed the kitchen extension before it could ring twice, trying to keep it from waking Mike.

"Nell?" It was Judy Connors' voice.

"Yes."

"I thought you'd want to know. I just got a call from the St. Luke's ambulance dispatcher."

"What about?"

"Cherilyn Howard. She's dead."

I stood there with the phone in my hand, and I didn't know how to react. What could have happened to Cherilyn? Had she committed suicide? Had a heart attack? Had Enid Philpott Howard decided to include her in the vengeance for her son's death and gone over and shot her?

But my big question was — how would Mike deal with this new disaster? Could I keep it from him?

Even as I asked myself the question, I heard an extra breath on the telephone, and I knew Mike already knew about Cherilyn. He'd evidently picked up the phone, and he'd probably heard Judy's announcement.

And I remembered what Mike had said the night before. Instead of goodnight, he'd said, "I'm sure someone is keeping an eye on Cherilyn Howard."

How had he known something might happen to Cherilyn?

I guess I'd been silent so long that Judy Connors had begun to think something had happened to me. She spoke again, and her voice sounded timid and worried. "Nell?"

"I'm here, Judy," I said. "I'm just taking it in. What happened to Cherilyn?"

"I don't know. They found her about a half-hour ago."

"Where was she?"

"At her parents' home. Eight-thirteen Birch. I'm on my way over there now."

"Surely it wasn't natural causes?"

"I don't know a cause of death yet. But natural causes don't seem likely, do they? Nell, I gotta go now."

"Thanks for the call."

"Sure." Judy hung up.

I almost ran from the kitchen to the bedroom. How was Mike going to take this new disaster?

He took it lying down.

When I looked at Mike, he hadn't moved anything but his eyelids. He was still lying on his side, with the air-conditioning-weight blanket pulled up to his chin, but now his eyes were open.

"You heard," I said.

"I was eavesdropping on your call," he said. "Are you going over there?"

"I guess so. I'm just too nosy to stay away. What about you?"

"Jim wouldn't let me in." He closed his eyes. "It's sure not my case.

I stared at him, troubled. This was not

typical Mike Svenson behavior. Mike Svenson wasn't all that shy about butting in on Jim Hammond's cases, any more than I was shy about butting in on someone else's story. Especially when Mike had made comments on the subject earlier. Comments I didn't understand.

"Mike," I said, "why did you think something might happen to Cherilyn Howard?"

His eyes popped open. "Did I think that?"

"Yes. You said something about it last night. Just as we got in bed. You said, 'I'm sure somebody is keeping an eye on Cherilyn Howard.'"

"I don't remember that," he said.

"You said it."

He turned over and adjusted his pillow. "Something I dredged up from my subconscious, I guess. I think I'll go back to sleep."

Go back to sleep. As if he'd ever been asleep. I stared at him, but I couldn't think of any way to rouse him. And I didn't know if that would be the right thing to do anyway.

I kissed him, got dressed and left.

Eight-thirteen Birch was in a plain, ordinary neighborhood, which backed up my feeling that Cherilyn had come from a plain, ordinary socioeconomic background. At least, I never heard of an old-money millionaire's daughter taking the beauty — I mean, "scholarship" — pageant route to success any more than I ever heard of a desperately poor family financing the gowns, voice or music or dance lessons and contest entry fees it takes to rack up pageant wins. Pageants are a middle-class phenomena.

The Carnahans lived in a white frame house with black trim. The attached single-car garage had been turned into a room of some sort, and a double carport had been tacked onto the front, overlapping onto the side yard. A big panel truck with a sign that read "Carnahan's Electric Service — Home and Commercial Repairs and Contracting" was parked under the carport, with a new-model mid-sized sedan next to it. A patrol car and Jim Hammond's plain vanilla sedan were at the curb.

People were standing around in the street, of course. But so far it seemed to be mostly neighbors, trying to see what the cops were doing at the Carnahans' house.

Judy Connors' talents as a police reporter included a remarkable ability to butter up the ambulance crews and dispatchers. She might have been the only reporter the ambulance dispatcher had called. For a moment I allowed myself to hope she had a clear beat. Then I saw the Channel 9 truck two doors down. The competition was already there.

Judy and the *Gazette*'s photographer, Bear Bennington, were standing near the Channel 9 crew, outside the yellow tape that outlined the yard at 813 Birch.

After all, I told myself, Cherilyn had worked for Channel 9. If they didn't have a pet dispatcher of their own, one of the neighbors had probably called them.

I walked over to the knot of news folks. "What's going on?"

Judy, Bear and the three Channel 9 people swung toward me. The TV cameraman — he was a ponytailed guy named Bert, and we'd stood around outside a lot of crime scenes together — answered me.

"Hi, Nell. What are you doing here? After yesterday I thought you'd be home taking Valium."

"Nope. I write until my personal traumas go away. Too bad Cherilyn couldn't do that. Do they think it's suicide?"

"Nobody's saying," Judy said. "Which makes it interesting."

We all looked wise. If the police thought it was suicide, somebody would probably have told somebody by now — some cop would have given some reporter a hint. "Found her in the back bedroom with a pistol in her

106

hand" or, "Looks like she took the whole prescription." A word would have been dropped.

Leaving the situation up in the air made it likely that either nobody knew what caused Cherilyn's death or that she'd been murdered.

Bert swung back toward the house, and I spoke again. "Who found her?"

"Her father," Judy said. "Her parents had been out of town. They drove all night to get back after they heard about Paul Howard being killed. Walked in to find Cherilyn dead, too."

"Rough homecoming. Where had they been?"

Bert answered that time. "Houston. Cherilyn's mother runs a beauty shop. She was at a big hair show."

I began to wish I had a second cup of coffee. And I reminded myself that Judy Connors was the *Gazette*'s crime reporter. I was just an onlooker. But maybe I could do something.

The three Channel 9 crew members began to mutter among themselves, so I took Judy aside and asked her if I could help her.

She frowned. "We don't know much yet," she said. "I'd better hang in here, waiting for the official word. Could you talk to the neighbors?"

"I'll try."

People were gathered in a yard across the street, but when I approached them, notebook in hand, they only had questions, not answers. None of them seemed to have any more information than the identity of the family who lived in the Carnahans' house.

"I've seen 'em carrying those fancy dresses of hers in and out," one said. "They're always pleasant, but they never visited much in the neighborhood."

So I moved on, to a driveway two doors down where a man stood alone, looking stoic and smoking a cigarette. He was a big, bulky guy with grizzled hair cut level on top.

"Hi," I said. "I'm Nell Matthews. From the *Gazette*. We're trying to figure out what's going on here. Do you live on this block?"

The man jerked his head toward the house behind him. "Lived here twenty-three years."

"Then you know the Carnahans?"

He nodded again and took a drag on his cigarette.

"Is Cherilyn their only child?"

Another stoic nod.

"They've had every right to be very proud of her," I said.

"Her dad says it's due to her mother," the man said. "She's the ambitious one. But I say, he footed the bills."

"I know Cherilyn's pageant talent was singing," I said. "Did she have voice lessons?"

"Voice and piano. Dancing. And she was in a bunch of plays in high school. Majored in speech and drama at Grantham State. We never had any kids of our own. Guess we took pretty much interest in her. Used to go see her in plays. Went to all her pageants."

He took another drag on his cigarette. "They spent a bundle on Cherilyn, but Joe always said he had nothing better to spend money on. I guess that's right. Taking care of your kids pays off. Or it usually does." He shook his head. "We all thought Cherilyn was right on top of the world — TV show, rich husband. But I guess it all blew up under her."

"Do you know what happened?"

"As much as anybody does, I guess. Teresa — that's Cherilyn's mom — she came running to our door before seven this morning. Yelling that something had happened to Cherilyn and that Joe sent her over to call the police. Didn't want to use their phone. Evidence, he said."

"That was probably smart."

"I think it was an excuse to get her away — you know, so she wouldn't be having hysterics with Cherilyn there on the floor. They're both sitting in our living room now, waiting for the cops to talk to them again."

He gestured toward the house. It was very similar to the Carnahans' house, except that there was a pickup truck instead of a van in the drive.

"I had to get away a minute," he said. "Teresa's getting a statement ready for the media."

I could feel my eyes widen. A grieving mother was preparing a media statement? Then I ducked my head to look at my notebook. Who was I to judge? And hadn't Enid Philpott Howard had much the same reaction? The minute she'd heard her son was dead, she'd rushed to the newspaper to tell her side of the story.

It made a weird sort of sense. Both the Howards and the Carnahans were Grantham celebrities. Even if they didn't seek publicity, it came to the Howards because of their wealth and position and to Cherilyn because of her beauty and television show.

But what should I do about Cherilyn's neighbor? He didn't seem to be disgusted at being confronted by a reporter. I knew from

experience that lots of people find it thera-
peutic to talk to the press at a time of crisis.
It lends importance to the terrible experience they've had. It's like telling everybody
about your operation.

I pulled my notebook into writing position. "I'm sorry, I didn't get your name."

"Rudy Schmidt."

"R-u-d-y? S-c-h-m-i-d-t?"

"That's right."

"Mr. Schmidt, my job here is to find out
what happened to Cherilyn. Can you tell me
what you know?"

"I know damn little," he said gruffly.
"Teresa said Cherilyn called them at the
hotel in Houston last night. Said she told
them Paul had tried to break into that shelter where she was staying. Said a policeman
shot him."

I nodded encouragingly. His story wasn't
quite straight, but it was close enough.

"Cherilyn told them she was leaving the
shelter, but she didn't want to go back to the
house she and Paul had — I always called it
'the big house.' I never liked it, and to tell
the truth, I don't think Cherilyn did, either.
She had a key to her folks' house, of course.
She told her mom she was coming here."

"Coming home."

I thought Mr. Schmidt was going to lose

111

his stoicism, but he gulped hard and held on. "If we'd have known she was there, we'd have gone over. Checked on her. Stayed with her. Then maybe — But Cherilyn told her mother she wanted a few hours alone. Said she had to decide what to do about something. So they didn't call us.

"Teresa and Joe just threw their stuff in the car and started back. They got in here around seven. Went straight to the house, of course."

I nodded.

"Joe says the first thing he noticed was that the front door was ajar. Well, Cherilyn wouldn't have forgotten to lock the door. That's one thing being a beauty queen teaches you — there's a lot of weirdos out there. She'd learned to be careful. So Joe says to Teresa, 'Something's wrong,' and he ran inside. So he was the one who found her."

He threw his cigarette down and ground it underfoot.

"I went over there and waited with Joe, waited until the ambulance and cops got there. There was a big puddle of blood on the living room carpet. And there were bloody marks on the wall in the hall. Cherilyn had run down there, I guess. Trying to get away. She was in her bedroom, her old bedroom. Lying in the door to the closet. All her dolls had been knocked off the little shelf I built for them. The vanity was turned over, and the mirror over the dresser was cracked. That big trophy she got for being Miss Grantham, it was all covered with blood. And Cherilyn — Cherilyn . . . her head . . . it was a mess."

He stopped talking.

I put my hand out to him. "I'm so sorry, Mr. Schmidt. Mr. Carnahan was lucky to have a friend like you to wait with him. Were the emergency techs able to do anything for Cherilyn?"

He shook his head miserably. "They said she'd already been dead several hours."

He pulled out a handkerchief and blew his nose. "Cherilyn was a nice girl," he said. "Real down to earth. She had the wife and me over to her new house, just like we were high society like the people the Howards mixed with.

"Here we thought she had everything, and all the time her husband was beating up on her."

He looked at me sharply. "She never told Joe and Teresa about that. Believe you me, Joe and I could have taken care of that jerk better than any shelter could have. I don't care how much money he had."

I ducked my head and smiled at my notebook. Cherilyn had certainly made a conquest in her old neighborhood. Rudy Schmidt's devotion was — well, sweet. I made sure my face was serious when I looked up.

"I guess she should have called on you," I said.

"Yeah. And not only was Cherilyn's husband a jerk, but some of her friends must have been crazy."

"Why do you say that?"

"Well, while Joe and I were waiting for the ambulance and the cops, I took a look around the house. I'm a carpenter, see. I've installed a few locks in my day, and I've been called in to do repairs after people had break-ins. Oh, I didn't touch a thing! I knew not to do that. But I looked at the front door. And at the back door. Checked all the windows."

He paused for dramatic effect, waiting for me to urge him to go on. I complied. "What did you find?"

"Nothing! There was nothing to find. The door hadn't been forced, and the chain was off. The windows weren't jimmied."

He leaned forward and punched a thick finger toward me for emphasis. "Nobody broke in that house. Cherilyn had to have opened the door for them."

I nodded encouragingly, and Rudy Schmidt crossed his arms and looked wise.

"Cherilyn let her killer into the house," he said. "She wouldn't have let a stranger in. The cops better be looking among the people she knew. One of them has to be crazy."

CHAPTER 8

I had been keeping an open mind on the possibility that Cherilyn had committed suicide, but Rudy Schmidt's description of the crime scene pretty well ruled that out. People don't commit suicide by beating themselves in the head.

No, it sounded as if Rudy was right. Cherilyn had let someone into the house, and that person had attacked and killed her.

A dark-haired woman wearing a robe called to Rudy Schmidt from the house then. I thanked him for his information and walked slowly back to the other reporters. A second Channel 9 truck had arrived, and I could see the new crew working the neighbors. I figured I might not have an exclusive on the information Rudy was handing out for very long.

But his information was certainly interesting. Who would Cherilyn have let in?

116

The possibilities were unlimited. Being an intelligent, talented, semi-famous beauty queen married to a wealthy man doesn't exactly make a girl unpopular. Cherilyn had known lots of people. Friends from high school and college, buddies of Paul's, relatives — of Paul's or of her own.

Enid Philpott Howard might have dropped by herself with a club stuffed down the leg of those casual slacks. Then there were fellow church members, coworkers —

I caught my breath. Coworkers. I was only twenty feet from a group of Cherilyn's coworkers. I walked on to the little group of reporters and photogs behind the yellow tape, ready to quiz the Channel 9 crew.

But could I get them to tell me anything? They were my rivals, after all. I decided a frontal attack was the best bet.

"Hey, Bert," I said, "did you work with Cherilyn often?"

All three of the Channel 9 people turned toward me. Bert shifted the camera on his shoulder and frowned. He was an older guy. The hair he pulled back into a ponytail was streaked with gray, and his face was heavily lined. The face looked as if he'd spent years smoking too many cigarettes, and his paunch looked as if he'd spent years drinking too much beer. But he'd always been

117

fairly friendly to me. My only problem with Bert was that he worked for the competition. It made us wary of each other.

Bert apparently was still wary, because he thought carefully before he answered. "I'd worked with Cherilyn a little," he said. "But I'm not the regular cameraman on her show, of course."

"Well, here I am interviewing neighbors, and it finally occurred to me that you all probably knew Cherilyn better than anybody here on the block where she grew up. Most people pal around with the people they work with. Did Cherilyn have close friends at the station?"

Bert's eyes cut left, at the young man reporter beside him. "Jeff knew her pretty well."

I followed Bert's gaze and quickly racked my brain for Jeff's full name. I'd seen him reporting on Channel 9 for a couple of years. He had that slick, television look with a firm jaw and improbably blond hair. He was wearing a nice linen jacket and striped tie, ready to go on the air — from the hips up. From the hips down he wore a faded pair of blue jeans, and he had dirty tennies on his feet.

His name came to me, and I spoke. "Jeff Donovan? I've seen your reports, of course."

Jeff shrugged. "TV pays better in notoriety than in money."

"The news biz is no way to get rich," I said. And that's true. Newspaper pay is terrible, until you get to the top levels, and television news pay is even worse — or so I've been told. Except for an elite group of anchors and national reporters, it's strictly a low-salary field.

"How'd you know Cherilyn?" I said.

"We were at Grantham State together. We were on the same team for a big project in news production class. I lost contact with her, of course, during the year she went to the Miss America Pageant and the year she tried to make it in L.A. Then we got to know each other again when she came to Channel Nine."

"Was this a dating thing?"

Jeff laughed. "If it was, I wouldn't admit it. Or I wouldn't have while Paul was alive. I wouldn't have wanted to mess up Cherilyn's life. Paul was one jealous dude."

"Was that the root of their problems?"

"I have no idea. Cherilyn and I had coffee together now and then — stuff like that. But she didn't tell me about her personal problems. I didn't know she'd gone to the shelter."

"What about this tale that she was doing a

personal investigation of the shelter?"

"First I'd heard of it was this morning, when I read Judy's story. And I noticed the station manager denied it."

"So she hadn't handed that story around the station?"

Bert, Jeff and the sound guy all shook their heads.

"Believe me," Jeff said, "if the words 'shelter' and 'Cherilyn' had come up in the same sentence, the news would have been all over the building before you could say, 'We interrupt this program . . .' After all, the Howards own a big hunk of Grantham. If we'd thought Paul was beating her up — " He whistled. "We might not have put it on the air, but it would have been hot news in the break room."

I nodded. "Then she never mentioned the shelter?"

Bert shook his head, but Jeff looked a little puzzled. "Not in a personal connection," he said. "But something came up about it. The United Way campaign chairman was going to be a guest on Cherilyn's show. The shelter was mentioned as one of the newer agencies while she was prepping for the interview. I remember Cherilyn sort of rolled her eyes.

"I kidded her. Something like, 'What's the

deal? You're in favor of battering women?' And she frowned harder. She said, 'No, I'm definitely against that. But that shelter — they've got somebody over there who's a real piece of work.'"

"She didn't say who?"

Jeff shook his head.

"Did she say anything about Patsy Raymond herself?"

He shook his head again. "No. She didn't mention Patsy. By name."

"Did you think she was talking about P — "

Suddenly all four of the people I was talking to erupted into speech. It was a hubbub. Judy, Jeff, Bert and the other Channel 9 crew member all started babbling at the same time. I looked from one to the other, completely perplexed.

Then Judy's voice rose over the others. "Hi, Patsy!" she said.

I shut my mouth so quickly, I could hear my teeth snap together.

And when I turned around, Patsy Raymond was striding toward me.

I gulped. "Hi, Patsy."

Patsy ignored me and launched an assault on the press.

"I'm sure you've all seen the charges in this morning's *Gazette*," she said, croaking like a frog ready to storm another frog's pond. "I'm referring to the report from Enid Philpott Howard, claiming that I had repeatedly called Paul Howard, challenging him to come to the shelter and attack me."

We all gaped. Her opening was so far from what we were all thinking that for that first minute, none of us seemed to know what she was talking about. The charges made by Mrs. Howard and written up by Judy for that morning's *Gazette* seemed miles away.

Patsy continued on her mental soapbox. "I did not call Paul Howard at all. I certainly did not call him repeatedly. I would never urge someone to violence — against myself or against anyone else."

She drew herself up proudly, and I thought she was going to make a dramatic gesture of some kind. She managed to restrain the gesture to a slight wave of the hand, but she kept on talking.

"I'm here to tell Cherilyn this myself," she said. "And to pledge a complete investigation into this matter."

We all stared — first at Patsy, then at each other — as it dawned collectively on the news media reps present that Patsy knew nothing about Cherilyn's death.

"And if I find out that someone else made calls to Paul Howard . . ." She paused and glared around at the assembled news folks as if we were the guilty parties. Then she continued. "Well, any person who threatens the shelter's operations with improper behavior is going to pay for it."

I realized that Bear Bennington, the *Gazette* photographer, had joined the group. Both he and Bert were taking pictures of Patsy making her announcement. I also realized that Patsy knew what they were doing.

"Now," Patsy said, "I'm going to try to see Cherilyn."

She stepped forward, through the clump of news folks, and came up against the yellow crime scene tape. For a moment I thought she was simply going to push it aside, but she hesitated, looking surprised, then stopped.

I decided it was time some of us stopped gaping and told the woman what was going on. I moved to Patsy's side and spoke.

"Patsy, Cherilyn has been killed."

Patsy's head slowly turned toward me. Her face was blank.

I went on quickly. "Her parents got here about seven this morning. They found her dead."

Patsy reached out and touched the crime scene tape gently. A look of horror began to creep into her face. When she spoke, her whisper was almost impossible to hear.

"Oh, my God! If only I'd been able to talk to her last night."

She turned around, looking panicky, and pushed her way through the news teams. She headed down the block at quick step. I headed after her, and so did Jeff Donovan, trailed by Bert.

"What happened last night, Patsy?" I said.

Patsy shook her head and walked on. She didn't say a word. She walked up to a dark blue Honda, unlocked the door and opened it. I was hard on her heels, but when I glanced around, I realized that Jeff and Bert had fallen behind.

As Patsy was swinging her fanny into the driver's seat, I caught up with her.

"Patsy, what happened?"

"I just made a complete fool of myself," she said.

"You mean you said the wrong thing because you didn't know Cherilyn was dead. That was an innocent mistake. I'm talking about the last thing you said. About if only you'd been able to talk to her last night."

Patsy shook her head.

"Did you call her last night?"

"No. I should have, I guess. But I took that darn sleeping pill and — "

"Did she call you?"

Patsy nodded. "She called the shelter. She left a message. Said I was the only one she'd talk to."

"So you don't know what she wanted?"

Patsy shook her head again, her face completely miserable. "I let her down. She needed help, someone to talk to. She called me, and I'd taken that darn pill . . ." Tears began running down her face. "She was so upset about her mother-in-law, about what she would say and do. I guess she just couldn't face it.

"I let her down! And now she's killed herself."

"But, Patsy — !" I began to speak, ready to tell Patsy the real situation. But she slammed the car door in my face, started the motor in a quick motion and drove off, nearly running over my foot.

I watched her go, frustrated and full of questions.

Why had Cherilyn called the shelter?

When had she done this?

Well, if Patsy wouldn't tell me about Cherilyn's call, maybe the shelter office staff would. I was sure they kept a phone log. Dawn Baumgarner could look it up for me. If it wasn't confidential.

And maybe Dawn could answer another

question, the one that had been bubbling around in my tiny brain since I arrived on the scene.

Why had Cherilyn been alone?

That's not the Southwestern way. When there's been a death in the family, people in our part of the world rally round. We bring food, we offer to sit by the phone, we hover until sometimes we drive the bereaved half mad.

But Cherilyn had apparently been alone in her parents' house.

Why?

Maybe Dawn Baumgarner could tell me that, too.

I walked back to the news media — two more radio reporters had arrived. Jeff and Bert were talking about something else. I decided that Jeff hadn't heard Patsy's final, excited comment. I took Judy aside and told her what I'd heard.

"I thought I'd try to get hold of the business manager," I said. "She might have a log — some way to figure out when and why Cherilyn called."

"Okay." Judy tapped her pager. "Beep me if you find out anything."

I drove to the shelter and pulled to the curb a half-block away. There was never any parking around the shelter, of course. That was one of the reasons the shelter staff and board were so pleased to be moving into a newly remodeled building.

The old building was awful.

It had started as a run-down bungalow in a run-down neighborhood with room for four women. As the community found out more about the shelter, and the shelter began to add more services — such as a crisis line for rape victims — the board was able to buy an adjoining run-down bungalow on each side. The three houses had been linked with donated building materials, which led to some odd architectural effects — they were painted puke green, a large and heavily draped picture window looked out onto a driveway, and the roof lines went every which way.

The three units were surrounded by a high board fence, and roofed walkways connected the buildings. But the staff and the clients sometimes had to go outside for a direct route through the mishmash. That was inconvenient and dangerous.

But the dilapidation was a worse problem. The old houses were about to fall down. The roofs leaked, despite temporary repairs. The windows rattled. The plumbing creaked and dripped, and the electricity was on the verge of being hazardous.

When you consider that people came there because they were in unsafe situations — well, it would be ironic if they took shelter from violence and the place caught fire.

I walked to the front door. At least that seemed secure. I had to identify myself via an intercom system and go through a complicated system of electronically locking and unlocking doors to get into the reception area.

To my surprise, Mary Baker was the official volunteer greeter.

"Do you live here?" I said. "The shelter seems to be working you much too hard for a volunteer. You worked all day yesterday and came back last night."

Mary chuckled. "I'm not a churchgoer, and Sunday mornings are hard shifts to fill. Besides, with the deaths of Paul Howard yesterday and Cherilyn Howard today — well, this isn't a normal day. Don't worry, I don't get pushed around. What can we do for you?"

"Does the shelter keep a phone log?"

"The hot line does."

"I saw Patsy, and she said Cherilyn called the shelter last night. I just wondered what time that happened."

Mary reached for a large ledger on the volunteers' desk. She opened the book to a page halfway back and turned it sideways. "Let's take a look."

I was surprised by her open attitude. The names of victims of violence were probably in this book. And she was letting a representative of the press read it.

"I thought there might be a rule against my seeing the records," I said.

Mary shrugged. "There probably is," she said. "But I'm afraid I've never been big on following the rules."

She craned her neck. "I see your fellow reporter, Judy Connors, called."

"She was trying to reach Patsy."

"But I don't see a call from Cherilyn."

I could feel my forehead furrow. "I wonder how Patsy knew she'd called."

"Oh, she probably left a message on the office answering machine. Go back to Dawn's office. She can tell you."

"Is Dawn here?"

"Yes, we all showed up. Don't know if we thought they'd need us to cope with the emergency or if we were simply curious."

Because of the makeshift arrangements at the shelter, Dawn's office wasn't next door to Patsy's, in the normal place I'd expect to find a secretary-bookkeeper. She was at the back of the building in a room so small, I suspected it had once been a linen closet.

And she wasn't alone. The tall, skinny Joe Bob — still in jeans and boots — was with her.

I paused in the doorway when I saw him.

"Come on in," he said. "I was just telling Dawn what I heard on television. About Cherilyn Howard being killed."

I was glad I didn't have to give Dawn the news. She already looked awful, as if she were about to collapse. There were deep circles under her eyes.

"Oh, Nell, isn't this awful!" she said. "I've been trying to find Patsy, but she's not here, and I don't know where she went. If you need a statement, I'll try to get Mrs. Doubletree."

"Patsy came by the crime scene," I said. "I imagine she'll be back at the office sometime."

"We need her here," Dawn said. She picked up a round brass rabbit that had been sitting on a stack of papers on her desk. "I skipped church to come in. Mama nearly had a fit. But I knew the press would be calling. And the volunteers. But Patsy came earlier than I did. She'd come and gone again by the time I got here. And then this news about Cherilyn . . ." She put the paperweight down and looked miserable. "If Joe Bob hadn't come by — I just don't know what I'd have done."

Joe Bob reached over her desk and patted her arm. His chest seemed to puff out. "Now, honey, I'm going to be here to take care of you. Don't you worry your little head a bit."

I felt slightly nauseous. Mike and I rely on each other, but I couldn't see myself making such an overt plea for his support. And I couldn't see him doing the "little lady" bit. He was considerate and reliable, but he treated me like a grown-up.

I decided I'd better stick to business before the atmosphere made me vomit. "Patsy was out at Cherilyn's parents' house," I said. "She said Cherilyn called her last night and left a message. I just wondered when she called."

Dawn's eyes grew round. "I don't know anything about that!"

"Mary Baker thought the message must have been left on the office answering machine."

Dawn glanced at the corner of her desk. A cheap answering machine sat beside the phone. "Well, if Patsy listened to it, it's been erased," she said.

"Would Patsy have left a note?"

Dawn looked more miserable than ever. "Any information like that would be strictly confidential," she said. "We can't possibly — Oh!"

Her startled exclamation alerted me to the presence of someone behind me. I turned in the narrow doorway and found myself face-to-face with Patsy.

"Hi, Patsy," I said. "I was just trying to find out what time Cherilyn called here last night."

"You can hear the message," Patsy said.

"But, Patsy!" Dawn looked as if she were going to wet her pants. "Those messages are strictly confidential — "

"I really don't give a damn," Patsy said. "The shelter is up to its hips in alligators. The worst thing we can do is try to hide something."

"Hide something? But you've always stressed confidentiality."

"Yes, but this call is going to be evidence in the investigation of two deaths. The police are going to have to listen to it."

"But Nell's not the police!"

"Right," I said. "Patsy, I was simply trying to get an idea of a time frame on all this."

"Then you don't want to know what Cherilyn said?"

"Of course I do! But, frankly, there's no reason you have to tell me."

Patsy pushed by me and went to the desk.

She leaned over and punched a button on the answering machine.

"As far as I'm concerned, you can hear the whole thing," she said.

The answering machine made a series of clicks and beeps. Someone breathed heavily. Then the machine clicked and beeped. It produced static. Click, beep, static, with the occasional deep breath thrown in.

"What is wrong with the damn thing?" Patsy said.

After about two minutes of clicking, beeping and static, with the occasional whir thrown in, the answering machine rewound itself, clicked a couple more times, then cut off.

"Damn!" Patsy said. She punched a button again. The entire process went on again. But no messages were recorded on the tape.

CHAPTER 9

"Hell and damnation!"

Patsy grabbed up the brass rabbit from Dawn's desk and slammed it down on the blotter. The desk lamp rattled and nearly went over, but Joe Bob caught it.

Patsy glared at us, and when she spoke, her voice rasped like fingernails on a blackboard. "Somebody called in three or four times and didn't say anything. All they did was erase Cherilyn's message."

Dawn seemed to shrink against Joe Bob. "Patsy," she said timidly. "Surely it was just an accident — "

"Yeah, sure." Patsy turned and pushed past me. "Four people called in a row and decided not to leave a message. Very likely."

"Patsy!" Dawn scooted around the end of the desk. She and I got all tangled up as she tried to follow Patsy out the door.

"Where are you going?" Dawn said.

Patsy's voice echoed from the hall. "Straight to hell!"

Dawn stopped in the doorway and twisted her hands together. "Oh, dear!" she said. "I wish she wouldn't blaspheme."

Joe Bob put his arm around her shoulder and made cooing noises. I decided it was time to leave. I scrunched past the lovebirds and started back to the reception room.

I wasn't quite ready to follow Patsy straight to hell, but I thought she was right about one thing. Somebody had deliberately erased Cherilyn's message. If the shelter's cheap answering machine worked like the cheap answering machine my roommates and I shared, once you had listened to a message, you had to tell it to "save" or the next message recorded over it. Obviously, after Patsy had listened to Cherilyn's message, the phone had rung on four more occasions and the caller had recorded nothing but heavy breathing. This had effectively erased Cherilyn's message.

I wondered if the police lab could make anything of the tape. That was a possibility, but it would take time. Time to do the lab work, but also time for the lab to get to it. The Grantham police lab and the state crime lab are both notoriously backed up. The DA frequently complains that he can't charge a suspect because the evidence hasn't been analyzed yet. I could write that possibility off for this week.

The whole episode seemed to add to the evidence that there was dirty work afoot at the crossroads.

But I'd come to the shelter seeking two pieces of information. First, the time when Cherilyn called trying to reach Patsy. That was apparently unavailable. The shelter answering machine didn't record the time a message arrived, and Cherilyn's message had been erased, so if she'd included that information in her call — "I'm calling at eleven p.m., and I'll be up until midnight" — it was gone now.

The second piece of information might yet be available. I had wanted to know why Cherilyn was alone at her parents' home. Why no friend had been with her. Why no shelter volunteer had stayed overnight.

And Mary Baker just might know that.

Mary was still out at the reception desk. She'd just punched the buttons that opened the door for a young woman with two little boys.

"Hello," she said. "How was Sunday school?"

One of the little boys — I guessed his age at five — held up a piece of paper. Crayon marks streaked up and down it.

"Oh, let me see, Jeffy," Mary said.

The little boy brought the sheet to her. "Tell me about it," Mary said.

The little boy stammered through an explanation. I didn't understand a word, but Mary hugged him and nodded knowingly as he talked. "Very good, Jeffy," she said. "You're quite an artist."

Jeffy's mom took the two boys down a back hall, reminding them that lunch would be ready soon and they needed to change out of their Sunday-school clothes. I sat down beside Mary's desk, thinking about what a nice person she was. "Grand-motherly" was the adjective I'd use if I had to describe Mary Baker. She looked like a grandmother, with softly curled white hair, bifocals and a frankly plump figure dressed in stretch pants and a comfortable over-blouse. She had a sweet, grandmotherly smile, and I'd never heard her say anything that wasn't kind, encouraging — loving.

So why had a wonderful, empathic person like Mary let a woman whose husband had been shot to death stay alone? Had Cherilyn been delighted that Paul was dead? Had she simply shoved Mary away?

"Tell me about last night, Mary," I said. "You were bucking Cherilyn up when she had to identify Paul's body. How did she take his death?"

"Well, she wasn't particularly sad," Mary said. "But she didn't seem relieved. She seemed to see it as another problem piling on her."

"Because of Enid Philpott Howard?"

"That was one reason, of course. But something else was bothering her."

"What?"

Mary shrugged her grandmotherly shoulders. "I really don't know," she said. "She seemed concerned about the effect on the shelter. I told her not to worry about it. After all, the shelter exists because of the threat of violence. We don't expect things to go smoothly all the time. We certainly don't want violence, but it reinforces our message."

"Did that calm her?"

"A little, I guess. She said she felt well enough to go over to her parents' house."

"Did you take her?"

"No. I brought her back here, so she could get her own car. She said she'd take herself on over there. I offered to find another volunteer to follow her over. But she said I didn't need to do that."

Mary leaned toward me. "Nell, is it true she was over there alone?"

"Yes."

She frowned. "Well, I guess she wanted to be alone then. Because I definitely had the impression her parents were home and would be with her. I'm sure she told me that."

I thought that over for a minute. Had Cherilyn given Mary the brush-off? Had she deliberately gone to her parents' house to be alone?

Who would know? Some friend? Who? Had Cherilyn had friends? What had the other women in the shelter thought of her? The shelter was communal living, of course. Had she had a roommate? Had Cherilyn made any friends in the shelter?

I asked Mary, and she frowned. "I don't think she was particularly close to anyone," she said. "Our clients change every day, of course."

"Could you ask?"

"Sure." Mary smiled again. Why did I feel that her smile wasn't quite as grandmotherly as it had been a few minutes earlier?

She rose from the desk and walked through the wall. At least that was the impression I got. I think the front hall of the original bungalow had an arched entrance to the dining room. The archway had been filled in with what looked like a sheet of plywood, and a door had been installed in the middle. It was a big old door, the kind my great-grandmother's house had, obviously scrounged from some house that was being torn down or remodeled.

Mary walked through this door. I caught a glimpse of the big window, heavily draped, which faced the street. It wasn't really suitable for a dining room. I speculated that it was another donation.

A hubbub of voices sounded as the door opened, then were dimmed as it shut. But when Mary spoke, I could hear her clearly through the wall. "Were any of you friends with Cherilyn Howard?"

More hubbub followed, and in a couple of minutes Mary came back out. "Sorry," she said. "Nobody seems to have done more than pass the time of day with her."

"With who?"

The question had come from another direction, and I turned to see Donna and her two little boys coming from the back hall. They'd all changed out of their Sunday-school clothes and were wearing cut-off jeans.

Mary didn't answer her, so I did. "Cherilyn Howard," I said. "Did you get acquainted with her?"

Donna shook her head. "Sorry. I knew

who she was — thanks to television. But she really kept to herself here. The only person she talked to much was that dark-haired girl. They roomed together, always sat together at dinner. You know, Mary — Bernice? Was that her name?"

"Bernie. She checked out." Mary's voice was abrupt.

"Oh?" Donna sounded surprised. "She was here at dinner last night."

Mary smiled, and again I had that feeling that the smile wasn't quite as sweet as it had been earlier. "Some friends picked her up late in the evening."

Donna shrugged and herded the two little boys through the door into the hubbub. Mary went back to her desk and her telephone.

"Bernie?" I said. "If she was friends with Cherilyn, she might be willing to talk to me."

"Sorry. She's gone."

"Where did she go?"

"That would be confidential, Nell."

"Well, I can understand that she wouldn't want you giving out her phone number. But could you call her and ask her to call me?"

Mary shook her head firmly. "Sorry. I don't know where she went."

"Would the office have a record?"

"No."

The answer was firm, and there was no touch of sweetness in Mary's manner now. I was mystified. I stared at Mary, trying to figure out why her attitude had changed so abruptly.

She smiled then. It seemed to require an effort, but she did it, and her face didn't crack.

"I'm sorry, Nell. Lots of the women who stay here go away with friends, but they don't leave forwarding addresses. I just can't help you."

And that was that.

Mary let me out of the shelter through the double set of electronically controlled doors, and I went to my car. I started the motor, turned on the air conditioner and thought.

If I couldn't get hold of this Bernie, who should I talk to?

The answer was Mike. He didn't know anything about Cherilyn's murder, but it was time for me to shift personas — from reporter to girlfriend. I was worried about him.

When I got to Mike's house, Wilda's car was parked in the drive. That wasn't surprising. Wilda was usually too busy to hover over Mike, but he was her only child. She had shown her concern for his situation the

142

night before, and I didn't think the twelve hours that had elapsed since then would have reassured her.

I used my key and went in quietly, in case Mike was finally asleep. Wilda was sitting at the kitchen table, surrounded by the debris of fast food hamburgers.

"Hi," she said. "I brought you a hamburger. We can put it in the microwave."

Suddenly I realized that I hadn't had either breakfast or lunch. "Sounds great," I said. I put the hamburger in the microwave and set the time for one minute. Then I leaned toward Wilda and spoke quietly. "Did Mike eat anything?"

She nodded. "Yes. Double cheeseburger and medium fries. Plus ice cream. He's getting dressed now."

I got a Diet Coke from the refrigerator and took the hamburger from the microwave. Wilda directed me to the oven for the leftover fries, and I seated myself at a spot where I could see the bedroom door. If we were going to talk about Mike, I didn't want him to creep up and catch us.

"How do you think he's doing?" I asked.

"He's not himself yet." Wilda made a face. "He said the psychologist is due back this afternoon."

I made a face back. We seemed to agree on

that topic. Time to introduce another subject.

"Did Mike tell you about Cherilyn's death?"

"I heard it on the television, but Mike hasn't mentioned it. That's one thing that's bothering me. Mike doesn't seem to care. He's not even curious about the case, and Mike is usually right in the thick of things. Just what happened to her?"

"Sounds like murder." I sketched out what I'd learned from the neighbor. Then I told her about Cherilyn's call to Patsy.

"Nobody knows when the call came in," I said. "In fact, nobody heard the message but Patsy."

"Patsy." Wilda's expression illustrated exasperation. She shook her head. "Patsy lives such a dramatic life."

It was the closest Wilda had ever come to criticizing Patsy. Was this my chance to find out what was really going on over at the shelter?

"Wilda, I haven't covered the shelter very long," I said, "but I keep getting an uneasy feeling about it."

"Oh, it's a great operation, Nell. I feel that it's one of the most worthwhile projects I've ever been involved with. There's no doubt that women are really turning their lives

144

around because of the help the shelter can give them."

Was her voice too bright and enthusiastic?

"I guess it's Patsy herself," I said. "The whole operation seems to revolve around her."

"I know. She's a wonderful leader."

"That's undoubtedly true. But . . ." I bit, chewed, swallowed and thought a minute. "I guess it's like going to a church because you just absolutely love the minister. Then he leaves, and half the congregation starts looking around for another church. The minister's not the church. The congregation's the church. But that doesn't mean the minister's not doing a good job. It's not necessarily his fault that his congregation has the wrong standards." I waved a french fry in the air. "I guess I'm not making any sense."

"I think you're making perfect sense. If you're going to a church only because of the minister, you're going for the wrong reasons. If people support the shelter only because they think Patsy Raymond hung the moon, they're doing it for the wrong reasons. Believe me, the board is well aware of this."

"Is that why I get this uneasy feeling? Are they thinking of letting Patsy go?"

"Oh, no!"

I decided not to say any more. I merely

chewed and wondered if I could outwait Wilda.

She gathered up paper napkins and burger papers, and stuffed them into a paper sack, appearing to concentrate on her task, shooting only the occasional glance toward me.

Finally she sighed. "Nell, the board is in a state of flux. Patsy founded the shelter, of course. The first boards, let's face it, were hand-picked by her. Now that she's getting some foundation money, the shelter's being pressured to expand its base." She tapped herself on the chest. "Like me. As you know, I only went on a year ago."

"Is the new board making Patsy nervous?"

Wilda laughed. "A herd of wild elephants headed up the front walk wouldn't make Patsy nervous. She's completely confident that she knows exactly what's best for the Grantham Women's Shelter."

"And completely oblivious to the new board's opinions?" I took another bite of my hamburger.

"That's overstating the case." Wilda said. "But you can see why I can't say much, Nell. Not for publication. And you can see why Cherilyn's death is a financial disaster for us."

She got up and moved toward the kitchen

146

trash while I was swallowing my bite, so I had time to think about what she had said. What had she meant by that remark?

I gulped my bite down and asked her. "A financial disaster? In what way?"

Wilda's head snapped toward me. "What do you mean, 'a financial disaster'?"

"That's what you said. That Cherilyn's death is a financial disaster to the shelter."

"No, no, no! I didn't say that. I didn't say 'financial.' I said 'potential.' It's a potential disaster! Potential! That was the word I used."

"That's not the word I heard."

Wilda set her jaw firmly. "It's the word I meant. Having someone murdered like that is potentially a public relations disaster for the shelter." She stuffed the lunch debris in the trash can with a vigorous shove, folded her arms, then stared at me. I felt she was daring me to make something of her slip of the tongue.

I decided to let it go. I liked Wilda, and I loved her son. I didn't want to quarrel with her. Besides, I was putting her on the spot. It's not fair for a reporter to cause friends and/or potential relatives heartburn by treating them as news sources.

Besides, I could probably get the information somewhere else.

So I shrugged before I spoke. "Who's the treasurer of the shelter board?"

"Lacy Balke," Wilda said. She said it warily. She could hardly refuse to answer a simple, direct question like that one, but she understood that I was planning to give Lacy the third degree because she herself had made a Freudian slip and allowed me to see that she was worried about the shelter's finances.

CHAPTER 10

If only life would let us worry about one thing at a time.

Wilda was worried about the effect Cherilyn's death would have on the shelter. I was worried about covering the shelter for the *Grantham Gazette.* We were both worried about Mike. And neither of us had time to worry about two things at once.

Mike emerged from the bedroom then, just as calm as he'd been since Paul Howard had died. He had on khakis and a brown polo shirt.

"Did you ever get any sleep?" I asked.

His shrug didn't answer my question. And neither did what he said. "Is there any more ice cream?"

Wilda looked surprised. "Mike! You had an enormous bowl!"

"And I may eat the rest of the carton."

I fought the impulse to jump to my feet

and get a bowl of ice cream for him. I don't usually wait on him, not in his own house, but right at the moment I almost felt that Mike was sick, that he needed special care and service. But I didn't move, and Wilda didn't get up, either. Mike didn't need to be treated like a cripple.

Wilda left while Mike was still scooping ice cream out of the carton, saying she wanted to check on one of the open houses her agents were running that afternoon. She gave Mike a concerned look as she went out the back door. He ignored her.

Mike took his ice cream into the living room and turned on the television, flipping through the channels until he found a baseball game. I threw my lunch trash out, then sat beside him. He didn't exactly ignore me, and he didn't seem hostile. But my presence didn't seem important to him, either.

What could I do to get him out of this passive state? It was unlike Mike. Or should I do anything? Maybe he needed to withdraw for a few days. Maybe his reaction was healthy. I'm no psychologist.

I finally decided I had to say something.

"Guess I'll have to go to the office pretty soon."

Mike didn't respond.

"I'll have to work with Judy. She's covering Cherilyn's death."

"Oh, yeah. Cherilyn's suicide."

"It doesn't sound like suicide. Jim hasn't said yet."

"Jim's out there?"

I almost clapped my hands in excitement. Mike had asked a question!

"Yeah, Jim's there," I said. "That's one thing that makes it sound as if Cherilyn did not kill herself."

As Grantham's most senior detective, Jim Hammond would not be involved in a routine suicide investigation. Mike and I both knew that.

Mike gave a very small nod. "He'll sort it out," he said. He almost visibly settled back into a catatonic state.

I wanted to shake him, slap him, scream at him. Anything to get him out of this inertia. The last time he'd sounded normal was the night before, when he asked me what Jim was keeping from him.

And I had told him. I'd told him that the man he had killed was a member of one of Grantham's most important families. He'd taken it in — said he remembered Paul Howard from YMCA League baseball. After that, nothing.

Maybe I shouldn't have told him. But how could I refuse? For one thing, I wouldn't lie

151

to Mike. For another, he would have found out anyway within a few hours, unless we figured a way to keep him away from newspapers, radio and television.

I was sitting there, fighting the impulse to whack Mike upside the head, when the doorbell rang. Mike didn't move, so I opened the door, and I was relieved to see Dr. Benson. Maybe a psychologist could get through the wall Mike had built around himself.

"Guess I'd better head for the office," I said. I bent to kiss Mike good-bye. "I've got a few things to contribute to the coverage of Cherilyn's death. Any suggestions?"

Mike shrugged. *"Cui bono?"* he said. "In other words, follow the money."

I was driving away before I realized his comment hadn't made sense.

"Cui bono?" That was Latin for "Who benefits?" I'm no Latin scholar, but it's a phrase detectives and lawyers have been known to use. And since it's just two simple words, I understand it.

It does not mean "follow the money." And Mike knew it didn't mean "follow the money."

If it hadn't been so hot, I would have pulled the car over and cried. Mike wasn't making any sense at all.

But if I stopped the car, my air conditioner wouldn't work as well as it does when the car is moving, and I was simply sweltering, so I blinked hard and drove on, down to the *Gazette* office.

Judy had gone to the PD to pick up the routine reports, so I wrote up what we'd gotten from the Channel 9 crew and added a few tidbits from Rudy Schmidt. I didn't go into the gory details — the puddle of blood in the living room, the trail down the hall. That's not *Gazette* style. We don't get graphic. I called it "signs of a struggle."

I zapped my story to Judy's computer file, then I looked up Lacy Balke's listing in the phone book and stared at it. Robert F. Balke. That had to be her. At least she had referred to her husband as "Bob." The address was in a new development. Wilda had told me it was a popular area for young couples who were headed up the socioeconomic ladder. She'd also been the one who told me Lacy Balke's husband was considered a comer in the Grantham banking world.

Could I call Lacy on a Sunday afternoon?

I reviewed what I knew about her. She was an attractive young woman whose career seemed to be shoving her husband up the ladder of success. She was probably volun-

153

teering at the shelter to make points with the Grantham Junior League.

It wasn't as if she kept office hours, I rationalized. I already knew that lots of the volunteers worked at the shelter on Sundays. I punched Lacy's number.

The phone rang a couple of times before she picked it up. After I identified myself, her answer was a hesitant, "Oh. Hi, Nell."

"I'm trying to talk to all the shelter board members," I lied. It was just a coincidence that I was beginning with the treasurer. Sure it was.

I went on. "Are you tied up tomorrow? I can meet any time."

"Just a minute," Lacy said. I heard muffled noises and deduced that she had put her hand over the receiver and was talking to someone. Her husband?

It was less than a minute later when she spoke again. "Nell? If you're working today — how about this afternoon?"

I was astonished, but that fit right in with my plans.

"I can come right over," I said.

"We're on the first cul-de-sac south of Angelfire Road," Lacy said. The phone line went dead.

I waved at Alan, who had just come in to his job on the copy desk, and left, full of curiosity. Why did Lacy and Bob Balke want me to come over? Obviously they had questions for me, just as I did for them.

The Balkes' house looked as if a banker lived there. Conservative. Red brick with white trim. The door was the only thing a bit different. It had been painted a bright blue. A blue ceramic planter on the porch was filled with blooming daisies.

Lacy opened the door before I could touch the doorbell. She invited me in.

"You have a lovely home," I said. "I love the front door. It takes courage to use those bright colors and make it work that well."

Lacy laughed. "In decorating, courage can be a substitute for money, I guess. Come on back to the den. As you see, the living room's not all that livable."

She waved at a room to the right, off the entry hall. It was empty except for a desk made of a door balanced on two filing cabinets.

"We should have put the den furniture in there, rather than leaving the living room until we can afford to get what we want," she said. "But we thought keeping the empty room might goad us into saving faster." She turned and led the way down the hall. "Bob refuses to borrow money or use charge accounts. I'm not sure that's a good sign in a banker." By then we'd reached a big room that was kitchen, dining area and den all together, and Lacy pivoted to face me. "How about some iced tea?"

I agreed to a glass, then walked past the kitchen counter and into the den area to greet a tall, lean and handsome guy with dark hair, a chiseled chin and strong eyebrows. I wondered if he planned to run for office. He and Lacy made a glamorous couple — the type that would appeal to voters.

But Bob's greeting killed that notion. He stood up stiffly, nodded stiffly, shook my hand stiffly and spoke not at all. His manner wasn't rude; it was timid.

Lacy made standard social comments from the kitchen. Bob said nothing. The thought of him working the crowd at a political rally was laughable.

But Wilda had said Bob Balke was regarded as a promising young banker. I decided he must be able to figure compound interest in his head. And I wondered why he had wanted to be present for this interview — which he obviously did, or they wouldn't have invited me over on a Sunday afternoon. Did he want to protect Lacy? Or was there some other reason?

Bob took an easy chair — which he made look decidedly uneasy — I sat on the couch, and Lacy perched on a cushion on the raised brick hearth. I decided I'd better grab control of the interview quickly. I allowed myself one preliminary question.

"Lacy, just how much time do you volunteer to the shelter?"

"Lately, quite a lot. The board assigned me to work with Dawn Baumgarner on the shelter's finances. Dawn — " She broke off. "You know Dawn's degree was social work?"

"She said something about that."

"Yes, Dawn came on the staff as a social worker. Patsy shifted her to administrative assistant after . . . after the board told her she needed more management help. Dawn's expertise is grant writing and making contacts with governmental agencies. She's not really a bookkeeper, but she has to do a lot of financial stuff anyway."

Enough background, I decided. Time for the real questions. "I've picked up a rumor that there's some financial problem at the shelter," I said. "Since you're treasurer, I figured you were the one to ask."

Lacy's eyes flickered toward Bob. "Mrs. Doubletree has to speak for the board," she said.

"But she's out of town," I said. "I hoped you could help me."

She shook her head. "I really can't tell you anything."

"Is there going to be an audit?"

"Not another."

I could see Lacy try to bite the words back, but they'd already slipped out. Aha! They'd already had an audit.

"This audit? Was it a routine audit?"

"Well, sort of."

"Sort of?"

Lacy didn't answer. She looked at Bob again. He didn't speak or appear to signal her in any way. I again wondered why he was there.

I decided to rephrase the question. "I mean, are the shelter's books audited every year?"

Lacy decided she could answer that one. "They will be," she said.

"Does that mean they weren't in the past?"

Lacy contemplated her cuticles. "Well, you know, Nell. That shelter's been pretty much a one-woman show. It's just in the past year or so that we've been trying to get it on a more businesslike basis."

I nodded encouragingly. "Yes, Wilda Svenson hinted at that to me."

"If we want to go for grants — and if we want state funding — things which could put the shelter on a much firmer basis financially . . ." Her voice trailed off.

"Then you've got to play by the rules," I said.

Bob cleared his throat. "Lacy — and Mrs. Svenson and several of the other new board members — are more knowledgeable about standard accounting practice than the original board members were," he said. "They've been trying to get things set up more formally."

I looked at him and nodded encouragingly. But he didn't go on, and I turned back to Lacy. "Does that mean there have been problems?"

"Oh, no! Not problems."

"Then the audit didn't find anything to criticize?"

"Auditors always find something to criticize," Lacy said. "That's their job."

She picked up her iced tea and took a sip before she went on. "Frankly, the board hasn't had time to go over the audit in detail. But we're going to recommend some changes in the operations over there. And you know Patsy — she's wonderful! But she wants to run the shelter her way. It's going to take real diplomacy to work things out."

She smiled again, looking slightly nervous, like a cat that's not sure it should head up a tree. "And I think that's all I'd better say!"

She was definitely antsy about something. I decided I might as well be blunt. "Did the audit find money missing?"

"Oh, no! No money was missing."

"Then what's the problem?"

Lacy darted the slightest little glance at Bob. When I looked at him, his mouth twitched triumphantly, and I felt sure I'd missed the point of Lacy's reply.

"Problem?" Lacy said. "I don't think there is a problem, Nell. It's simply a matter of procedures. And, please don't go to Patsy and tell her the board wants to reorganize the shelter. She's fully aware of the situation, and we won't make any changes without her full cooperation."

Period. End of sentence. Lacy's voice put a firm end to the discussion. I sipped my own iced tea, looked at my notebook and wondered why I was there.

Why had Lacy and Bob wanted me to come over? She must have known I was going to quiz her about the shelter. If she wasn't going to tell me anything, why did she agree to talk to me at all? She could have told me on the telephone if she wasn't going to make any comment. But, no, she'd asked me to come out to her house.

So what was coming next? I decided to push a bit and see what happened.

I flipped my notebook closed decisively and picked up my handbag. "Well, thanks for seeing me," I said. "Bob, it was nice meeting you. I'll get out of your hair now, leave you part of your Sunday afternoon."

Lacy nearly panicked, and Bob almost changed his expression. "Oh, don't run off!" Lacy said. "Finish your tea."

I moved forward in my seat. "The tea is delicious on a miserably hot afternoon like this one, but I mustn't impose on you any further."

"I was hoping we could get a little better acquainted," Lacy said. "Are you a native of Grantham?"

"No, I grew up in Amity," I said. I stood up. I was determined to make 'em beg. "I've lived here nearly three years."

"Please, don't go for a minute," Lacy said. She looked at Bob, and he finally spoke.

"Miss Matthews, I'm sure you know that I'm associated with Grantham National Bank. Some really strange gossip has been going around the bank staff, and Lacy and I thought you might know the truth of the matter."

He still had his timid look.

"As a reporter, I try to deal in facts, not

gossip," I said. "And, as I just told Lacy, I'm not a native of Grantham. A lot of the local gossip simply goes over my head."

"Please, let us talk to you just a minute," Lacy said.

I sat down again. "Just don't tell me anything off the record," I said. "I'm too forgetful to remember what's on and what's off, so I don't work that way."

I tried to look encouraging, but neither of them spoke.

"This must be a really hot rumor," I said. "Is it about Cherilyn? Or Paul?"

"Both, I guess," Lacy said.

There was another silence.

"If we're gossiping," I said, "I've got a question for you all. Did anybody at the bank know that Cherilyn had gone to the shelter?"

"Oh, no!" "Absolutely not!" They both answered that one.

"We had no idea," Bob said.

"Well, something I heard . . ." I recalled Mike starting to say something about Paul Howard. Then he'd refused to explain.

"Had Paul ever been in trouble? For any sort of violence? Fighting?"

Bob's deadpan cracked slightly. "It was pretty well hushed up, according to what I heard at the bank," he said. "He was arrested in the bar at the Lincoln Avenue Ramada three or four years ago."

"How'd he get off?"

"I have no idea just what happened. But no charges were ever filed."

"Fighting?"

"He punched a guy. This was before he married Cherilyn, of course."

Lacy leaned forward eagerly. "After the arrest — or so we were told — he went into treatment for alcoholism."

I nodded. "They probably paid off the guy, so he wouldn't file charges. Then, if Paul agreed to seek treatment, the cops would probably let the case drop. But his mom, or somebody, must have really buttoned it up. It's hard to keep cops from talking about things like that."

"We all thought he'd straightened up," Bob said. "A couple of months after that, he started dating Cherilyn. He began to be a lot easier to work with."

"What kind of a guy was he?"

"Oh, not bad. The old-timers at the bank tell me he was alternately spoiled and disciplined when he was growing up. You know, Mrs. Howard tried to keep from being too lenient with him, but it's hard — and his father was an alcoholic. They say it's inherited."

"Had he been drinking recently?"

Bob's jaw clenched. I'd brought him back to the present, and he didn't want to be here. "I hadn't heard that he had."

I decided it was time to get down to business. "Okay, Bob, you hadn't heard that Paul was drinking again, and you hadn't heard that he'd been beating his wife. So, what had you heard?"

He took a deep breath, then spoke. "It was on our doorstep this morning. A picture. That's what started the talk."

"May I see the picture?"

Bob looked at Lacy. Lacy looked at Bob.

"Look," I said. "It's touching to see a couple so close, they communicate without speaking, the way you two do. But you wanted to consult me about some gossip, and now you won't tell me what it is. Let me see the picture."

Lacy went to a desk in the corner and brought back an ordinary white, legal-sized envelope.

"It was tucked into the door when I went out to get the paper," she said.

I opened the envelope and found a piece of $8^{11}/_{42}$-by-$11^{11}/_{42}$ paper, folded like a letter. I unfolded the top flap and found a murky, black-and-white picture of a couple. The dot pattern showed that it had been copied from a publication of some sort. Maybe a year-book.

The people in it could have been anybody. I had to read the caption to find its significance.

"During the Senior Sneak to the Grantham-OU football game, Cherilyn Carnahan had a reunion with an old friend, former CHS football great Mike Svenson."

CHAPTER 11

What the hell else was going to happen?

And how could it all be happening to Mike?

I stared at the picture dumbly. It was a picture of the man I planned to marry with a beautiful woman. But I didn't feel jealous. Mike hasn't been described as a "former Central High football great" since he was 22, and he's now 32. He'd never mentioned knowing Cherilyn, but if they'd gone to Grantham Central a few years apart, it was entirely possible that they'd run into each other. Romantically, the picture was a washout. Whatever Cherilyn had been to Mike, she was now ancient history.

But she was also dead. What did the picture have to do with that fact?

I looked at Lacy, then at Bob. "Is this supposed to prove something? I knew that Mike and Cherilyn grew up only a mile apart. So they went to the same high school. Even the cutline on this picture indicates that they weren't at Central at the same time."

"Look at the rest of the sheet," Lacy said.

I unfolded the final third of the page. Scrawling letters were hand-printed across the bottom. I read them twice before I got them to make sense.

"Where did Mike Svenson get that pistol?"

The room rocked for a minute. The picture of Mike with Cherilyn was snide. But the words were vicious.

I said the word out loud. "Vicious. This is vicious." I looked at Bob, and I hoped my voice sounded firm and confident.

"The picture — "

"The picture is Mike and Cherilyn. That's true. But look at the hair. Mike hasn't had hair that long since he became a cop. And Cherilyn's dress is pretty dated, too. I wore one of those big collars to my high school graduation."

Lacy was nodding. "I noticed that."

"Mike has never mentioned that he knew Cherilyn, but Grantham is a small town inside a city of a third of a million inhabitants. Everybody tends to know everybody."

"The part about the pistol — " Bob's voice was timid again.

"That's really rotten, because it's related to the truth without being true," I said. "It's a part of the police investigation, and when the facts are clear, it will appear in the *Gazette.*"

Neither Lacy nor Bob said anything, and I went on, covering the story of the pistol beginning with the reason Mike didn't have his own pistol — I had accidentally hidden it from him — to how Mike had found another and ending with the fact that I was sure Jim Hammond would find out who had brought it to the shelter.

Bob pursed his lips, and Lacy leaned forward earnestly. "Nell, I don't know Mike all that well," she said, "but he seems like an awfully nice guy."

"He is."

"But this" — she pointed at the sheet of paper I still held — "this is clearly saying that he was involved with Cherilyn somehow."

"Yes, and it goes beyond that. It hints that Paul's death was an ambush, rather than a case of self-defense. Which I can testify was the true situation. I think this sheet should go straight to Jim Hammond, the detective in charge of the investigation into Cherilyn's death."

"Of course," Lacy said. "He can have our copy."

It took a minute for the implications to sink in. "Your copy? How many copies are there?"

"We know of four," Bob answered.

"Oh, no! Who got them?"

"Bank officers. And the executive director of the Howard Foundation."

"Not shelter board members?"

"No," Lacy said. "As far as we know, they went to bank people."

"How about Enid Howard?"

Bob kept his deadpan. "I don't know if she got one or not. I haven't called anybody who would know."

"Who would know the names and addresses of bank officials?"

"Anybody. Anybody who can read." Lacy pointed at the Sunday *Gazette*, piled up on the table at the end of the room. "The bank ran an ad with pictures of most of the officers today. Most of them are in the phone book."

I stared at the photocopy in my hand and at the message scrawled across the bottom of the page. I was willing to bet any amount of money that Enid Philpott Howard had a photocopy of this piece of nastiness and at that very moment was conferring with her attorneys about it.

It seemed that everything was stacking up

against Mike. And I wasn't helping the situation.

"I shouldn't have touched this," I said. "There might have been fingerprints on it."

I asked Lacy and Bob a few more questions. How had the photocopy been delivered? Answer: It was tucked inside the storm door. Anybody could have come up on the porch at dawn and stuck it in. Who else got one? They told me the names, and I wrote them down.

I recommended that they call the detective bureau, and I left.

I was convinced that Jim Hammond should be told about the photocopy, and I decided to try to find him. I'd go to wherever he was, I decided, then I'd wait until he had time to talk to me. Jim would know what to do.

Not that Mike was in any danger of being arrested. Jim wasn't going to arrest somebody because of an anonymous photocopy. No responsible law official would do that. Besides, Jim knew Mike, and he hadn't even hinted that he didn't think Mike's story — corroborated by both Patsy and me — didn't make perfect sense.

But a rumor that Mike had been involved with Cherilyn — it was the kind of thing

170

people love to believe, even if it's completely untrue.

The *Gazette* office was between the Balkes' house and the Carnahans' house, so I stopped in there to use the phone, trying to locate Jim Hammond. There was no sense chasing out to the scene of Cherilyn's death if Jim had already left there.

Peaches Atkins, the secretary in the detective bureau, was off on the weekend, as usual, but she had obviously trained her stand-in. The woman who answered gave me an answer as curt as any Peaches would have supplied. And she didn't identify herself.

"Captain Hammond is interviewing Mrs. Howard's parents," she said. "He won't have time to talk to the press today." Slam. End of conversation.

Apparently Jim was still out at the crime scene. I gathered up my notebook and started for the back door. But Alan waved at me, and I stopped.

I haven't gotten used to having a father. Oh, I had Alan — then known as "Daddy" — until I was eight. He disappeared from my life because of problems that I had only recently learned about. My grandfather had filled in for the next few years, until he died. After that I had managed without a father

171

figure until a few months earlier, when Alan and I had found each other.

Our relationship was still tentative. We got together for coffee or dinner several times a week. Certainly we hadn't thought of sharing a domicile. And it rarely occurred to me to go to Alan for advice.

But I felt happy when he waved at me, and I willingly sidetracked across the *Gazette* newsroom to speak to him.

"How's Mike?" he said.

"Not too good. And the situation seems to be getting worse."

Alan frowned and turned to Jack Hardy, who was on the city desk that night. "I'm going to take a break," he said.

Jack nodded, and Alan and I left the newsroom and headed downstairs to the first-floor break room, the one with all the junk food machines. On the way down, I filled Alan in on the day's events and Mike's lack of reaction to them. By the time I got to the photocopies being passed around to officers of Grantham National Bank, we were sitting at a Formica-topped table and Alan had a cigarette going.

"I'm willing to bet that Enid Philpott Howard got a similar photocopy," I said.

Alan frowned. "I wouldn't worry about it. If Jim Hammond is in charge of the case — "

172

"I don't have any serious worry that Mike is going to get in legal trouble over all this. But looking ahead — oh, Alan, you know Mike is ambitious. Fifteen years from now — or twenty — he'd like to be chief. I don't mean that he politics around, trying to get promotions — in fact, he has a lot of contempt for people who rely on that sort of finagling, instead of working hard. But a rumor like this could ruin everything for him, even if the rumor is completely unfounded."

"I'm sure Jim will do a complete investigation."

"I hope he understands what's going on, because I don't. Has Jim given Judy a statement?"

"Very brief. Cherilyn's dead, and it's definitely homicide. That's all she got. How about you? What angle are you working on?"

"I cover non-profits, remember? I'm trying to stay out of the homicide coverage. I just cover the shelter."

I'm sure my disgust showed, because Alan grinned and patted my hand. "I remember. And I remember why you got the job."

Non-profit organizations are not usually hot news, and this wasn't a beat I'd wanted. I'd spent seven years on the violence beat — police, sheriff's department and fires. Then

I'd fallen hard for Mike Svenson, a cop. This forced me to ask for a new assignment, since the *Gazette* wisely has a policy that reporters can't cover topics or people they're personally involved with.

I had spent six months as an assistant copy editor. And when I went back to being a reporter, I'd been assigned to non-profits.

I'd been hoping for city hall or the courthouse. After seven years spent chasing fires and killers, the Salvation Army, the Red Cross and the Cancer Society sure seemed like a comedown. I'd felt as if I'd been demoted. Writing up fund-raisers and doing features on self-righteous philanthropists and the grateful needy had seemed a dull prospect.

But the city editor, Ruth Borah, took me aside and told me the bosses did not want puff pieces. In fact, she said, the editors were concerned that the *Gazette* hadn't been treating non-profits tough enough. Nationally, there had been a number of scandals about non-profit organizations, and if something happened in Grantham, we didn't want to find out about it from television.

Ruth didn't want me to take the do-good groups at their face values. She didn't want me to run them down, but she did want to make sure they were actually doing good.

"Cover them as if they were governmental agencies," she had said. "Find out how much of their budgets go to administration and how much actually help their clients. Find out how much those budgets are. Find out who makes the decisions, who picks the board members, who spends the money. It's the public's money, remember."

So I'd started on a series on volunteerism, which gave me an excuse to take an in-depth look at four or five different agencies. The shelter had been the first, and right away I'd run into petite, peppy Patsy and her one-woman show.

Alan patted my hand. "Ruth is counting on you to take a hard look at the agencies on your beat, including the Grantham Women's Shelter."

"I knew non-profits would be hard to dig facts out of — their budgets aren't approved by an elected body, the way the police or the park department are. But I hadn't counted on running into murder."

"Then Cherilyn's death has to be connected to that crazy attack by Paul Howard?"

"What else can it be?"

"Prove it to me." He took a drag from his cigarette and put on his devil's advocate expression.

I felt annoyed. The whole situation was plain as day, and Alan knew that. But maybe he was right. Maybe I needed to go through it, step by step. I sighed and started.

"First," I said, "according to Enid P. Howard, someone had been calling her son from the shelter's phone, claiming to be Patsy. In retaliation, Paul goes to the shelter and tries to kill Patsy. In a series of events which no one could have predicted, Mike shoots Paul. With Paul dead, Cherilyn leaves the shelter and goes to her parents' house. Someone follows her there. She apparently lets that person in. He or she kills her. Then the killer puts these photocopies incriminating Mike in the doors of people who will be in a position to make trouble for Mike."

"Okay. That's clear. Now, why did each of these things happen? First, the phone calls."

"I can't imagine. All they would do is cause trouble for the shelter and for Patsy."

"Okay. We put that one aside. The next question is, who would have known Cherilyn had gone to her parents' house?"

"Anybody connected with the shelter could have. Anybody who was at the shelter Saturday afternoon or evening."

"Or anybody who talked to one of those people."

"Yes. Word spreads fast."

176

Alan nodded. "Now, who would Cherilyn have let into the house?"

"Hundreds of people! Friends, relatives, neighbors — "

"And people she'd known in the shelter."

"Yes. Among others."

"And who would have known about the yearbook with Mike and Cherilyn's picture in it? Who would have had access to such a yearbook?"

"Five or six hundred people who graduated from Grantham Central with Cherilyn."

Alan grinned. "Plus five or six hundred who graduated the year after."

"And hundreds of teachers, librarians, spouses — anybody who could have seen such a yearbook."

"Yeah, but I'd bet on someone in Cherilyn's class or the class right after it." He wagged a finger at me. "But none of this is your business."

"I know. It's Jim Hammond's case, and Judy's story, and my story is the shelter. In fact, that's the reason I went to see Lacy and Bob Balke. To ask questions about the shelter's finances. And both Lacy and Wilda make me think there's some financial problem over there, more by what they won't say than by what they will."

"So, what do you do next?"

"Next I make sure Jim Hammond knows about that photocopy. Second, I get ready to quiz Patsy Raymond early tomorrow." Then I gasped. "Oh, I forgot! Tomorrow is moving day."

Alan looked blank.

"For the shelter," I said. "Tomorrow was supposed to be the day when they moved into the new building. I made a photo assignment for ten a.m. But now — I wonder if the move's still on."

Alan smiled and snubbed out his cigarette. "Guess I'd better get back to work. I don't suppose it would do any good to tell you to go get a good night's sleep."

"I will. Just as soon as I check on the move and get hold of Jim Hammond."

He walked me to the back door and gave me a hug. "Take care, kid," he said. "Don't find out too much. Promise me you'll let Jim handle the murder part."

I promised. Then I went by the Carnahan house. Jim was still inside, but a patrolman agreed to ask Boone Thompson to come out and talk to me. I told him about the photocopy, and he said that Bob Balke had already left a message, and that he'd be sure somebody got in touch with him right away.

Then I stopped at a pay phone — I keep meaning to get a cell phone, but I haven't

178

had time to shop for one — and called the shelter's hot line. I identified myself to the volunteer who answered.

"Is the move still on?"

"I really have no idea," the volunteer said. She had no interest, either, I realized. Her shift ended at midnight. What happened tomorrow was someone else's problem.

I called Patsy's daughter, but there was no answer.

So, just in case, I drove by the new shelter. I parked on the side street and peeked through the gate in the high wooden fence that surrounded the parking lot. I could catch just a glimpse of Patsy's red car, the one with the antiviolence bumper sticker. It was one of three or four cars and a couple of pickups parked in the lot.

I walked around the building to the front door and punched the bell. Nothing happened until I had punched it three times. Then the intercom over my head crackled, and a voice said, "Yes?"

"It's Nell Matthews. From the *Gazette*. I need to talk to Patsy."

"Oh!" The electronic voice sounded faint, but a loud buzz sounded, and the door opened. I went through it, and it closed behind me. I found myself imprisoned in a closet, a closet with a door at each end and a video camera mounted over my head. I had to wait for thirty seconds before another buzz sounded, and the door in front of me opened. Through it I found the reception area. Like the one in the old shelter, it was a tiny room, with closed doors in three walls.

Its only furniture was a desk, a desk chair and two straight chairs of the type that might be found in a poorly-furnished dentist's office.

Joe Bob Zimmerman was standing behind the desk holding a hammer. Dawn was beside him.

"Praise the Lord," he said. "I was praying that you'd come by. Help me convince this silly little Dawn that she's got to tell the police she's being threatened."

CHAPTER 12

"Threats?" I said. "What are you talking about?"

Dawn was standing behind Joe Bob, wearing another one of her white blouse and dark skirt outfits. "We get threats all the time," she said meekly.

"But you don't have two killings all the time," Joe Bob said. "You should tell the police. Shouldn't she, Miss Matthews?"

"I don't want to decide anything for Dawn," I said. "What kind of threats do you get 'all the time'?"

"Oh, you know. 'You're hiding my wife over there, and I want to see her — or else.' That kind of thing. We don't worry about it unless they get real specific. And unless they seem to know where we are."

"Are these new threats different?"

"Well, they seemed to know who I was," Dawn said. "But that's stupid. I'm nobody around here."

"What did they say?"

She twisted her hands together. "Oh, a bunch of nonsense about I was helping women get away from their families. I keep these people on my prayer list. And I know that God is watching over me."

"God may well disapprove of somebody coming after you with a gun, but He might not send a lightning bolt to stop the bullet, Dawn. You do have to remember that Cherilyn's killer is on the loose. If he thought you knew something — "

"I don't! I don't know anything! I barely spoke to Cherilyn Howard while she was here. Patsy dealt with her. Personally."

I moved closer and dropped my voice. "How about those mysterious phone calls?"

"Phone calls?" Dawn twisted her hands again.

"You know. The ones Mrs. Howard claims her son got from Patsy."

"I don't know anything about that. I can't believe Patsy would do anything like that. She's not dumb!"

Dawn gathered up some file folders from the desk. "And I've got to get back to my filing," she said. "If you need Patsy, she's back in the west wing."

Dawn reached under the desk and a

buzzer sounded. She went through the inner door and into the office.

Joe Bob twirled his hammer nervously. "Maybe I should insist that Dawn get out of here," he said.

His attitude annoyed me.

"Dawn has to decide for herself," I said. "If she doesn't like it here, if there's too much stress, she could always get a job someplace else."

"She's afraid Patsy would ruin her chances anywhere else."

"Why?"

"Jealousy, maybe? I don't know. Patsy's not a real professional, you know. She's gets a lot of things done, but she just walked into this shelter deal. Dawn has the degrees, bachelor's and master's in social work. She really runs the place."

I looked at him narrowly. He seemed perfectly sincere, and, in a sense, I saw his point. Dawn was probably the person who kept the shelter going on an everyday basis. But she was not making policy decisions.

Patsy really decided how the Grantham Women's Shelter functioned, I thought. Her enthusiasm provided the momentum to keep the agency moving. Dawn just typed the letters and made the bookkeeping entries. She didn't "run the place."

I decided Joe Bob's opinion was based on his admiration for Dawn, rather than the real situation. And I wondered just what he saw in her. "Mousy" was a one-word description of Dawn. Which doesn't mean she wasn't a nice person. She was the type of woman who could have been pretty, if she'd bothered to fix herself up; who could have been interesting company, if she had the nerve to speak out; who could have been a lot of fun, if she had just forgotten to be afraid of everything and let herself go.

Maybe Joe Bob could bring out Dawn's potential. She seemed to be highly appreciative of his attentions, and Joe Bob wasn't unattractive. He paraded his religion too much for my taste. But he seemed to have a pleasant personality, even if he did overdo the chivalry shtick. He wasn't repulsive physically, and he owned his own business, which indicated that he had something on the ball. He had a lot going for him.

I moved toward the door into the shelter's inner reaches. "Dawn's fortunate to have a friend like you to rely on," I said.

I'd meant that as a comment that would close our conversation, but Joe Bob took it as an invitation to continue.

"Oh, no! I'm the one who's been blessed,"

he said. "I need someone like Dawn in my life."

"Then I'm glad you were lucky enough to find each other."

"There was no luck about it. It's all part of God's plan."

That made me pause. God as a celestial matchmaker? I started to ask how Joe Bob had uncovered that particular part of God's plan, then decided not to. He was obviously ready to "testify." I didn't particularly want to hear it.

"How wonderful," I said. "Joe Bob, could you open that inner door for me?"

Instead of punching the button for the inner door, Joe Bob kept talking.

"A person like me doesn't deserve a wonderful woman like Dawn," he said. "I've been a terrible sinner. Women, drinking, partying — I admit it. It broke up my first marriage. But that pursuit of pleasure never brings true happiness, Miss Matthews."

"I'm sure that's true," I said.

"I was an empty vessel, searching for Living Water to fill the void in my life."

"And Dawn does this?"

"The Lord does this. I gave my life to the Lord a year ago."

"I'm sure your decision has given you real fulfillment."

"Yes, my life became fuller and richer. But there was still a void." He leaned across the little reception table and spoke seriously. "It is not good that the man should be alone; I will make him an help meet for him," he said. "Genesis 1:18."

"And God picked out Dawn for you?"

"I believe that He did, Miss Matthews. She was an answer to my prayers from the first time we met."

"That's wonderful!" I smiled. It was easy to smile at Joe Bob. And I don't mean smirk. Although I didn't share his simplistic outlook on life and religion, I respected its meaning to him. "Did you meet Dawn at church?"

"No. Here at the shelter. I went by to pick up the specs for the remodeling project. And there she was, sitting in that old office. She escorted me over here so I could look at this building. I was knocked clean in a heap. Of course, it was several months before I could get up the nerve to ask her out. We've only been seeing each other a few weeks."

"That's a nice story!"

Joe Bob nodded. "She's everything that I admire. A good Christian, takes care of her mother and helps her with her little home-based business, works here at the shelter helping people who really need help. It was just like the Lord drew me to her."

I was beginning to wonder how I was going to get away from Joe Bob. He had me trapped. I wanted to figure out a polite way to tell him I'd heard enough of his testimony and wanted him to release me. I snatched at his final sentence.

"Did the Lord draw you into working on the shelter project?"

Joe Bob looked taken aback. "Not exactly," he said. "I'd done some remodeling on rent houses owned by Wilda Svenson, and she told me about the renovation project. So I bid on it."

"Well, you've certainly turned out to be a blessing for the Grantham Women's Shelter," I said. "Did you install this electronic entry system?"

"Well, no. Four-A was our electrical sub." Then he smiled. "You want me to open the door!"

I smiled back. Good. He wasn't angry at having me interrupt his testimony.

He felt under the lip of the desk and a buzzer sounded. Then he stepped over to the inner door and opened it for me. "Sorry. My life has made such a change that I can't help talking about it."

"I admire that, Joe Bob. I'm sorry my concerns are more worldly right now. I do want to catch Patsy."

"Sure! I understand." As I passed him to enter the door, he leaned close and almost whispered, "Don't tell Patsy what I said about Dawn running the place."

"I won't."

His voice grew even lower. "Patsy may be close to leaving, you know."

Then he held the hammer to his lips in an exaggerated "shhh" and let the door shut between us.

I was tempted to turn back and ask him what he was talking about. So far two board members, Wilda and Lacy, had both told me Patsy was in no danger of losing her job. Had Job Bob heard something different?

But the door shut with a click, and I turned to survey the interior of the new shelter. I'd entered a spacious reception room. It looked attractive and homey, though I knew the furnishings had been selected to stand up to hard use by children.

One of the pieces of advice shelter workers give clients who are thinking of leaving an abusive situation is to take their children. Kids may be in danger if they're left behind. And leaving them may be construed as abandonment; the fleeing mother may never get them back. So the shelter houses a lot of kids.

The office where we'd been working the day before was through a door on the left. I shuddered as I remembered sitting there in an office chair, with blood on my shoes, as we waited to make our statements. But I gritted my teeth and put my head through the door to the office. Mary Baker was winding up the cord to a carpet cleaning machine.

"Mary! Don't they ever let you go home?"

A smile crinkled up her grandmotherly face. "I think I live here, Nell. But it won't need such long hours as soon as the move is over."

"Is the move still on for tomorrow?"

"Oh, yes."

"What about the kitchen?"

"Wilda sent a cleaning crew over. At her own expense! We'd never function without people like her. And she brushes off any thanks."

"Wilda doesn't undertake something like the shelter board halfheartedly," I said.

I watched Mary winding the electrical cord around the carpet cleaner, and I wondered about her. One of the privileges of being a reporter is that you're certified as nosy. So I pulled out my notebook.

"Mary, you know that I'm working on a story about volunteerism." She nodded, and

I went on. "I asked you once why you volunteered at the shelter, and your answer was a little vague. Can I ask you again?"

"Sure. But my answer's likely to be just as vague. I don't really have a reason except that I enjoy it."

"What do you enjoy? Surely not cleaning carpets."

"Of course, the action of cleaning carpets is not a lot of fun. But if you see it as a piece of the larger picture of making a safe and comfortable place for women and children who need one — then it's satisfying."

"What got you interested in women and children who need a safe and comfortable place?"

She smiled her grandmotherly smile. "I read about the shelter in the *Gazette*. And I read about the problem in *Time* magazine. And I read a novel about an abused wife."

"Did Patsy influence you?"

"Not directly. I like Patsy, of course. But I was sold on the need for a shelter before I ran into her."

"I see. How does your family feel about all the time you spend down here."

"They're glad it keeps me off the street! My children are grown and have their own homes. I'm a widow. I need something to keep me from feeling sorry for myself. This does it."

"Then you have no personal reason? No personal experience with spousal abuse."

"Like Patsy? No, I was never an abused wife. My husband was an awful nice guy. He volunteered here, too, before he died three years ago."

She laced the heavy cord for the carpet cleaner in a twist that would have kept an ocean liner tied to the dock. "No, I just come for my own pleasure. But maybe I have a sick reason, too."

"A sick reason? What do you mean?"

"I'm not proud of it. But I find it rather exciting to be around people who are threatened, who have faced violence. Even horrible events like yesterday's are fascinating, if not pleasurable! I guess that I'm like people who stop to look at accidents, or who cluster around murder scenes. Being on the periphery of violence is exciting to me. On the one hand I'm truly sorry for the shelter's clients, and I want to help them. On the other, I'm fascinated by the terrible events that drove them here."

She thumped the carpet cleaner firmly. "So you see that I'm no saint. I'm basically a ghoul. I suppose you can't understand that."

"I understand it very well," I said. "I spent five years as a crime reporter! I loved the excitement on that beat."

We both laughed.

"Thanks for the info, fellow ghoul," I said.

"That's fine. And I need some information from you."

"Sure."

"Did you tell the detectives about Bernie?"

I had to stop and think. "Bernie? Do you mean the woman who had been friendly with Cherilyn?"

"Yes, the one who checked out the night Paul Howard was killed."

"You said no one knew where she went. I decided I couldn't get hold of her, so I never gave her another thought. Did the detectives ask about her?"

"They were just trying to find her. Some man named August."

"Sergeant August? Sorry. I don't know anything about the investigation. You're sure she can't be reached?"

"I'm sure."

Mary's voice brooked no argument. I said good-bye, turned and crossed the reception room. I had entered the hall leading to the bedrooms before I remembered who Sergeant August was.

"Missing persons," I said aloud. "August is assigned to missing persons."

I opened my notebook to the back page, where I keep a to-do list for reference when I get back to the office. I wrote "Missing persons? August? Bernie?" Then I snapped the notebook shut and went back to the bedroom wing.

I'd prowled around the new shelter several times since I took over the non-profit beat, getting ready to write a story about its opening, a feature scheduled to run on Tuesday's Metro page. We wouldn't put the address in the paper, of course, but we'd run interior shots and would describe the new facility.

As a former nursing home, the building had been changed into a shelter with a minimal amount of work. The dining room and largest reception area were merely repainted in a soft cream color. Hallways led to the bedroom wings. Each bedroom had a bath, in contrast to the old shelter's lack of facilities, and the clients no longer had to stand in line, taking turns using residential-type bathrooms.

Each bedroom had been repainted — the shelter must have bought a tanker-load of that cream paint — and was furnished either with twin beds or with bunk beds and a twin. New mattresses and springs had been purchased, I knew, but as I glanced in the open doors, I saw every type of furniture. The shelter had a special drive, asking Grantham residents to donate unused dressers, mirrors, chests of drawers, bedside tables and desks. When one of our roommates moved out, Martha and I had donated her dresser and headboard.

As I walked from room to room, I concluded that many had also given chairs. The place looked like a secondhand store.

More accurately, it looked like my grandmother's house. By the time she died, Gran had accumulated furniture over a period of nearly sixty years. And she had inherited some that was even older. Every style, shape, color and size was scrambled together in the house where I grew up. The shelter had the same atmosphere.

But nowhere in this mishmash did I find Patsy. Was I in the wrong wing?

"Patsy! Are you here?" I called.

A dark head popped out of a door at the end of the hall, and Patsy's voice croaked. "Hi, Nell! I'm here in the storage room."

I walked back and found Patsy in a room filled with clothes. Dresses, slacks, shirts and children's clothing hung on long racks. Shelves along the walls held underwear and shoes. Most of it was used, of course. The shelter collects and sorts cast-off clothing to provide emergency wardrobes for clients. The room was a vivid reminder that women often leave everything they own behind when they come to the shelter.

"How's Mike?" Patsy asked.

"Fair," I said. "How are you?"

"Shaky. But I'm making it. How about you?"

"Oh, I'm fine. What are you doing?"

Patsy crossed the hall and opened the door to a room that was crammed with eight baby cribs. Rollaway beds and cots, folded up, were against one wall.

"I'm trying to get the rooms ready," Patsy said. "We have four crib babies in the shelter right now." She tugged at a crib, but its leg was caught behind the crib next to it.

"Here. Let me help," I said.

It took us a couple of minutes to untangle the baby beds. Then Patsy pulled the crib out the door. "It's sure nice to have these extra-wide doors," she said. "At the old shelter, we had to take the beds apart to move them from place to place."

"Then the move is still on?"

"Right. The trucks are supposed to be at the old building at nine a.m."

"And I'll have a photographer there at ten a.m."

"No pictures of the clients!"

"I know, I know! I thought it would be a good opportunity to get some shots of the board members and volunteers. Anybody you'd like to see get a little credit?"

"Let's see. Dorothy Doubletrce is out of town. Her mother's having cancer surgery, and she had to go to California. And Lacy Balke called and said she'd be late. I thought it might be something about her husband's job. I guess he's having to clear up the mess Paul Howard left."

"What kind of mess was that?"

"Maybe it's just routine. Paul was trust officer, she said, and Bob is an assistant trust officer. I guess the bank does a complete audit when someone dies."

Patsy whirled the bed around and started through the door of one of the bedrooms. "Just between you and me," she said, "Lacy seems pretty excited. I wondered if Bob hadn't gotten the word that he was getting Paul's job. Moving up to trust officer."

I hadn't thought about the bank angle of Paul Howard's life. I wondered if Paul had done any actual work at Grantham National. Or had Bob Balke been taking care of business right along? Who else had benefited by Paul's death?

Then I reminded myself that Paul was an

accidental victim in all this. It didn't matter who benefited from his death. He wasn't supposed to die. He had tried to kill Patsy, because of the phone calls which someone had made claiming to be her. Mike had killed him.

That knowledge, and my knowledge of how the death had affected Mike, turned my stomach into a lump of lead. I quickly finished up with Patsy — we decided to try to get Mary Baker in a picture — and left the new shelter. I needed to check in on Mike.

I was concentrating on getting over to Mike's house as quickly as possible. I walked swiftly to my car, unlocked the door, opened it and nearly jumped out of my skin as an ungodly racket broke out.

CHAPTER 13

I jumped about four feet off the ground, and before I landed, I saw what had made the noise.

It had been produced by a large plastic bag loosely filled with aluminum cans and light bulbs.

I examined how it had been fastened to my car. Someone had stuffed the bag — it had once held twenty pounds of potatoes — with cans and light bulbs. A piece of heavy string had been tied to the sack. The cans and bulbs had been stuffed under my car. The string had been taped to the lower outside corner of the driver's side door with ordinary black electrician's tape.

When I swung the car door open vigorously, the string dragged the bag out from under the car. And all hell broke loose. On the quiet side street, on an afternoon so hot that everyone was inside under the air conditioning, the aluminum cans had sounded like a car wreck right under my feet. A couple of the light bulbs had popped, sounding like gunshots.

My heart was still pounding as I picked up the bag and ripped the electrician's tape off the car door.

"Stupid joke!" I said. I felt like a fool. The only good thing was that nobody had seen me.

I looked around to see if the shelter had an outside trash can. I didn't find one, but I did see something else. A piece of paper was tucked under my windshield wiper.

I pulled it out. It was a piece of $8^{11}/_{42}$-by-$11^{11}/_{42}$ paper, folded in thirds.

"Great," I said aloud. "I got one of those photocopies."

But my sheet was different. Instead of a high school photo of Mike and Cherilyn Howard, it was only a note, scrawled in what looked like the same printing that had been on the photocopy Lacy and Bob Balke had shown me.

"SURPRISE!" it said. "It wasn't a bomb."

I unfolded the rest of the sheet and found more writing. "It might have been," it said. "Butt out, or you could get hurt."

I tossed the note and the sack of noise-makers into the trunk. I didn't feel I needed to call the bomb squad out to check the motor before I left. Oh, I admit that I was a bit nervous as I turned the ignition key over, but mainly I was angry.

I headed for Mike's house. Should I tell him about this?

I was extremely relieved when I saw Boone Thompson's car in front of Mike's house. Maybe I could inveigle Boone outside and show him the booby trap. And "booby" was the right word. "Booby" as in stupid. It was the dumbest thing I'd ever seen.

I didn't understand why it scared me so much.

My plan didn't work out. I used my garage door opener, drove inside and came in through the kitchen. Boone and Mike were sitting in the living room. Mike still had some ball game on, but the stands were going wild and he was sitting there like a lump of Silly Putty, so I didn't think he was paying a lot of attention to it.

I greeted Boone and kissed Mike. I got more reaction from Boone. At least he looked in my direction and spoke to me.

Then I enticed Boone away from Mike and into the kitchen by asking him some question about the beer supply, but my efforts were wasted. I had barely begun to whisper to him when Mike roused himself and came into the room. He looked suspicious.

"Talking about me?" he said.

Maybe Mike was improving. Paranoia might be a step forward from catatonia.

"No, we're talking about me," I said. "Somebody played a stupid joke on me."

I told both of them about the cans, bulbs and note, and the three of us went out to see the remains. I will say that Boone looked serious, and Mike became more animated than he'd been for twenty-four hours. If you call anger animation.

He scowled at me. "What are you up to?"

"Not a double dadgum thing! I'm simply going along covering the shelter. I haven't messed in the murder or the murder coverage at all. It's Judy's story."

"I wonder if she's had any threats."

Boone put the booby trap stuff into a paper sack. Mike and I went back inside, and I called the *Gazette* and was told Judy had gone home. When I reached her at home, she said she hadn't been threatened.

"At least not more than usual," she said. "Hal the jerk Johnson threatened to call the publisher over a drug arrest."

I rolled my eyes in disgust. Hal Johnson is a local defense attorney, and he's continually threatening to sic the publisher onto the police and court reporters. Apparently it has never occurred to him that the reporters are guided by a set of policies that are approved by the publisher. The editor and the publisher might have the authority to make exceptions — which they rarely do — but the reporter won't get in trouble for following the rules. And we all know from experience that the publisher hates Hal Johnson like poison. Hal's threats had nothing to do with the shelter killings.

"So," Mike said. "Can we assume that this bomb threat is aimed at you, Nell, rather than at the *Gazette*?"

"Not really. Maybe I was just the only *Gazette* staffer handy."

"I've got to get back to work," Boone said. "I'll try to find time to walk that block, see if any of the neighbors saw anybody tie this thing to your car." He left.

I followed Mike back into the living room. "Have you eaten dinner?"

"I've been snacking all afternoon."

"We could go out to Hu Nan Village. Or El Gordo's."

He shook his head.

"Or I could bring something in."

Mike scowled. "Why? Are you the baby-sitter?"

"No," I said. "I'm hungry."

"I'm not."

I picked up my purse and walked back out to the kitchen. I stood at the sink, staring out the window at the backyard. The sun was going down, and the shadows were making the outdoors look deceptively inviting. I knew it was a million degrees hot out there.

And I didn't know what to do about Mike. I had been eager for him to move out of the passive state he'd been in. But I hadn't expected him to get mad. Should I just leave?

Then I realized Mike was behind me. "Listen," he said. "I know you and Boone and Jim are all my friends, and I appreciate your concern. And Dr. Benson and Mom are just doing their jobs — but you're all driving me crazy!"

"I hadn't noticed. When you don't say anything or change your expression or even move any muscle except the thumb you use on the remote, it's kind of hard to understand what's going on with you. Like trying to solve a mystery without a clue."

"You don't need to solve anything. Not the mystery, not me. I don't want to be understood. Okay? Just let me alone."

"That's kind of hard. I've seen you every day for around ten months. You've become a habit."

"Work on breaking that habit, okay? Get a hobby!"

He went out the door into the garage and slammed it behind him.

I'd simply have left, but my car was in that garage. To get to it, I had to walk out that same garage door. Would Mike be standing there? Would he yell at me again? I realized that tears were running down my cheeks.

Then I heard rattles and thumps from the garage. Now what was going on?

I decided I had to beard Mike in his garage, get my car and go. I dried my eyes with a paper towel, blew my nose, picked up my handbag and went out the back door.

Mike was at the back of the garage, standing on a ladder and taking painting supplies off the top shelf of a steel storage unit.

"Here. Take this," he said. He thrust a paint tray in my direction.

I put my purse on the hood of my car and took the tray. "Where do you want it?"

"Anywhere. Try the work bench."

Silently he handed me a folded plastic drop cloth, a new paint roller, several old brushes. I put all of them on the work bench. When I turned around, he was coming down from the ladder.

"What are you going to do?" I asked.

"I've been meaning to paint the back

bathroom. If I'm stuck at home for the next few days, I might as well get it done."

"Do you have the paint?"

He hefted a gallon can. "I think there's enough left from when I painted the kitchen."

"And you don't want help."

"No."

"And you don't want dinner."

"No."

"Or anything else."

"No."

I pulled my car keys out of the side pocket of my purse and punched the button that opened the garage door. "Call me if you change your mind within the next week," I said.

Mike didn't answer. He didn't even look around as I drove off.

He'd sure left me at loose ends for the evening. I drove without thinking about where I was going, and when I came to myself, I was in the *Gazette* parking garage, parked opposite the employees' entrance.

I rested my head on the steering wheel and cried. Didn't I have anywhere else to go? Mike and my job. They'd been my whole life for the past ten months. When I left one, I automatically went to the other. Didn't I have any other life? Maybe I did

205

need to get a hobby.

I was still sitting there, with my head on the steering wheel, when someone rapped on the window. It was Alan.

Once again I'd forgotten I had a father. I rolled the window down.

"What's wrong?" he said.

"Oh, Mike and I had a fight. I don't think it's the end of the world."

"Just feels like it, huh? Have you had dinner?"

I remembered then. I was hungry. "Get in the car," I said. "Is Goldman's okay?"

I drove the two blocks to Grantham's favorite downtown deli. I told Alan about the fight, and he made it clear he was on my side. It's amazing how much good you can get out of a bowl of chili and a half-hour with a guy who thinks you're still his special little girl.

"I like Mike," Alan said, "and I know he's having a bad time. But he doesn't need to take it out on you."

"Oh, he's not really mad at me as much as he's mad at the whole situation. But it's harder for him to yell at Boone or Jim. They don't love him."

"Well, he could yell at the psychologist. That's what that guy gets paid for. Where is he while all this is going on?"

"He was over this afternoon." I took a last drink of my iced tea. "I guess Mike is just moving through the stages of grief. What are they? Denial, anger, something else I can't remember, and, finally, acceptance."

"If he doesn't get past anger pretty quick, you can just tell him to stuff it."

Alan's annoyance wasn't scary, the way Mike's anger had been. In fact, it made me feel fondly amused. "Well, enough about my problems," I said. "How are things on the copy desk?"

"The usual Sunday. Slow. But the shelter showed up in a story today."

"Oh? A story about what?"

"Missing person."

"We don't usually do missing person stories. So often they turn up on their own."

"I know. But this case has developed into a 'wanted' story. This woman's mother-in-law says she ran off and took a family heirloom. She's filed charges."

"How did the shelter figure in it?"

"That was the last place she was seen. She told a friend she was going there. She claimed her husband had threatened her life."

"Hmm. And now the mother-in-law says she is actually a thief?"

"Yep. Pretty suspicious. Maybe the

mother-in-law is in cahoots with the husband, trying to get her back. And in an interesting sidelight, husband is a deputy sheriff out in Washington County. And this Bernadette — "

"Bernadette!"

"Bernadette Fitzgerald. Did you meet her?"

"No! But a woman named Bernie was identified as the person who knew Cherilyn best at the shelter."

My mind went racing around. Mary Baker had said Bernie left "with friends." She also swore that the shelter didn't know where Bernie went or how to contact her. A glimmer of an idea came.

I began to gather up our dinner debris. "I'm coming back to the office with you," I said. "Maybe there's something in the files."

I think it's a pity that the traditional newspaper "morgue," the place where past stories and future obituaries are filed away, is itself dead. But the morgue is a casualty of the computer age. Old stories and future obituaries are still on file, but now they're in a computerized "library." Some newspaper libraries are even accessible through the Internet. And those libraries are run by librarians — professional information handlers. It's efficient, as long as the computers aren't down, but it's not very colorful.

I went straight to the *Gazette*'s library, and I searched the system for three words — "missing" and "Grantham" and "shelter."

Stories about five cases came up. Five cases from over the past seven years. All of them were about women who disappeared and who were last seen at the Grantham Women's Shelter.

There was Adelina Kane, who came to Grantham by bus from Wichita Falls, Texas. She took a cab to the Grantham Women's Shelter. The driver remembered taking her there, but the shelter had no record that she ever entered. Her husband had arrived in Grantham only minutes after she left the bus station. He was described as very worried about her welfare.

I'll bet he was.

There was Norene Canby, whose disappearance was covered in two paragraphs. "Last seen at the Grantham Woman's Shelter, Canby is five feet four inches tall, and weighs 175 pounds. She has brown hair and her right arm is in a cast." Or so she was described in the second paragraph.

Jimmie Sue Threadwick was a noncustodial parent who disappeared after kidnapping her two children. She had been staying at the shelter, but had left it for visitation with the kids. None of them were seen again. Her ex-husband was questioned closely about their whereabouts, but no bodies were ever found and no charges were ever filed.

And then there was an assault case. Two years earlier an irate husband, Abdul Munawar, had waylaid a volunteer as she left the shelter. He gave her a black eye before help came. Munawar claimed that the shelter had hidden his wife, Carol Jones Munawar, from him. Carol had earlier filed a peace bond against Munawar, claiming that he had threatened her and that she feared he was planning to kidnap their children and take them to his Middle Eastern native land. In turn, Munawar had filed missing person reports for his wife and children.

Mary Baker had been identified as the last person to see Carol Jones Munawar at the shelter. She had also been the person Abdul Munawar had assaulted.

And now Bernadette Fitzgerald had disappeared after she left the shelter "with friends." And Mary Baker had been the last person to see her.

I'm not a great detective, but the situation pointed strongly toward one conclusion.

"Hell's bells!" I said aloud. "That shelter is a station on the underground railroad."

CHAPTER 14

Lots of people know that the modern underground railroad exists, but few know much
about it. It was the topic of some magazine
articles and an Associated Press series a few
years ago. But I always wonder if the people
who are willing to talk to reporters about it
really know very much.

Today's underground railway is an un-
official — or maybe the word is irregular —
equivalent of the Federal Witness Protection
Program. Just as the pre-Civil War underground railway helped slaves escape, the
modern one helps battered wives and
abused children hide out.

For example, if a mother is convinced that
her ex-husband is sexually abusing their
daughter during court-ordered visitation,
she can go to court and try to get the visitation ended. But if she can't prove anything,
and the judge won't believe her, what can

she do? One woman who claimed she was in that situation sent her daughter abroad with her parents while she herself served years in prison for contempt of court.

But what if the ex is threatening to kill them all? What if he's really clever, and she can't get the evidence that he's planning murder? What if the ex is a judge himself? What if he has millions, and she gets along on minimum wage? What if he's a cop? What if — what if — what if — ?

There are a million scenarios out there, and in some of them, the women or children involved decide to flee. The underground railroad helps them.

It's a nationwide network. I don't know how the women who need it find a station where they can get on board, but I believe it exists.

And the police report I'd discovered sure made it sound as if the Grantham Women's Shelter could be involved.

Did the cops know about this? I thought about it and decided they probably did, although the cases wouldn't be likely to arise very often. But they very likely knew about it and were winking at the situation.

Only the fluke of pulling up missing persons reports linked with the shelter for a ten-year period had given me a clue. But the police computers probably stored data in a different form. They very well might know that people were disappearing from the shelter.

Not all that many women disappear in a mid-sized city like Grantham over the course of a year. And when they do, they're often prostitutes, drug addicts, or others who live irregular lives and may be apt to simply take off for parts unknown without bothering to tell their families or friends or landlords.

Besides, many of the women who disappeared wouldn't be listed as missing persons. If you leave a note for your mother, saying, "So long and don't try to find me," she probably won't report your departure to the police.

My impulse was to ask Mike. Then I remembered our less-than-friendly parting. No, this wouldn't be a good time to discuss the underground railroad with Mike. If he knew anything, he wasn't in the mood to talk about it.

Besides, if the Grantham PD didn't know about it, it wasn't my place to tell them. I was sympathetic to the women and children who used this method to flee. At least I could see that it might sometimes be the only way out. I didn't want to upset that particular applecart.

On the other hand, the irregular railroad could certainly be open to misuse. If I committed a crime and thought the cops were getting close to arresting me, I might try to convince the underground railroad that I needed protection. Once in the system, I could resurface clear across the country with a new identity.

No, I decided, Patsy was the key. I needed to ask Patsy about the connection. And there was no point in trying to do that until the next day.

I closed out the computer, said good night to Alan and went home. On the way, I realized that I was exhausted. I'd been running on adrenaline all day. I wanted a shoulder to cry on, a shower and bed. In other words, I wanted Mike.

And he was painting his bathroom.

My landlord, Rocky, had the kitchen full of delicious aromas when I came in the back door. He was creaming butter and sugar, and wonderful smells were coming from the oven.

"Hi, Nell, you just got a phone call," he said. "I wrote the number on the pad. It was that Boone guy."

I wasn't in the mood to talk to Boone, but I sighed and reached for the phone. "Better get it over with," I said.

Boone had canvassed the residential street across from the new shelter, but nobody had seen anyone fooling around with my car.

"One person saw a gray-haired lady walking out there," he said. "He thinks she's connected with the shelter. But she wasn't seen stopping beside or touching your car."

"Gray-haired lady? That could have been Mary Baker," I said. "I left the shelter before she did. Besides, I can't imagine Mary doing something like that booby trap." I thanked Boone for the call and hung up.

Mary Baker? Could she have booby-trapped my car? It was hard to picture a person so wholesome defying the law. Besides, she was too intelligent to pull a dumb trick like that one. Wasn't she?

"Penny," Rocky said.

I returned to the real world and realized Rocky was offering me a penny for my thoughts.

"Sorry," I said. "I was off in a cloud, wasn't I?"

Rocky is more than six feet tall and balding, though he's still in his thirties. He's usually around twenty pounds overweight — an appropriate problem for a restaurant professional.

Rocky is a partner in Grantham's most respectable gay bar, and he acts as its manager. Since the bar doesn't make a whole lot of money, he also works as a waiter during the noon rush at the Garden Path, a popular restaurant near the Grantham State campus. But what he really likes to do is cook.

Oh, he offers some interesting hors d'oeuvres at the bar — Canadian meatballs or the artichoke squares that I want to put on the list when I plan my last meal — but in both his jobs, his opportunities to cook are limited. So my roommates and I get the benefits of his real creativity. At home, Rocky goes into the kitchen and cuts loose.

"What are you making?" I said.

"I was in a down-home mood," he said. "Brownies, just the way my grandmother made 'em. Plus oatmeal refrigerator cookies."

"May I share?"

"Sure. I'll have the brownies iced in about half an hour."

"Can I help?"

Rocky turned around and looked at me. "You look all done in. Why don't you put your jammies on, then come back down. I want to hear all about the big story."

I laughed. "Comfort food and an intelligent interest in my job. Rocky, you're going to be hard to leave."

"Mike'll cook for you."

"He makes a mean BLT, true."

I went upstairs. Moving out of Rocky's house was another problem I had to face. I'd thought I had it figured out, but now I wasn't so sure.

I'd moved into the big house near the Grantham State campus nearly three years before, sharing the rent with three college friends who had also landed in Grantham. After six months, one of us got married, and the rest of us started looking for a replacement. We put up a notice on the bulletin board at our favorite restaurant. Rocky had been our favorite waiter there, and he'd seen the notice. He'd asked to move in because the house was only a block from an AIDS hostel where his long-time lover had just been forced to move.

We'd all had some qualms about allowing a man to move in, even one who wasn't interested in women and who'd tested negative for AIDS, but Rocky had worked out great. He regarded himself as a big brother to us — a big brother who liked to cook. He took the downstairs bedroom, which had its own bath and a tiny sitting room, and Martha, Brenda and I took the three upstairs spots, sharing a bathroom and an improvised sitting room on the landing. We all

217

used the downstairs living room and kitchen.

When Rocky's boyfriend died, he left a bit of money to Rocky, and Rocky invested it by buying the house we were living in and a partnership in the Blue Flamingo bar. So he'd become our landlord.

And now we were being evicted. Brenda had gotten married two months earlier, and Martha was about to finish her MBA. I had been thinking about a joint future with Mike. Rocky wanted to remodel and turn the upstairs into a separate flat with an outside entrance. I surmised that his new romantic interest, Jamie, would be moving in. It was time for me to move out.

Before Paul Howard and his knife turned Mike's life upside down, I'd had the idea that Mike and I would be getting married before long. In fact, he'd been pushing me toward the altar. Only my refusal to wear an engagement ring had kept our status from being official. But now this didn't seem like a good week to start shifting my computer, clothes, bed and bookshelves over to Mike's house. I didn't want to overreact to Mike's temper fit, but he was obviously rethinking his life. He might not even want to include me in his future.

I didn't know what I was going to do. So I

got in the shower, stood there and sulked. Then I got out, dried my hair, put on a pair of shorts and a T-shirt and went back downstairs. Rocky had made iced tea and was moving brownies to a plate.

"Yum," I said.

Rocky sat down and handed me a napkin. "I give you down-home food. You give me information about the big crime."

"If I have any. I'm not really working on the story about Cherilyn Howard's death. What do you want to know?"

"Was she definitely murdered?"

"Looks pretty likely. Somebody chased her down the hall with a club."

"Yuck. But it wasn't her husband?"

"No, being dead gives a guy a great alibi. Why did you think of him?"

Rocky chewed and swallowed before he answered. "Paul Howard used to eat at the Garden Path a couple of times a week." He took another bite.

"So? Was he one of your regulars?"

"God, no! If he sat in my section, I paid somebody else to wait on him."

"Lousy tipper?"

"I was afraid he'd remember me if he ever got a good look at my handsome puss."

He started to put a brownie in his mouth, but I grabbed his arm. "Okay!" I said. "Stop eating and tell me what the heck you're talking about. Why would Paul Howard have remembered you and why would that have been bad?"

"I was tending bar the night of the Flamingo fight." Rocky grinned. "I was one of only a couple of people who caught on to Paul's identity."

"Tell me about it."

He chewed his bite with considerably more vigor that the brownie really required. "This was before I took over as manager. Back when I worked as relief bartender. Paul came in with a tour group."

"A tour group?"

"You know, a bunch of frat guys who wandered over from the campus to look at the queers."

Rocky's voice had a bitter edge, and I could understand why. Rocky and his customers didn't like to be laughed at.

"When was this?" I asked.

"About three years ago."

"Paul Howard would have been too old for fraternity life three years ago."

"Yes, he was older than the guys he was with. I guess he was the token alum. They were already tight when they came in. I got the idea they'd been at some fraternity event and hadn't wanted the evening to end.

Believe me, I checked everybody's ID. That's how I caught onto just who was honoring us with a visit."

"And Paul got into a fight?"

"Yeah. He was loud and disruptive the whole time he was there. He embarrassed the younger guys, I think. They all got quieter and quieter."

"What was there to see? Every time Martha and Brenda and I come by the Flamingo, it looks just like any other bar. Or are the customers on their best behavior for us?"

"No, what you see is pretty typical. We're a gray bar."

"A gray bar?"

"We appeal to an older crowd. We're not one of those nude dancers on the table places. That's why Paul was so out of place. Our customers aren't boisterous. But he was."

"What happened? You said there was a fight."

Rocky nodded. "Something happened out back."

"What?"

"I don't know. Certainly the stories the participants told didn't match. Paul had gotten up to go to the men's room. Somehow he wound up out in the alley with a guy

221

named Lyn. He swore he just stepped out for a breath of air, and that Lyn came on to him. Lyn said Paul initiated . . . whatever happened. Anyway, Paul punched Lyn out — or rather, in. Lyn fell right in the back door. The door flew back and slammed, hard. It made a big noise. Not something I could pretend wasn't happening."

"Oh, gee! What did you do?"

"I went back there on the double, and, of course, I had to beat my way through the gawkers. When I got to them, Paul was up and Lyn was down. Paul was kicking Lyn in the head."

"Ouch!"

"Ouch is right. He could have killed him. Maybe he would have if one of our regulars who's a bodybuilder hadn't helped me grab him. You'd have laughed to see us. I grabbed Paul around the neck, the bodybuilder grabbed him around the waist — we hauled his rear out the back door."

"I take it he didn't go quietly."

"No, there was a lot of kicking and screaming involved. That's why I said the stupid thing, the thing I regretted ever since."

"What was that?"

"I had him around the neck, see? And his ear was near my mouth." Rocky rolled his eyes roguishly and went on in a singsong voice. "And I said, 'Naughty, naughty, little man. We're going to have to tell Mommy.'"

I laughed.

"Actually a pretty dumb thing to say," Rocky said. "I mean, the creep can't help who his mother is. Anyway, he stopped struggling, and when we put him down, he turned around and gave me a look that nearly froze my innards."

"I can see why you didn't want to serve him a Reuben when he dropped in for lunch at the Garden Path. Did he get arrested?"

"No. Nobody ever called the cops. Lyn wasn't as badly hurt as we had feared. I made him an ice pack for his face."

"And naturally, he didn't want to press charges."

"You can see why," Rocky said defensively. "Lyn's parents didn't know about his real life in those days. He certainly didn't want to land in the *Gazette*."

"And Paul Howard certainly wouldn't have wanted to make the news."

"Weirdly enough, I think I was the only person there who realized who Paul Howard was."

"What about the frat guys he'd come with?"

"I told you he was embarrassing them.

When he went to the men's room, they all split out the front door."

"So they missed all the excitement. Then nobody else figured it out?"

"Some guy came around the next day. He was very nervous." Rocky raised his eyebrows and shrugged. "He said he'd heard we had a fight the night before. He said 'one of the people involved' wanted to make sure the second one wasn't hurt. Offered money for any damage. Cash."

"A little payoff, huh? Did you take it?"

"I took some to give Lyn for ice packs. Then the guy asked — real casually — if I knew the name of the straight involved in the fight."

Rocky looked at me seriously. "I lied," he said.

"You mean you said you didn't know him, but you'd actually made him when you checked the IDs?"

Rocky nodded. "Maybe I didn't actually lie. I said something like, 'I never saw him in here before.' I sure didn't want to get mixed up in that deal. The Howards have a lot more lawyers than I do."

"So Paul got away with a spot of gay bashing."

"That's the interesting thing," Rocky said. "I don't think it started out as gay bashing."

"What do you mean?"

"I guess you had to see Lyn to understand. Lyn is about five-foot-two, with a really sweet figure. He was wearing his red sequined sweater that night, with a blond wig and some black slacks that really showed off his cute little ass."

I gasped. "Lyn is a cross-dresser?"

"Right. And he looks . . . realistic. There's nothing butch about him. I think Paul was too drunk to realize he was a man until things got really hot and heavy back there. That's when the kicking and punching started."

"You think he and Paul were — well, let's call it making out. And when Paul realized Lyn was a man, he lost it and got violent?"

"Yeah." Rocky pushed brownie crumbs around his plate for a minute, then spoke again. "Whatever was bugging Paul Howard, Nell, I don't think it was hatred of gays. I think it was more like self-loathing. I think Paul took his anger at himself out on Lyn."

"What do you mean?"

"When I came up behind Paul — when the bodybuilder and I were trying to grab him — he was muttering. But not what I'd expected to hear. He wasn't saying 'You faggot' or anything like that. He'd say 'I am not!' Then he'd kick Lyn. 'You take that back!' Kick. 'That's a lie!' Kick.

"I think Paul Howard — whether he recognized it or not — was either gay or bi."

CHAPTER 15

After I went up to bed, I thought about Rocky's experience with Paul Howard. It didn't really give any new revelations of Paul's character, I decided.

Oh, if you considered that Paul was likely to be either bisexual or homosexual — and that he wouldn't face it — it certainly might explain the rage he must have felt, the rage that expressed itself in violence against Lyn and later against Cherilyn. He was married to a beautiful woman, and he must have been the envy of all his pals, yet he himself might not have had much interest in her. His mother had probably nagged him to carry on the Philpott-Howard line. He'd already had a leaning toward violence, as shown by his attack on Lyn and by the Ramada Inn episode that Bob Balke had heard about — and which I was willing to bet Mike had heard about, too. Paul's problems with

Cherilyn had led to more violence.

Then he'd had the calls by someone pretending to be Patsy Raymond. He'd already been teetering, and those calls had pushed him right over the edge.

It was sad. Sad for Paul and sad for Cherilyn, who certainly had no idea of what she was letting herself in for when she married him. Or had Cherilyn known and not cared? Had she married Paul only for his money and position?

I doubted it. Cherilyn could have had her pick of the eligible men in Grantham. She surely wouldn't have selected a dangerously unstable mate, no matter how wealthy, if she'd had any idea of his potential for violence.

With Paul and Cherilyn's romantic problems settled in my own mind, I thought about my own. A major decision had to be made. Should I call Mike? Or not?

Or not, I decided. I was still smarting from his behavior that afternoon. If he didn't want me hovering over him, I'd cease to hover. See how he'd like that.

I turned out the light early and promptly fell asleep. Woke up at eleven, when Martha came in. Read until two in the morning before I fell asleep again. Woke up at four. Read until six. Fell asleep again and slept through the alarm and didn't wake up until Martha knocked on my door at eight-thirty. It's hard to get a good night's sleep when you keep having nightmares about guys with knives and guns when you're asleep, and when you worry about the most important person in your life when you're awake.

After Martha woke me, I jumped up and headed out in a hurry, blessing the fact that I'd had a shower the night before. I had a photo assignment at 10:00 a.m. Moving day at the Grantham Women's Shelter.

I struggled into panty hose, longing for my days on the violence beat when I could wear slacks all the time. Covering the non-profits, I had to visit offices where people wore more businesslike attire, so I dressed up a bit more these days. I decided a linen skirt and plaid blouse with mid-heeled pumps would be dressy enough for a summer Monday in the sizzling Southwest.

I stopped in the kitchen long enough to eat a bowl of Rice Krispies, and looked at the *Gazette* that Martha had left on the counter. The Howard family was all over the front page again, with a major story about Cherilyn's death, accompanied by a picture taken the night she was a runner-up in Atlantic City. A little box advised the reader, "See related news, Page 1B." One-B was the cover page for Lifestyles. They were doing a recap of Cherilyn's career.

I got to the office an hour late, but I'd worked over the weekend, so no one seemed upset. I stopped at the newsroom switchboard to check on messages. To my surprise, I had two, both from the executive director of the Grantham United Way, C. C. Cecil. He'd been at his desk early.

I returned his calls immediately. Since I was covering the United Way campaign, which was due to kick off in two weeks, I needed to get along with him.

C. C. Cecil should have been a minister. The "C. C. Cecil" he used to answer the phone reverberated along the phone lines like organ pipes with all the stops out.

"Hi," I said. "This is Nell Matthews, returning your call. Happy Monday."

"After the events of the weekend, this can hardly be a happy day."

"True. But I keep hoping. What can I do for you?"

"I hope you can help us meet this crisis."

"Which crisis?"

"Two violent deaths associated with one of our agencies! Scandal! That seems like a crisis to me."

"Yes, but that was yesterday's crisis. I was afraid some new disaster had happened.

How does the United Way fit into the deaths of Paul and Cherilyn Howard?"

"The Grantham Women's Shelter is one of our agencies."

"But their problems are not necessarily associated with the United Way."

"I'm afraid you're mistaken there. Particularly since both of the victims were related to Enid Philpott Howard, who is a former chairman of our board of directors. We simply must play the entire scandal down. The affair is tragic, but I hope the news media will not overreact."

I didn't answer for a moment, trying to figure out what C. C. wanted. "The *Grantham Gazette* can't ignore a crime," I said.

"Certainly not! But it doesn't have to be sensationalized, either. It doesn't have to be all over the front page!"

"Where else can we put it? Cherilyn was one of the most famous people in Grantham. And Paul Howard was — "

"Paul was a member of a family that has never been mixed up in a scandal. I know Enid Philpott Howard would be most unhappy with this — this — this overdramatic coverage."

"Mrs. Howard came by Saturday night and talked to the managing editor personally," I said.

"Oh." That stopped him. But not for long. "I'm concerned about the United Way, of course. For one of our agencies to be the scene of such events is terrible public relations."

Public relations? Two people were dead, and he was worried about public relations?

"Actually, I would have thought it was good publicity for the shelter," I said.

"Good! How can it be good?"

"The shelter only exists to protect women from violence. A demonstration that violence does occur — "

"Nonsense! We simply can't have stories that tear United Way agencies down. This has to be stopped."

Well, he stopped me. If he thought the *Gazette* could ignore the murder of one of Grantham's most famous citizens because it might give the United Way drive bad publicity, he had to be living in another world. I took a deep breath and tried to remember that a soft answer has been known to turn away wrath.

"Mr. Cecil, I don't make decisions about the way news is handled," I said. "And I don't cover crime stories anymore. I will pass your concerns on to the city editor and managing editor."

"You mean Jake Edwards?"

232

"Yes. He and the city editor, Ruth Borah, decide how stories are to be played."

"Played?"

"They decide on the relative importance of each news item. What sort of stories will be used to cover it. Which page it will go on. How big the headlines will be. Is that what you're concerned about?"

"We simply can't have bad publicity right now," C.C. said angrily. "Not before the drive. Let me assure you that any problems at the shelter are being worked out."

He hung up. I hung up, too, feeling blanker than blank. Why did I have the feeling we'd been talking about different subjects? I'd been talking about a crime story. But C. C. Cecil had referred to "problems at the shelter." Had C. C. Cecil been talking about the killings of Paul and Cherilyn? Or about the financial problems Wilda and Lacy had refused to reveal? Was something serious going on at the shelter?

The woolly face of Bear Bennington, our most bearded photographer, appeared over the top of the partition surrounding my cubicle. "Ready to go out to the new shelter?" he said.

"Maybe I'd better take my own car," I said. "I may have to hang around out there for a while."

Bear and I parked down the block from the new shelter. The parking lot was full of cars and trucks; no room for the press. For once, the front doors were propped open, and Bear and I simply walked in without going through the security rigmarole of inner and outer doors and corresponding buzzers.

I found Lacy Balke in the main office, shoving file folders into a drawer in one of the two desks. The picture of Bob identified the desk as her work area, just as the brass rabbit on the other desk identified that one as Dawn's.

"Hi, Lacy," I said. "I thought Patsy said you were going to be late."

"I just got here. Bob and I had an appointment. We have the most wonderful news!"

She stopped work on the desk drawer and waved her hands in the air like a song and dance man. "Oh, Nell! I'm so excited! I'm telling everybody."

"Then tell me."

"We're getting our kids! Our Russian kids!"

"What!"

"We've been working for eight months to adopt two kids from a Russian orphanage. And as of today, it's all been approved. We leave next week to pick up Olga and Nick."

I squealed. I hugged her. She hugged me. She jumped up and down. I jumped up and down. Her delight was infectious.

"What lucky kids!" I said.

"No, we're the lucky ones." Then she wagged a finger. "Of course, they haven't met us yet. We have to bond with them. If they don't take to us, then the deal's off."

She pulled out a picture of two beautiful blond children. The little girl had a big bow in her hair, and the boy wore a sailor suit. "Olga is three, and Nick is five," she said. "I've already talked to the schools here about the ESL program." When I looked blank she said, "English as a second language. They seem to have a really good program. And we've met three other couples here who adopted from Russia."

"Sounds as if you're well-prepared. But two kids at once! Do you know what you're getting into?"

I heard a chuckle from the door, and Mary Baker came in and gave Lacy a hug. "If any parents knew what they were getting into, the human race would cease to exist in around thirty years," she said. We all laughed.

"I can see you won't be working around here so much," I said. "Olga and Nick are going to keep you too busy."

"Oh, I'll still work with the shelter's accounting," Lacy said. "I can take that home and work on it in the evenings. I want to keep my hand in. In a year or two Olga and Nick will be settled, I hope, and I'll be looking for a real job again."

"What do you do?"

"I thought you knew. I'm a CPA. That's why they put me on the shelter board. I quit working when we moved to Grantham because I wanted to concentrate on the adoption. The shelter board has been a godsend. It lets me keep my hand in the accounting world without tying me down to a nine-to-five job. And I've made a lot of good contacts, too. Like Wilda."

I could see Bear pacing outside the office, and I decided the glee had to wait.

"I guess we'd better get our moving day photo before Bear wears a trench in your new carpet," I said. "We want to show off how nice the new shelter is. How about the Victorian parlor Patsy mentioned? Is the furniture in there yet?"

My question brought all jubilation to a halt.

My grandfather used to do a trick, run his hand up and down over his face, from above his head to below his chin, then back the

236

other way. When the hand had gone up, his expression was happy. When it was below his chin, he looked sad. I thought it was terribly amusing when I was five years old.

Lacy had apparently had a grandpa who did the same trick. In the time it would have taken to move a hand in front of her face, her expression changed from jubilant to dismayed. "No, n-no — " She began to stammer.

It was Mary Baker who reacted firmly. Her face had changed, too, from happy to deadpan. But she didn't panic. When she spoke, her voice was calm.

"The Victorian furniture hasn't been moved in yet," she said. "How about a picture of one of the bedrooms?"

I agreed, and she led Bear and me into the wing opposite the one where I had met Patsy the previous afternoon. And with every step, I wondered what I had said to cause Lacy and Mary to give me that unusual reaction. I'd definitely dropped a bomb.

Bear got his picture and left, and I went looking for Patsy Raymond. I found her in almost exactly the spot where she'd been yesterday.

"It's looking good, Patsy," I said.

"I think I'm caught up. The moving van

left the old place ten minutes ago."

"Then they'll be here any minute."

"Right. We're moving three bedrooms of furniture — the furniture that's pretty good. Plus all the living room furniture, and the pots and pans and kitchen equipment. Not to mention the office. It's awful how much stuff it takes human beings to live!"

"What's the deal on the Victorian parlor?"

Patsy didn't panic, but she looked wary. "What do you mean?"

"I suggested a picture there, and Lacy and Mary acted — well, weird."

Patsy looked away. "The Victorian furniture donated by Mrs. Bateson is still in storage."

"How did she come to give that furniture to the shelter?"

"She inherited it, I believe. From an aunt. She had it in her own home for years, but when she moved to an apartment, she gave it to us. Until now we haven't had anyplace to put it. It's not the sort of furniture you can let pre-schoolers bounce around on. Which reminds me — have you seen our new playroom?"

The playroom was truly delightful, painted in primary colors, with a hopscotch pattern laid into the tile and lots of shelves for games and books. Two little girls and their mother were putting the toys away. The mother wore a trendy outfit, and the kids had shirts marked with the most fashionable logo around. I assumed they were volunteers, but after we left the room, Patsy told me they'd been staying in the shelter for a week.

"It's their third stay," she said. "Daddy always swears he won't get violent again, and Mama wants to believe him. He makes $100,000 a year, but he claims he can't afford counseling."

I peeked back through the door at the trio. The mother's shoes had cost enough to feed a family for a couple of weeks, I realized. She and her little girls certainly didn't fit the stereotype of a poor, lower-class family, which most people associated with family abuse.

Which reminded me. The underground railroad. I wanted to ask Patsy if there was any connection with the shelter. But how could I do it?

Patsy prattled on as we walked back to the main lounge, describing the decorating committee and its efforts, but I didn't take in much of what she said. I was rolling phrases around in my head. How could I ask about the underground railroad in a way that would entice Patsy into commenting?

By the time we reached the lounge, I had decided to use a technique that I've found very useful in my years as a reporter. I'd use plain English.

"Patsy," I said. "I want to change the subject abruptly."

She looked cautious, but she nodded.

"I was looking up an old article about what I call 'the underground railroad.' The network that hides abused women and children."

Patsy's face was something to see. Emotions were flitting over it like clouds running before a wind. But she didn't speak.

"I've wondered," I said. "How on earth does someone who wants to get aboard that train find a station?"

"I don't know!" Patsy yelped out the words. She whirled around, headed toward the office. Then she whirled back toward me. She flopped her hands sideways. She threw her head back and went into massive contortions through her shoulders. She was so loud that Dawn, Mary and Lacy popped their heads out of the office door to see what was causing the commotion.

I'd thought Lacy and Mary had acted odd over my question about the furniture, but their reactions had been nothing to Patsy's response to my question about the underground railroad.

Talk about using plain English. Patsy might as well have simply said, "We're a station. Climb aboard." The nerve I had touched was so raw that an innocent — well, semi-innocent — question had sent her into a fit.

I was afraid she was going to bust a gusset. My grandmother used to say that, but I had never known what it meant. Now, looking at Patsy, I understood.

Finally she grabbed my arm. She leaned close. "Nell, I don't know anything about this!"

"It's all right, Patsy! I just asked. I'm not going to write an exposé or anything!"

"I am careful not to know anything about this."

"I understand. I imagine that's a wise policy."

"I just can't tell you anything, because I don't know anything. The shelter is not involved."

"Right."

"But if you really want to know about this pistol, I'll see if somebody can find out."

She turned and almost ran into the office. I followed her, nearly tripping over Dawn as I went in the door.

"Patsy!" I said.

She headed into her own private office, but she yelled back over her shoulder. "Maybe Bernie can call you!"

Bernie?

Bernie? Did she mean the Bernie who'd been Cherilyn's pal? The one who had left the shelter the night Cherilyn was killed? The one the GPD missing persons investigator was looking for?

I didn't know anything about Bernie. I had no interest in Bernie. I didn't care about Bernie.

So why did she keep popping up? First Mary Baker had mentioned her again — wanting to know if I had told the police about her — and now Patsy had.

And what was this about the pistol? Did Patsy mean the one Mike had used to shoot Paul Howard?

Then I heard a roar from the back of the building. It was the sound of a big truck. The moving van had arrived.

CHAPTER 16

My impulse was to give Patsy the third degree about her remarks about Bernie and the gun, but that simply wasn't possible on moving day. I decided I'd either have to start hefting boxes or get out of the way.

I borrowed the phone in the office to call in and ask the *Gazette* switchboard if I had any messages. If there were none, I planned to go by to see Mike before I went back to the office.

But there was a message. I was to call Peaches Atkins, the secretary and chief mover and shaker for GPD detectives. I dialed the number with a sinking heart. Peaches was rarely good news.

Her raucous voice answered. "Please hold!" she screeched.

The receiver began to deliver the idiotic music the city provides as background for its phone system. I have a theory that they use it to lull taxpayers into a state of dull resignation.

"Detective Bureau!" Peaches was back.

"This is Nell Matthews, Peaches. I had a message to call you."

"You get over here to sign your statement." Peaches never requested; she gave commands.

"Sure. I'd forgotten that detail. I'll come now."

"And Jim wants to talk to you." She hung up. Nobody ever accused Peaches of wasting city time with chit-chat.

I let the assignments editor know where I was, then headed for the PD. On the way, my imagination anticipated the worst.

Signing the statement was routine, but why did Jim want to see me? Jim was close to Mike. Did Jim know something about Mike that I should know, too? Had something happened to him? Should I have called last night? I had worked myself halfway into a snit by the time I walked in the door of the Detective Bureau and faced Peaches.

"Where's Jim?" I said.

Peaches glared, resettled her bulk in her chair, and thrust a short stack of typed pages at me. "Jim's got somebody with him. You sit down and read this. Read it twice."

Her reaction was a letdown, but I sat

down and read the statement I'd made Saturday. I had time to read it three times, make two slight changes, initial each change and each page, then sign it before Jim escorted his caller out of his office.

The caller was Lacy Balke. She must have left the shelter while I was looking for Patsy. We spoke briefly — saying, "How'd you beat me down here!" in unison. Then she left.

Jim beckoned me into his cubbyhole, a notoriously neat area. Jim's one of those people who keep every pencil lined up, all papers neatly stacked, the phone exactly parallel to the Rolodex.

He spoke before I could sit down.

"What do you know about this pistol?"

"What pistol?"

"The one Mike used to shoot Paul Howard."

"I don't know anything about it. I assumed from the first that he took it from that closet where Patsy has all the weapons stored."

"That's what he says."

"Okay. Our stories match. Mike had put his own pistol in my purse. And I'd stuck the purse in a drawer in the kitchen. When he needed his pistol, he couldn't find it. So he took that one."

"Mike says he took it because it was like

his. He had a clip for his own pistol in his pocket."

"That makes sense. A gun's not much use without a clip. Saturday night some officer out at the scene was speculating that the spare was a Grantham PD issue. I remember wondering which of your guys had sent his wife to the shelter and let her take his gun along."

"The pistol wasn't one of ours. We're going to have to go to the manufacturer to trace it."

"The manufacturer? Don't the shelter records say where it came from?"

"Shelter records?" Jim laughed humorlessly. "The shelter records on weapons are a joke."

"Surely they keep a list, a register of some sort, for the weapons they're locking up."

"They give the client a receipt."

"Then you can look in the receipt book."

"There is no record for this particular pistol in the receipt book."

I stared at Jim. "Patsy Raymond — "

"Patsy Raymond seems to be in Never-Never Land most of the time, as far as the day-to-day operations around there go."

"Then Dawn — "

Jim was shaking his head. "She swears she knows nothing about the pistol."

"I guess a lot of volunteers work in the office. One of them might know something."

He shook his head again. "Lately it seems they've only had a limited number of volunteers working in the office. This Mrs. Balke, she's been there every day."

"She told me she'd taken over the bookkeeping and accounting."

"She's doing more than that. She's setting up a whole new records system for them. But she says she hadn't gotten to the weapons closet yet. And that Mrs. Baker answers the phone a lot. Neither of them will admit knowing anything about that pistol. And none of the clients will claim it."

"Maybe it had been there a long time."

"Possibly. But that doesn't help us. And it's complicating things for Mike. We've ought to be able to explain where that pistol came from before he can be officially off the hook."

I took that in, sitting silently. I certainly wanted Mike to be officially off the hook. But I didn't understand why the shelter's poor records on the pistol were a problem for Mike. Then the light dawned.

"It's that photocopy, isn't it? The one that went to Lacy and Bob Balke. Plus a whole bunch of other people. Has Enid Philpott Howard decided Paul's death was a plot?"

"No!"

Jim's denial had been a little too vehement. It made me mad.

"Jim," I said. "If Mike was going to commit cold-blooded murder, I assure you he'd do a better job than this. You know what a tricky mind he has. He'd come up with an alibi that proved he was in Anatolia when the murder was committed — and make it look like an accident anyway. And he wouldn't rely on two eyewitnesses whose credibility could be attacked."

"And just why are you and Patsy Raymond poor witnesses?"

"We're not. We're good witnesses to the truth. But Patsy Raymond is a flake. She handles the truth pretty well, but if you asked her to lie, she'd get so confused, she might say any damn thing."

"That leaves you."

"Yes. And my testimony would be discounted because I would say anything Mike wanted me to. I happen to be in love with him."

I got up, turned on my heel and angrily stalked out of Jim's office. Then I nearly fainted from surprise as a big, red-headed guy grabbed me and pressed my nose against his polo shirt.

"Thanks for the confidence in my ability

to commit murder and get away with it," the giant said.

"Mike! What are you doing here?"

"Got tired of being cooped up and came down to harass Jim. But it looks as if you're handling that for me, too."

Jim came out of his office. "Nell knows I'm in your corner, Mike. Come on. Let's all go to lunch."

"Okay," I said. "Then I've got to get back to the *Gazette* and find out what else is going on in the world. The Grantham Women's Shelter is only one of the things I cover."

"That's another thing I wanted to talk to you about," Jim said.

I looked at Mike closely as we settled around a table in the back room at Goldman's, a deli two blocks from the *Gazette*. He was conspicuously silent, but he didn't seem to be spoiling for a fight, the way he had been the night before. I decided to act as if nothing had happened — at least until we could ditch Jim. So I kicked off the conversation, between bites of a tuna salad sandwich.

"Jim, if you're willing to publicly identify yourself as 'in Mike's corner,' doesn't that sort of skew your investigation of Paul Howard's death? And maybe of Cherilyn's?"

"Yep. Everything I do is going to be double-checked by the state police. Then it goes to the DA's office and they check it again."

"Oh. So we have to make all these statements over?"

"Probably not. And I'm still in charge of the investigation of Cherilyn's death. Which brings me to the question I wanted to ask you. What's your assessment — as a reporter — of that shelter?"

I bit, chewed and swallowed before I answered. My brain was working madly. What should I tell Jim? What *could* I tell Jim? What was speculation on my part? How about the underground railroad bit? Did he already know? Did I know? I decided to be cautious.

"I think the shelter does wonderful work, Jim. Could you be a little more specific?"

"What do you think of Patsy Raymond?"

"Patsy Raymond *is* the shelter. She lives and breathes the shelter. She would do anything for the shelter and its clients."

"Anything?"

"Such as commit a crime?" I chewed and swallowed again. "I doubt it. Too much chance of getting caught — and getting caught would reflect poorly on the shelter. But she'd shade the truth to favor the shelter."

"White lies?"

"They'd be white to her — or she'd convince herself that she was telling the truth. She'd probably pass a lie detector test with flying colors."

I looked at Mike. "And you don't need to tell your mother I said this, but I think they may have had some problems over there. All the board members keep talking about this big reorganization. Sort of defensively. But everybody gets real vague when I ask about what inspired it."

Mike nodded grimly. "I picked up on that, too," he said. "Something like, 'Now we have strict accounting procedures.' With just a slight emphasis on the 'now.' But Mom hasn't told me a thing."

"Even if we're right," I said, "that doesn't mean there was anything going on that was illegal, or even unethical. It may simply mean they're changing their methods so they can go for more grants. Both the government — where their clients need to get food stamps and aid to families with dependent children — and big private foundations are picky about that kind of thing."

Jim frowned, and I quickly asked him a question about his family. He took the bait, and the subject was changed. The butterflies in my stomach gradually settled down. I'd gotten out of that one without having to mention my suspicion that the shelter was a station on the underground railroad. We didn't let the shelter or the Howard family intrude on the rest of our lunch.

We'd each driven our own vehicle as we left the PD for lunch, and I'd parked at the Gazette and walked to the deli. Mike walked me back, holding my hand.

"I want to apologize for snapping at you yesterday," he said.

"We'd all been looking at you as if you were a bomb about to explode. You probably felt better after you did blast off."

"Not really." Mike sounded grim. "I'm still mad as hell."

I squeezed his hand. "I could take a couple of days off — "

"No. I've got to work this out myself." We walked on for half a block before he spoke again. "I guess I'll paint the bedroom," he said. "What color would you like?"

Maybe he did think I'd be living at that house. I started to suggest "cream," as a paint color, but that reminded me of the shelter, so I tried to call it something different. "Off-white," I said. "A real light beige? Could you live with that?"

We parted at the Gazette's employee entrance — platonically, thanks to the other employees going in and out — and I ran upstairs, checked my messages and went to my desk. I returned two calls. Luckily neither of them was pressing. Then I wrote a 15-inch story about moving day at the shelter, plus cutlines for two of the pictures Bear had taken. I checked my mail, which was mostly newsletters and news releases, marking items that were worth stories.

By then the afternoon was half gone, and I didn't have time to go on my beat. So I made phone calls to some of the other agencies I covered, mainly asking for more information about items I'd discovered in my mail. It's not the best way to cover a beat, but it'll do in an emergency.

If there's anything that makes me mad, it's hearing a reporter complain about some story he'd missed, whining, "They didn't tell me about that." Another thing that makes me mad is hearing reporters say, "They didn't even put out a news release," or, "I typed in the news release."

It's not the news source's responsibility to give out the news. It's the reporter's to dig it out. And it's a reporter's responsibility to write it, too. Not "type it in."

I guess my attitude was the reason the editors had wanted me on this beat. The previous reporter was a fine feature writer, but in covering routine news he had simply taken what the non-profits handed out and "typed it in." He hadn't dug around, or asked nosy questions, or followed up, or checked on things personally. I was used to the crime beat, where the reporter frequently has to cajole news sources into giving out the facts. I'd been forced to develop a more aggressive style.

And the first step of an aggressive style of reporting is following a routine. The reporter has to show up in the news source's office every day, every week or every couple of weeks, unannounced. He has to get to know the director or PR person personally. He has to become a familiar face to the secretary. He has to know what's going to be on the agenda for the board meetings — and he may have to attend them.

By focusing on the Grantham Women's Shelter, I was neglecting the Red Cross, the Cancer Society, the homeless shelter and forty or fifty other non-profits the *Gazette* covers. So I spent a couple of hours playing catch-up.

It was nearly quitting time when the phone rang. "Nell Matthews," I said.

The voice on the phone was calm and cultured. "Ms. Matthews, this is Enid Philpott Howard."

I turned a gasp of surprise into a polite cough. "Yes, Mrs. Howard."

"I've decided I should meet Patsy Raymond face-to-face, just informally. You seem to be the only mutual acquaintance we have. Can you arrange it?"

Then I did gasp. And I blurted out a response. "Why?"

Mrs. Howard didn't answer, and I found myself apologizing. "I'm sorry," I said. "That's none of my business, of course. You just surprised me."

"After you heard me accuse her of all sorts of nefarious deeds, I can understand your concern about arranging this. But several people — including the police — have assured me that it's unlikely that Mrs. Raymond made the phone calls to my son. Perhaps I've been duped." She gave a strange little laugh. "I don't plan to bring a gun or anything. Or even my lawyer. I simply want to talk to Mrs. Raymond."

"When?" I said. "Where?"

We settled on the next afternoon at two p.m., at Mrs. Howard's office in the Grantham National Bank Building. I warned her that Patsy Raymond wasn't always easy to find.

"If she can't meet tomorrow, then Wednesday," Mrs. Howard said. "The funeral won't be until Thursday."

As soon as she hung up, I called Patsy.

Patsy's voice grew raspier than usual. "What does she want?"

"She apparently wants to ask you about those phone calls."

"I don't know anything about those phone calls."

"I guess she just wants to hear it from you."

"I doubt she wants to write me a check. But I guess I'd better see her. Wouldn't I love to get in with the Philpott Foundation! They've always turned us down."

I told her Mrs. Howard had promised not to bring either a gun or a lawyer. Patsy was not amused.

"Will you be there?"

"I'd sure love to, Patsy, just because I'm so darn curious. But I don't see how I could go to a private meeting between two private individuals. Now, if you and Mrs. Howard want to grant me an interview — "

"Who knows what will happen?" Patsy hung up.

I called Mrs. Howard's office to confirm the meeting. Then I called Mike, offering to cook dinner for him. He accepted, so I went by the store and picked up some steaks, plus baking potatoes and salad fixings. We had a pleasant enough dinner, since we didn't talk about the shelter, Cherilyn's murder or the shooting of Paul Howard. But the situation still hung over us like a cloud, and Mike was making a visible effort not to snarl. He was still angry over the whole thing, though he'd apparently realized I wasn't willing to be used as an emotional punching bag. He got jumpier and jumpier as the evening went on.

When the ten o'clock news came on, I offered to go home. Mike seemed relieved. So I got a good-night kiss and left.

One of the things I'm not crazy about is the backyard at the house where I've lived for two years. The house, the one Rocky now owns, is near the Grantham State campus, in a neighborhood that grew up long before the city had rules about how many parking spaces a multi-family dwelling must offer per apartment. Since most of the single-family houses in the area have turned into multis, parking is really tight.

Rocky, Brenda, Martha and I had dealt with this by graveling the backyard and turning it into a parking lot with four spaces. Last person in gets the space farthest from the house — the third one, since Brenda

257

moved out. That night, it was mine.

There's a light on our back porch, but there are also lots of trees and bushes to block the light. So the area is usually quite dark.

That's why I didn't see the person with the club.

CHAPTER 17

I guess Joe Bob Zimmerman would have said it was a miracle of God that the attacker didn't get me.

Maybe it really was divine intervention. Or maybe it was poor muscle coordination. Because just as I got out of my car, I dropped my keys. I felt them hit my foot, and I immediately ducked down to feel around for them.

At that same moment some sort of a club slammed into the roof of my car.

I don't think I screamed right away. I was startled by the motion over my head and by the crack of the club hitting the car, but it didn't occur to me that I was being attacked. Then I looked up and saw the club being drawn back for another whack. And I realized what was going on.

I was all crouched down, so my impulse was to jump up. By the time I was halfway erect, still off balance, the club was coming down again. I threw my arms up. My purse went flying, and I sat down, hard, on the gravel.

The blow I'd been dodging missed me. And I finally found my voice.

"Help!" Not very original, but it got the message across.

The club was coming again, and I began to scream. All sorts of shrieks, hollers and gurgling began to fill the air. My larynx made sounds I wouldn't have thought possible. The occasional word was thrown in — I think I remember squealing, "Nine-one-one!"

The noise didn't make any difference to the club.

I knew there was a person wielding it, but I couldn't look at the attacker. All I could see was this heavy stick rising and descending.

And I knew I couldn't keep it from hitting me for many more blows.

It came at my head again, this time from the side, and I dodged by dropping flat on my back on the ground. And there I found the hope of a refuge. From that position I could see under my car.

I swung my head and shoulders to my right and pushed them behind the back wheel.

I couldn't roll over and get under the car. The little Dodge was too low to the ground. I had to scrabble my way under, digging my heels into the gravel and shoving along like a mechanic on a creeper, but without the creeper.

My yells declined to a gurgle as I struggled, but I stuffed nearly all of myself under there. Only my left leg was sticking out when the club whacked into my thigh.

I shrieked in pain, and I yanked that leg under, too.

I kept yelling — aware that noise might be the only thing that could save me — but no more blows descended. Then something hit my left side, and I realized the attacker was punching at me, using the club like a pool cue.

When the next punch came, I grabbed at the club. To my surprise, it had sharp corners. I didn't get hold of it, and it was withdrawn. I steeled myself for another punch.

Then I heard the most beautiful sound. It was a deep, loud voice. "Nell! Nell! The cops are coming!" it said.

The back door slammed, and I realized that Rocky was coming, too. Help was on the way.

I tried to warn Rocky. "Watch out! It's a big club!"

But the club was in retreat. The gravel scrunched both to my left and my right. On the left I heard Rocky come down off the porch and walk cautiously across the parking area with a slow "scrunch, pause, scrunch, pause, scrunch." On my right, the attacker ran toward the back gate with a fast "scrunch, scrunch, scrunch, scrunch." The sound faded into the alley.

"Nell? Is that you?" Rocky said. "Where are you?"

"Under my car! Is he gone?"

Rocky couldn't find any signs of the club wielder, so I began to inch out from under the little Dodge. It was a lot harder getting out than it had been getting in. Adrenaline had deadened my sense that the gravel had sharp edges that were digging into every inch of my back.

Adrenaline had also kept me from panicking because the underside of the car was only inches from my face. I don't cope with small, enclosed spaces very well. But while I was being poked at by a club, I hadn't stopped to consider just how small and enclosed the space under a car is.

Rocky helped me into the kitchen, where I sat and shook. Martha hugged me and held my hand, while Rocky hovered, offering to make hot chocolate and other comfort foods. They had just finished watching a videotape, they said. Rocky had gone to the kitchen to rinse out a popcorn bowl, so he was handy when I shrieked.

"I wasn't sure I'd heard you at first," he said. "I had to listen carefully."

In our climate, houses are kept tightly shut in the summer, so the air conditioning won't escape. It was a miracle he'd heard me at all. Maybe there *had* been divine intervention.

After he'd become convinced someone was being attacked in our backyard, Rocky had yelled at Martha to call 911, then opened the door and yelled. And my attacker had fled.

The Grantham PD car pulled up within five minutes. A patrolman came in and asked me if I felt up to making a statement. I think he thought someone had tried to mug me.

Then all hell broke loose.

It began with banging on the front door that sounded like Vikings taking a ram to the drawbridge. The doorbell began to chime like Big Ben striking twenty. And I heard yelling.

It was Mike.

Martha ran and opened the front door. Later she said Mike almost flattened her against the foyer wall as he flung the door back. I heard him roar.

"Nell! Where are you?"

Before I could answer, he came racing into the kitchen and grabbed me. As soon as I assured him I wasn't seriously hurt, he shook me like a rag doll, glaring with every shake.

"What have you been up to?"

The patrolman grabbed his arm. "Calm down, buddy!"

Then Mike turned on him. He dressed the poor guy down. You'd have thought he was a detective in charge of a crime scene, and the patrolman had sprinkled alien cigarette ash all over the place. Which was pretty close to the way Mike saw it, I guess. He had reverted to his days as a detective on the Chicago force, and he was assuming control of the crime scene.

This was not a smart thing for him to be doing. With one temper tantrum, he could wipe out two years spent building a base of support and camaraderie on his hometown force.

"Mike," I said. "Mike!" He didn't pay any attention to me. Finally I tapped him on the arm and raised my voice. "Officer Svenson!"

Mike froze. He seemed to realize that he was bawling out a fellow officer who was of equal or higher rank than he was. He shut his mouth so fast, his teeth clicked.

He gulped twice before he spoke again. "Sorry. This lady is really important to me."

I put my arms around him, and he held me close and murmured in my ear. "Oh, God, Nell! If anything happened to you . . ."

He rested his chin on the top of my head, and in a moment it moved. I realized he was speaking to the patrolman. "Sorry," he said again. "Next time I take a call, and some family member bawls me out, maybe I'll be more sympathetic."

The patrolman looked confused. "Who are you?" he said.

Mike didn't look much like a cop, true. He was wearing his painting clothes — ragged jeans and old T-shirt — and he had paint in his hair. But he calmed down enough to tell the patrolman and his partner who he was, who I was, that I was a witness to the shooting of Paul Howard and that I'd been threatened earlier. He was quite tactful by the time he suggested there might be a connection with the other two cases and that they call for Boone Thompson or for Jim Hammond himself.

Jim did me the honor of coming by to hear about what had happened, and Boone led the search of the backyard.

Mike took me through my statement, questioning me about just what had happened. It wasn't until later that I realized Mike had again taken his detective role.

But even Mike's skillful questioning didn't uncover much information. I had no idea if the person who had set up the ambush in my backyard was a man or a woman. The attacker had seemed to me to be a disembodied club. He or she had said nothing. The gravel was unlikely to show footprints. The alley was paved and the weather had been dry, so footprints probably wouldn't be found there, either.

Because of the possible connection with the death of Cherilyn Howard — "Used a bludgeon. Same M.O.," one of the patrolmen said wisely — our backyard was ringed with crime scene tape. All the neighbors came out to gawk. The crime lab crew took a preliminary look and promised to come out for a closer one the next morning.

But they were not likely to find any physical evidence. Even I could see that. Unless the attacker smoked cigarettes and threw the butts in the grass, or ripped a hunk from whatever garment he or she was wearing, or dropped a snot-stained hanky that would provide DNA evidence.

But I didn't care. I was almost euphoric.

I was alive. And so was Mike.

After two days of zombie-like indifference to everything happening around him, Mike was now alert, interested — much like himself. Oh, he was still angry. I wasn't dumb enough to think he had completely snapped out of the black reaction that had hit him after the death of Paul Howard. But he wasn't locked away from me anymore. I held his hand tightly. I didn't want him to slip away again.

It was Martha who asked the next question. "How did you know about this, Mike? I didn't have time to call you."

"Alan called me," Mike said. "I guess they heard it on the scanner at the *Gazette*."

Sure enough, in about a half-hour my dad came in, and I was once again hugged, petted and generally made to feel that people were glad I was alive. It was a good feeling.

But Jim Hammond picked up on the same theme that Mike had. Mike had shaken me and demanded, "What have you been up to?" Jim was less physical, but he asked the same question in different words.

"Just where have you been poking your nose?"

"Jim, I swear, I have not been looking into the deaths of Paul Howard and Cherilyn at all. I have been leaving it strictly alone."

"Okay, we know what you've not been doing. But what *have* you been doing?"

"Just my job. I've had to spend a lot of time on the new shelter — just because it's new. I've written a story about the move. I've tried to understand just what's going on with the organization. That's what the *Gazette* pays me for."

"Have you found out anything?"

"Nothing I could print."

Mike butted in right then. "Have you quizzed my mom?"

Jim and I answered in unison. "No." We'd each thought we were the one he was asking.

"Mom's on the board," Mike said. "If there's anything illegal over there, she's supposed to know about it."

"She hasn't been threatened, has she?" Jim's voice was sharp.

"She hasn't mentioned it." Mike went to the phone and called his mother's house. I thought he looked a bit relieved when she answered. A few questions confirmed that she was all right and that she had not been threatened. And she hadn't heard of any of the other board members being threatened.

"Well, lock up tight," Mike said. He hung up and looked at me. He was still angry. I knew his anger wasn't directed at me, but at whoever had attacked me. Still, I was getting tired of being glared at.

"Nell," he said, "what do you know that the board members don't?"

"Nothing! That shelter has been hell to get information out of. Patsy talks all the time and never says anything. The board president has been out of town ever since I was assigned to the non-profit beat. And everybody else says she's the only one who can talk to the press."

"But you've been hanging around over there."

"Oh, I know a lot about the shelter, true. I know how many bedrooms the new building has, and how many people it will hold. And how much the project cost, and who the major donors were. I know that it's a one-woman show, with Patsy as star performer. But I don't know where any of the bodies are buried. Unless they're in that Victorian parlor they're supposed to have. Nobody will talk about that."

Jim and Mike looked at each other sharply. "I hadn't heard about that," Mike said.

"Somebody donated a lot of Victorian furniture to the shelter some time ago," I said. "It's in storage. But they're supposed to set up a beautiful Victorian parlor — make the shelter feel less institutional. Some decorator donated some fancy swagged draperies. Those are in place, but the furniture isn't. And when I asked Lacy Balke about it, she stuttered. Not exactly enough to hang an exposé on."

Mike was still glaring. "Anything else that people won't talk about?"

"No. Nothing they won't talk about." I sighed and decided I had to mention the elusive Bernie, who had been Cherilyn's roommate and who had disappeared the night Cherilyn was killed. "But there's one thing they keep talking about when I haven't asked."

I quickly described my casual question about Cherilyn's roommate and my resulting suspicion that she was listed as a missing person. I didn't follow this up with my conclusion that Bernie had entered the underground railroad, and that her boarding station had been the Grantham Women's Shelter.

That's when Alan cleared his throat and produced a printout of a news story.

"This will be in the *Gazette* tomorrow," he said. "I knew Nell had been interested in the missing persons report on this Bernie, so I made a printout to bring her."

He passed the page around. I read it over

Mike's shoulder. It said that Grantham police were aiding the Washington County Sheriff's Department in looking for the wife of a Washington County deputy sheriff. The wife had disappeared a week before, leaving most of her clothing and other personal belongings behind. Her husband had no idea where she could have gone, but she had previously lived in Grantham, and he was asking if friends had seen her. Theft charges previously filed by her mother-in-law had now been dropped, the story said.

The missing woman's name was Bernadette Fitzgerald, and her nickname was Bernie.

It was a five- or six-inch story, quite routine.

But when Jim Hammond read the story, his reaction was anything but routine.

He jumped to his feet and waved the printout in the air.

"Mike!" he roared. "This could be where that pistol came from!"

CHAPTER 18

Jim left, apparently headed to a city phone to call the Washington County sheriff, and the rest of the crowd drifted away, too. Alan and Boone went home, Martha went upstairs, and Rocky went into his own sitting room and turned on some late night rerun of a formerly prime-time sitcom. We could hear the canned laughter at intervals.

Mike and I sat on the living room couch and held each other.

Things didn't get too passionate; neither of us was really in the mood, but I wanted to be sure he was there. Maybe he felt the same way. For a long time neither of us said anything.

Finally my curiosity won. "How are the nightmares going?" I asked.

"Haven't had a one."

"Oh." I wasn't sure that was a good thing. If Mike wasn't having nightmares, it might mean he wasn't making any progress in dealing with the killing of Paul Howard.

"How are you sleeping?"

He shrugged. It felt like "Not good" to me.

"How about Dr. Benson?"

"He seems like a nice guy."

"Oh."

"I'm more worried about you than about me," Mike said. "Nobody's trying to kill me."

"Mike, honest! I don't know anything that would cause anybody to kill me."

He kissed my forehead. "Nell, is there anything — anything — you didn't tell Jim?"

"Nothing. Not really."

"I know a wish-washy answer when I hear one. Spit it out."

"I have no evidence. It may be all in my head."

"There're a lot of smart ideas in that head."

Flattery can get Mike anywhere. So I told him. First about Bernie's mysterious disappearance in the night, and the shelter's claim that she couldn't be reached. Then about the missing persons detective coming out. Then about my computer search of the *Gazette* library, which revealed similar cases in which other women disappeared after

273

staying at the Grantham Women's Shelter. And my deduction that the shelter was a stop on the underground railroad.

"But it could all be coincidence." I sighed. "And now I've put you on the spot. You probably have to turn them in for running some kind of an illegal operation."

Mike shook his head. "Like you say, there's no concrete evidence. And if Bernadette Fitzgerald left the shelter of her own accord, it's probably not illegal, no matter who took her away."

I contemplated that. "I guess I really don't want to know if it's true or not," I said. "I don't know how I feel about all this, Mike. Is what they're doing — if they're doing it — wrong?"

"I don't know. If a woman — Bernadette, for example — feels that she can't fight someone who's threatening her life — and I admit that can be a problem if she's married to a cop — then she may not have much choice but to run. And if I felt sure someone was mistreating a kid, and I couldn't find any legal way to stop it, then I can understand taking some desperate action."

"Of course, there's a lot of room for abuse in the underground railway. It would be a great way to escape arrest."

"That's possible, too." Mike's embrace

tightened, and we sat there a moment.

"Patsy was very firm when she told me that she didn't know anything about it," I said.

"Which means she's blinking while someone else over there runs the system."

"I didn't want to put you on the spot."

"You haven't. I don't know a thing."

"Maybe I can ask around — "

"No!" Mike sat up straight, and I thought he was going to shake me again. "You're going to drop the whole thing. Don't go near that shelter!"

I didn't argue. The memory of that club rising and falling was too clear.

Mike stood up then. "Guess I'd better go," he said.

I batted my eyelashes in a parody of seduction. "I imagine you could stay," I said.

"What about your 'no overnight boyfriends' rule?" Martha, Rocky and I had this agreement, and Mike knew it.

"We can close the door, and I'll sneak you out at six a.m. As usual." Mike and I had broken the agreement before, and Martha pretended not to notice as long as she didn't meet Mike in the bathroom.

"I don't think you're feeling too passionate," Mike said.

"I wouldn't mind company, either

275

passionate or impassionate." I waggled my eyebrows like Groucho Marx.

Mike laughed. "I've got to be up and doing," he said. "But thanks." Then he left.

"Up and doing." I wondered about his phrase as I made sure all the doors and windows were locked, then headed upstairs. Maybe Mike wanted to work on his nightmares by himself.

I took a long, hot, relaxing shower and washed the gravel out of my hair. I admired the vivid bruise that was developing on my left thigh. I set my alarm. Then I held a book in my lap, stared into space and thought.

I thought about the shelter, about the people I'd met over there, about the things I'd learned, about the possibility that the shelter was doubling as a station on the underground railway.

I abruptly fell asleep. When the alarm went off, I knew what to do next.

I'd call Mary Baker. She knew everything that happened at the shelter. And I couldn't suspect Mary Baker of being the person with the club. She was simply too full of kindness and common sense. I got up and grabbed clothes out of the closet.

I had to invade the crime scene area in my backyard to get my car out. Boone was already there, along with the GPD crime scene team and the Chevy van that held their portable lab. They agreed that they were through with my car and let me drive away. The dent in the roof didn't look too serious.

Further down the alley I passed one of the techs. He was kneeling, taking photos of something. As I drove past, I looked at him. He was photographing a board, maybe a two-by-four. It looked as if someone has tossed it aside, and one end had landed up against a fence.

Was that the club the vague figure had wielded? It was the right shape — I remembered the rectangular feel of it as it was poked at me from the side of the car.

My teeth chattered the rest of the way downtown. That two-by-four could have brained me in a minute. But I had to go to work. I could not let fear take over my life.

I went up to the newsroom, fielded a dozen questions about the night before, assured Judy Connors I didn't want to write a first-person account of being attacked by a club-wielding masked person, and sat down at my desk. Today, I vowed, I'd act like a real reporter. I'd actually go on my beat.

But first I called the shelter. Luckily, Mary Baker was there.

"Hi, Mary. How about lunch?"

"Why?" Mary's voice was cheerful, but curious.

"I just wanted to talk about the shelter with someone who seems levelheaded."

There was a pause before she answered. "I usually eat with the clients."

"I can offer the Trellis Room. My treat."

Mary paused again, then laughed. "Offer me cheesecake and I'll follow you anywhere. What time?"

We settled on noon, which would be before the fashionable hour for ladies lunching, and while there was plenty of cheesecake left. I called to reserve a table. Mary may have thought I was bribing her with cheesecake, but I was really picking a place so public that I'd feel safe. If anyone walked into the Trellis Room wearing a ski mask and carrying a two-by-four, one of the lunching ladies was sure to notice.

Then I went on my beat. I hit the Red Cross office and talked to the public information specialist, attended a ten o'clock meeting of the Cancer Society board to check on their plans to sponsor a city-wide colon cancer screening, then dropped by the Health Department to introduce myself to the director. He'd been on vacation since I'd taken over the beat. He wanted to talk, so I was nearly late for my luncheon date.

Mary arrived at the Trellis Room wearing a denim jumper, plaid shirt, and loafers. It was the first time I'd seen her in anything except slacks, a tunic top and tennis shoes. I speculated that she'd gone home and changed.

Mary ordered a bowl of vegetable soup and asked the waitress to put aside a serving of chocolate caramel cheesecake. I went for the spinach salad and the raspberry cheesecake. We both had iced tea, since it's the official drink of the American Southwest.

I opened the conversation. "Is the staff settling in to the new building?"

"Oh, sure. The cook is ecstatic over the storage space and the new stove."

"Who's in charge of the housekeeping over there? I know the clients have to clean their own rooms."

"They clean the common areas, too. Which may mean they're not always spotless. These gals have a lot on their minds."

"Who decides what's to be done on a given day?"

"Dawn. She's basically the administrator."

"I thought she ran the office."

"That, too. Since she left the counseling staff. She has a master's in social work from Grantham State." Mary raised her eyebrows. "Phi Beta Kappa, or so her mother always says."

"I thought Patsy did a lot of the counseling."

"Patsy does a lot of the inspiring. There are two professionals to lead group sessions, get people on welfare — the other social work type things. Patsy's not a professional counselor, but she's extremely intuitive."

"Reads minds?"

Mary chuckled. "Sometimes she seems to. I can remember — well, maybe I'd better shut up."

"Tell me. You don't have to name names."

She contemplated her tea glass, and I wondered if she were editing the story. "Well, this woman called in one day. Said she was closing up her mother's house, and she wanted to donate all the sheets and towels to the shelter. So we gave her the address, and she came by. I was on the desk, so I let her in. Patsy just happened to be standing there, and she gave the woman the glad hand."

Mary stopped. "Was the woman impressed?" I prompted.

"I thought that Patsy had picked her as a potentially hefty donor. She was reasonably well-dressed." She gestured at the women around us. "You know, looked like she was on her way to lunch here. Maybe a little more formal than most of the people are here — more like church. But she kept standing there, talking about how she hated to see her mother's linens going to waste, and Patsy kept egging her on, telling her about the shelter and about other things we could use — food, clothing, toys.

"Then Patsy began to say things that had nothing to do with that. I kind of tuned her out, I've heard it so often. She began to cite statistics — from a third to a half of all women are abused at some time in their lives, that abuse can happen in all socioeconomic classes, that the abusers are fearful people who have to be in control — and she said something like, 'And we're so glad you came to us.' And she gestured toward me, and she said, 'Mary, I think Mrs. So-and-so would like a Kleenex.' And I looked up, and this well-dressed, poised woman had simply dissolved. She was standing there, just openly weeping. And she said to Patsy, 'What am I going to do? He's waiting in the car.'

"And Patsy put her arms around her and said, 'You're not going anyplace where it's not safe.' And Patsy went outside and told this guy that his wife was going to stay — and she made it stick."

Mary shook her head. "Patsy is unbelievable. I would have simply brushed the woman off — not intentionally, but her facade would have fooled me completely. Patsy caught on."

"Is it because she was an abused wife herself?"

"I'm sure that encourages people to talk to her. But — she simply looks people in the face. Like I said, I think it's pure intuition."

Our food came then. Mary buttered a roll, and I poured Russian dressing over my spinach. I led the conversation to Mary herself, talking about how long she'd worked at the shelter and about her four daughters and eight grandkids. All of them lived in Grantham.

"I think they're the real reason I keep so busy over at the shelter," she said.

"Why?"

"I'm not the greatest grandmother. Little kids make me really nervous. But my daughters seem to think I just live to baby-sit. I don't mind helping them out in an emergency — if one of the kids is sick or something. But having a commitment at the shelter gets me out of a lot of routine hassle. I didn't really enjoy it when my kids were little, and I don't want to do it all over again."

I waited until the cheesecake arrived before I introduced my real topic of conversation.

"Mary, I'm going to go into my blunt mode," I said.

"Okay. I've been wondering why I'm here."

"I've been reading articles about what I call 'the underground railroad.' I want to know if the Grantham Women's Shelter is a station stop."

Mary didn't flinch. "Is this for publication?"

"I'm not planning to do a story," I said. "Not unless it gets tied up with the deaths of Paul and Cherilyn Howard."

Mary frowned, and I pressed the point. "Mary, two people are dead. One of them has been killed in circumstances that point to someone from the shelter being the killer. There are not going to be any secrets if Cherilyn's death had anything to do with that underground railway business."

"It didn't."

I'd made a breakthrough. Mary had confirmed that the underground railroad did exist.

"Can you be sure?"

"The 'underground railroad' — I call it 'the tunnel' — was never a possibility for Cherilyn Howard. She didn't want to leave her life here behind."

"A woman who would do that would have

to be pretty desperate."

"There are a lot of desperate people out there. Women whose husbands are sexually abusing their daughters — or their sons. Kids who are on the streets because they don't dare go home. Women whose husbands are abusive but so plausible that the police never believe the women's stories."

"Wives of cops?"

"Sometimes." Mary laid her fork down. "I saw the story about Bernie Fitzgerald in this morning's *Gazette*. Are you talking about her?"

"She disappeared. She could have been the latest to leave Grantham by that 'tunnel.' Is it just a coincidence that she was Cherilyn's only friend in the shelter?"

Mary nodded. "If we'd known Cherilyn was going to be killed, she wouldn't have left that night. It's complicated everything."

"Patsy claims she knows nothing about this."

"Oh, no! Patsy would be the last person we'd involve. She's too vulnerable."

"Vulnerable?"

"Oh, yes. Patsy would do anything to protect or advance the shelter. Threaten to close her down or offer her a big grant — she'd blab everything. We'd never tell her anything."

"She told me she'd see if she could get Bernie to call me."

Mary grimaced and took a bite of cheesecake. "Once they leave, Nell, I really don't know where they are."

"Surely you could trace along . . ."

Mary looked grim. She chewed and swallowed. "I'll work on it," she said. "But don't say anything to Patsy, okay?"

I promised. We finished our cheesecake, I paid the bill and we left. When we reached Mary's car, I turned to her for one last question.

"Mary, why are you doing this?"

"What do you mean?"

"You've denied that you yourself were an abused wife. You made it clear that none of your daughters are in that situation. What made you become active in this — railway or tunnel or whatever we call it? You could go to prison!"

Mary looked at me, and suddenly her eyes were sparkling.

"That's it," she said. "The risk! My husband was a very interesting man, full of intellectual curiosity, always ready to try something new. Without him — things got too dull."

"So you got involved in something of dubious legality?"

"That's what makes it fun! Illegal isn't always immoral. This is a job that needs to be done. These women need help. And what have I got to lose? I've lived a full and happy life. Besides, who's going to send a grand-mother to jail?

"I always wanted to be a spy, pictured my-self leaving secret messages at the third lamppost from the corner, dodging the KGB. Now I can do something along that line. I'm having a great time!"

She thanked me for the lunch, still sparkling, got in her car and started the motor. As I went to my own car, she pulled up beside me and rolled her window down.

"Remember, Patsy's the weak link over there. Don't tell her a thing!" she said. And she drove away, grinning happily.

CHAPTER 19

My grandmother used to say, "First deny-er, first liar."

I thought of that as I drove away from the restaurant. Was Mary being too firm in her denial? Was she covering up Patsy's involvement in the underground railroad?

Or was I giving Patsy credit for a subtlety she didn't really possess?

Actually, everything I had seen of Patsy indicated she was a straight-ahead, forward-march kind of person. She might be intuitive in her readings of people, as Mary had said, but she wasn't tricky. She was thinking about the shelter's viewpoint every minute. In justice, this included how the shelter could best serve its clients, not only how she could get money and other help for it.

I wondered idly how Patsy was going to get along with Enid Philpott Howard that afternoon. If I knew Patsy, she would not only convince Mrs. Howard that she herself hadn't made strange phone calls to Paul Howard, she would also convince her that the Philpott Foundation should pay off the shelter's mortgage. And maybe pay to get the Victorian furniture out of storage.

Of course, Patsy wouldn't know how much either the mortgage or the storage bill amounted to. She brushed off minor details like that.

Mike's house was just two blocks off my route, so I stopped by and punched my garage door opener. As the door swung up, I saw that his truck was gone. Where could he be?

I went inside, but Mike hadn't left a note giving me a hint. The painting gear had been tossed into the garage, so maybe he was through with the redecorating therapy. But what was he "up and doing"?

I used Mike's phone to call the office and talk to the assignments editor, telling her I was going by the United Way office before I came in, and giving her an estimated length on the story I planned to write about the cancer screening. She would report all this to Ruth, the city editor, when Ruth got there at four o'clock, so Ruth could begin allotting space.

The United Way office was in a building

just a few blocks from the *Gazette,* and I parked in the newspaper's parking garage and walked over. To my disappointment, the United Way director, C. C. Cecil, was not in. I'd wanted to mend a few fences after our rather acrimonious conversation the day before, but the receptionist said he was out for the afternoon. The public information officer was there, she said, though he was tied up at the moment. I said I'd wait and sat down in the reception area, glad that the United Way had seen fit to spend funds on comfortable chairs, local artists and a couple of trees in big pots.

I opened my notebook and began to try to write a lead about a mass colon cancer screening. It wasn't easy to get people to be checked for colon cancer. It's an embarrassing test. "Don't die of embarrassment." How was that? Not in good taste? Maybe it would be better to play it straight with, "A community-wide screening for colon cancer is being planned by the Grantham Chapter of the American Cancer Society."

Before I came to a decision, a voice caught my ear.

"No! The deadline is tomorrow," it said. "We can't make exceptions."

It was a woman's voice, deep and reverberating. I didn't recognize the voice, but I was willing to bet that whoever it was sang contralto solos.

I looked around and decided the voice was coming from an open door straight across the reception room. The plate to the left of the door read "Muriel Harmon, Executive Secretary."

I hadn't met Muriel, though I knew she was second-in-command to C. C. Cecil. I'd had no idea she had such an interesting voice.

"You're making a big deal out of nothing," the voice said. "It's only a routine report. Look in your files for the one you did last year, then update the numbers."

I had assumed Muriel was talking on the telephone, since I hadn't heard any reply, but now something moved beyond the door frame. A neat black pump began to bounce up and down nervously. Then I heard a small, whispery voice, so faint that I wouldn't have noticed it without Muriel's ringing tones to draw my attention.

I couldn't understand what the voice was saying. "Whisper, murmur, whisper," it went. And the black shoe pumped up and down nervously.

Muriel's voice boomed again. "Lost? How can the files be lost?"

More whispering.

"I'll bet Mary knows where they are."

Whisper, whisper.

"Yes, I can understand that you'd rather not go to her, but you'll have to. We will be forced to postpone your next allotment if we don't have that report on time."

Whisper, whisper.

"I'm sorry." Muriel sounded exasperated, not sorry. "I know the move has confused things. But we can't make exceptions, Dawn."

Dawn. Oh, my gosh! Muriel had been reading the riot act to Dawn Baumgarner. I couldn't get away from that shelter, no matter where I went.

I felt panicky for a moment. I felt sure Dawn was going to come out of that office, and I did not want her to know I'd heard the scolding she'd gotten from Muriel Harmon. I looked around the reception area. Where could I hide out? I saw a little arrow that pointed to rest rooms down the hall. I grabbed my notebook and purse and stood up quickly.

But before I could take more than a step toward the rest room, the receptionist spoke. "Nell Matthews?"

"Yes?"

"You have a phone call."

I took the call at a desk in the corner —

apparently unoccupied. It was the assignments editor, the *Gazette* staffer I had just spoken to from Mike's house.

"Glad I caught you," she said. "Can you head on over to Enid Philpott Howard's office?"

"What! What's going on?"

"Apparently she and Patsy Raymond put their heads together, and they have a statement. They want you to come over to pick it up. They asked for you."

I was hanging up the phone when Dawn came out of Muricl Harmon's office. She looked almost scared when she saw me, turning to glance back over her shoulder and hesitating before she walked forward.

At least I'd been over near the phone when she came out. I didn't think she could have figured out that I'd overheard Muriel scolding her.

I told the receptionist I'd have to come back to talk to the PIO another time and left. Dawn and I rode down in the elevator together, but I didn't pay much attention to her. I was thinking about Patsy and Mrs. Howard. A statement? What had those two cooked up? If the two of them got behind something — anything — it was a done deal. With Patsy's charisma and Mrs. Howard's money, they could take over the country in about a week.

Suddenly I realized Dawn was talking to me. I jumped all over.

"I'm sorry, Dawn. What did you say? I got some unexpected news on the phone, and I'm still off in a cloud. I wasn't listening."

"I just said you had a narrow escape last night."

"I was very lucky," I said. "Joe Bob would probably say it was a miracle."

"Joe Bob is definitely a pietist."

I looked at Dawn. A pietist. I remembered the term from some long-ago Sunday-school class. It's often used to refer to a person who emphasizes a personal relationship with God, as opposed to corporate worship.

Well, that summed up Joe Bob. I would have thought it summed up Dawn, too. At least, she'd referred to her "prayer list." But she wasn't acting as if she saw herself as a pietist. I decided not to ask any more, but Dawn spoke again.

"Joe Bob is a young Christian," she said in a condescending tone. "Young in the faith. I'm sure he'll develop a more mature religious viewpoint."

"He seems completely sincere, and I admire that," I said. I was surprised to hear myself defending Joe Bob. I decided it was time to change the subject. "Do you have to come up to the United Way office often?"

"Paperwork," Dawn said. She sighed. "I know they need it, but I don't know why they can't keep things straight."

Her comment made me have trouble keeping my face straight. For Dawn to imply that the United Way office had their paperwork in a mess when she herself had just been called on the carpet — well, it was laughable. Luckily, the elevator door opened then, and we were on the first floor. I fled out the door and up the street, waving goodbye to Dawn.

Enid Philpott Howard's offices were in an elegant skyscraper just two blocks further down Main. First National Bank of Grantham, now absorbed into Grantham National Bank, had built the building in the 1920s, and it was Art Deco to the teeth. The main bank lobby now swallowed up the few people who came in to write checks and make deposits, and the upper floors were given over to consumer and commercial loan departments and to the corporate headquarters for GNB Holding. I didn't know how many branches GNB had. Seems they opened a new one every few days.

I was studying the building's directory, trying to figure out which floor Enid Philpott Howard had deigned to occupy, when an elevator opened and several people emerged. I didn't look at them until a hand was clapped on my shoulder.

The touch came too quickly after I had been attacked by a guy with a two-by-four. I dodged away and whirled around.

It was Jim Hammond.

"What are you doing here?" we said in unison.

"I didn't mean to startle you," Jim said. "I've been talking to Mrs. Howard and Patsy Raymond about their new scheme."

"What is it? They called me over to give me a news release on it."

"You'll find out. Where's Mike?"

"I don't know. He's not at his house. Last night he said he had to be 'up and doing.' But he didn't say what he planned to get up and do."

"He called this morning, asked me a lot of nonsensical questions."

"What about?"

"A bunch of stuff. The Grantham State University Alumni Association. Patsy Raymond's ex-husband. Flea markets. Paul Howard's job at the bank."

"That doesn't sound very focused."

I guess I looked worried, because Jim patted my arm. "Mike's okay," he said. "Last night he seemed to snap out of that awful lethargy he'd been in since — since — "

"Listen, Nell, Mike's not going to get over this right away. I've known guys — sometimes they break down and cry, sometimes they're shaky for months. I've known one or two who started hitting the bottle."

"I know, Jim."

"But Mike's not one of these who tries to hide his feelings — from himself, I mean. It's the ones who say they're okay that I worry about. They're usually not. But Mike will be fine. It's just going to take time. Hang in there, gal."

He gave me a final pat and went out the front door. I decided to head for the GNB corporate offices on the top floor. And I worried all the way up.

The previous night, when Mike had finally decided to be "up and doing," I'd felt that there was hope that he'd break out of the depression that had hit him. Now apparently he was wandering around asking questions that Jim saw no sense to. I hoped he wasn't going to step on a lot of toes needlessly. Patsy Raymond's ex-husband? Was he in prison? Had he been in prison? Why had Mike wanted to know? Grantham State Alumni records? Flea markets? Paul Howard's job? It was a strange combination.

As the elevator door opened on the top floor, I tried to forget Mike's situation, which was up to him, and focus on something I could influence — my job. What did Patsy and Mrs. Howard want with me?

At least I felt sure it would be worth a story.

An attractive woman — mid-thirties, dark hair, beautiful suit — sat opposite the elevator door. She gave me a smile. After all, this was the parent company of Grantham National, whose slogan was "The Friendly Bank."

"May I help you?" she said, managing to make me feel that I had made her day by dropping by. When I identified myself, she nodded knowingly.

"Mr. McNeal wanted to know when you arrived."

"Mr. McNeal?"

"Our marketing director."

"Oh." One black mark against GNB, as far as I was concerned. The duties of public relations director and marketing director are not the same. Too many businesses, and even entities such as hospitals or professional associations, try to combine them. This leads to news releases which can't be told from ads. Then the marketing directors get all bent out of shape because their news releases are either completely rewritten or not used at all.

I took a seat and checked out the reception area while I waited for Mr. McNeal. The room was all dark colors, plants and antique furniture — furniture that had been the latest thing when Grantham was settled in the late 1800s. Of course, Grantham's early settlers hadn't had fancy furniture. This had been brought from elsewhere by some decorator determined to make Grantham National seem like an old established bank.

Actually, or so I'd learned from the *Gazette*'s business editor, Grantham National was formed as a suburban bank in the mid-1970s when Edna Philpott Howard's father, Anthony Philpott, got mad at the president of First National. It had been only ten years since Grantham National acquired First National and its Art Deco building. Speculation was that Anthony Philpott turned over in his grave at the thought of the price the directors agreed to pay his old rival. And they'd paid a pretty price for the office decor of the corporate HQ, too. At least, the furnishings looked like genuine antiques.

I didn't have time to look the furniture over in detail, because a smooth-looking man, fifty-ish and wearing a gorgeous pin-stripe, came out from an inner sanctum.

"Miss Matthews? I'm Steve McNeal." We shook hands. "Please come on back to Mrs. Howard's office."

"Back" was the right term. I think we walked clear to the back of the building, which was half a block deep. And on the way, Steve McNeal told me he was a former reporter for the *Gazette*.

"Jake Edwards and I covered trials together. How's Jake doing?"

"Fine, as far as I know. We're not in the same coffee klatch, but he keeps up with what goes on in the newsroom."

"Jake bawled me out when I quit. Called me a sell-out."

I smiled, but my mouth felt stiff. I didn't know what to answer to that comment. Most real newspaper types — like my dad and like Jake Edwards and maybe like me — consider public relations only a baby step from selling yourself on the streets.

McNeal seemed to understand my silence. He chuckled. "I went back to school, got a master's in marketing," he said. "Changed my whole focus. But sometimes I still miss chasing fires."

He walked past a young woman at a desk, rapped lightly on a beautiful carved door, then opened it. He waved me ahead of him. "Here she is, Mrs. Howard."

Mrs. Howard's office had been outfitted by the same decorator, again from the same late 1800s era, but it had a lighter, less ponderous color scheme, and the furniture was smaller in scale.

Mrs. Howard wasn't behind the library table that apparently served as a desk. She was seated in a curvy chair, alongside an equally curvy love seat. And on the love seat was Patsy Raymond.

Both of them had been crying.

I didn't mention the tears. Mrs. Howard motioned me to a place beside Patsy and took a sheaf of papers from Steve McNeal. McNeal didn't leave, but he moved across the room, leaving the three of us apparently secluded. Which didn't mean he wasn't hearing every word.

"Ms. Matthews, Patsy and I have come to an understanding," Mrs. Howard said. "I've discussed what I'm about to tell you with a representative of the Grantham Police Department. Steve has prepared a news release, which will be distributed to the media this afternoon, but we wanted to talk to you directly."

"Why me?"

"Because we felt that your close association with these tragic events entitled you to a full explanation."

I picked up my pen. "Just what have you decided?"

"First, I'm withdrawing all my remarks about Patsy Raymond calling my son, and I'm extending a full apology to her."

Patsy put her hand on Mrs. Howard's arm before she spoke in her hoarse whisper. "I fully understand just how Mrs. Howard came to feel I had made those terrible phone calls, and I don't blame her at all for her reaction."

It was a regular love feast. I nodded and scribbled.

Mrs. Howard turned to me. "After meeting Patsy, I see how her personality and dedication have the capability of aiding abused women. She's made me see the scope of the problem in much broader terms — " She seemed to struggle to go on. "It's important to break the cycle of abuse — it's a mother's responsibility."

She stopped and gulped, then took a glass of iced tea from the end table and sipped it. In a minute, she seemed to regain control, and she spoke again.

"Secondly, I'm offering a reward for information that leads to the arrest and conviction of the person who killed my daughter-in-law, Cherilyn Carnahan Howard. Her death was the end of a beautiful and promising life. I join Cherilyn's parents in grieving for this lovely young woman."

It was getting deep in there. I kept scribbling.

But Mrs. Howard sat back in her chair. She looked at Patsy, and she might as well have been a folk singer saying "Take it" to her partner.

Patsy took it. "Mrs. Howard and I have gone over the entire situation with the phone calls," she said in her raspy voice. "Apparently someone took advantage of the way my voice sounds, and the fact that many people know it sounds that way. That person called Paul Howard repeatedly, telling him it was me. He believed the caller and was manipulated into making the attack that led to his death."

Patsy and Mrs. Howard exchanged glances and quick nods. I was afraid the sisterly feeling was about to stain the carpet.

"Because of the circumstances of the calls," Patsy said, "to my horror, I have had to accept the knowledge that the calls were made from the Grantham Women's Shelter.

"Therefore, I intend to work very hard, to exhaust every opportunity to identify who made them. Staff members, volunteers and even clients will be quizzed."

Her face grew grim, and she did not look to Mrs. Howard for support or agreement. "Nell," she said, "I'm going to find out who used the shelter this way or die trying."

CHAPTER 20

As I walked back to the *Gazette*, I considered that my assessment of Patsy's powers of persuasion hadn't been far off. First she had convinced Mrs. Howard that she hadn't made the phone calls to Paul Howard. Then she had convinced her that the shelter's work was worthwhile.

The night Paul had been killed, Mrs. Howard had referred to the "fad" of aid for abused wives. Three days later, she seemed convinced it was a genuine need. Patsy had not only cleared her name with Mrs. Howard, she'd taken a giant step toward getting the shelter on the list for Philpott Foundation backing.

As to the reward Mrs. Howard was offering for conviction of Cherilyn's killer — well, I didn't know how much good that would do. We weren't talking about a street crime, a crime in which a witness might turn up or in which the killer might brag to friends. I supposed it was possible that some of Cherilyn's parents' neighbors might have seen a strange car in the neighborhood or someone walking along the street at the time of Cherilyn's death. But they surely would have told the police about it already. The Carnahans lived in an ordinary middle- and working-class neighborhood, after all, not the kind of area in which people are afraid to talk to cops.

I thought the reward was largely symbolic.

When I got to my desk, my voice mail was blinking. The message was from Mike's mom. That frightened me, since I was still worried about Mike, but when I reached her, she simply invited me over for dinner. Mike had called, and on the spur of the moment, she had asked him to come.

"I'm getting carryout something-or-other," she said. "Nothing fancy. How about your dad? Could Alan come, too?"

"I'll be there," I said. "But Alan's on the copy desk tonight. How was Mike when you talked to him?"

"He seemed awfully absentminded. But not comatose, the way he was Sunday. That was scary. See you around six-thirty."

I wrote the story about the meeting be-tween Patsy and Enid Howard, leading with the reward. I got hold of Jim Hammond to ask for a statement on the reward and on the progress of the investigation. By the time I turned the story in, it was five o'clock, and I told Ruth I was putting the colon cancer story off a day.

"No, you're not," she said. "Sorry, but I've already got it dummied in on my health page. Six or eight inches ought to fill the hole."

I went back to my terminal. So much for changing clothes before I went to Wilda's. Which reminded me — how was I getting to Wilda's? I called Mike, but got his answering machine. I decided I'd better not wait to hear from him, and told the machine I was running a little late and that I'd see him at his mom's house. Not that he'd indicated that he planned to pick me up.

I was clicking away at the colon cancer story, frantic to finish and get out of there, when the phone rang again. I wanted to answer with "What the hell do you want?" but instead I said "This is Nell Matthews."

"Oh, Nell, I'm so glad I caught you." It was Mary Baker. She was her usual cheerful self. "I hope you can get free tonight."

"Why?"

"Bernadette Fitzgerald is going to call."

"Oh! When?"

"Ten o'clock. I know it's late, but — well, it may not be late where she is."

"Where is she?"

"I don't know. And I don't want to know. But she's agreed to call the old shelter phone."

"The old shelter?"

"Yes. The person who called me said she was willing to call only to that phone, because she knew it doesn't have caller ID"

I gave a scoffing chuckle. "Well, we won't use caller ID if she doesn't want us to, but we could plug a different phone in there."

"Actually, you couldn't. That house is so old that the phone connections are the originals — wall connections, not phone jacks."

"I'm surprised that there's still a phone hooked up there, now that the shelter's moved."

"Dawn still has some filing cabinets in that office, and she's doing some work over there, so the phone is still working."

I barely hesitated before I assured Mary I'd be at the shelter office shortly before ten, ready to talk to the mysterious Bernie. Three hours should be long enough for dinner at Wilda's.

Actually, now that we'd established that Bernie was the person who brought the mysterious police issue pistol to the shelter

307

and left it there — at least, it had been established to my satisfaction — I really didn't have a lot to ask her. But she apparently was the last person to talk to Cherilyn on a friendly level. Maybe she'd know something about her that the public would want to read.

I finished the colon cancer screening story, hung over Alan's shoulder while he copyread it, then told him I was headed for Wilda's for dinner.

"You were invited, but I told Wilda that you were on the desk."

"Maybe someday I'll get a regular daytime job."

"Ha! You'd hate it."

"Probably." He shook a finger. "Young lady, you go home early and get some rest. And be careful!"

"Yes, Daddy."

He laughed. "Have a relaxing evening," he said.

Wilda lives in a town house in one of Grantham's most exclusive areas. Her place offers high security, a marvelous view of a golf course, beautiful furniture and decor, plus comfort. She met me at the door wearing a knit tunic and trousers in a golden brown that blended with the shade of blond she'd picked for her summer hairdo. Gold lamé tennis shoes matched her chunky gold necklace and earrings.

I'd run by the house and taken off my panty hose, substituting khaki slacks for my linen skirt and leaving on the tan-and-rust plaid shirt I'd worn all day. For jewelry I wore a gold wristwatch and some gold stud earrings. Wilda always makes me feel like a fashion nincompoop.

What the heck, the rust in my shirt made my hair look really red, I told myself. And I'll never be able to wear clothes the way Wilda does. I'm average height, after all. She's four inches taller.

I'd arrived at Wilda's determined to follow my father's instructions and have a relaxing evening — at least until time to go take Bernie's call — but Mike sabotaged me. He got there five minutes after I did, and from the moment he said "No, thanks" to an offer of a beer, I knew relaxation was not on his agenda.

Wilda's idea of "carryout" had been to call Mike's favorite Mexican restaurant for a dozen enchiladas — three each of beef with chili sauce, chicken with sour cream sauce and chicken with salsa verde — plus rice, beans and tortilla chips. Normally, a bottle of Mexican beer would be Mike's beverage of choice with this meal. It was mine. But

Mike made himself a glass of instant iced tea.

Mike was obviously keyed up. After his three days of passively sitting by while things happened around him, it was a relief to see him taking an interest. But that evening, I wanted to be passive. I was tired. I had had a bad scare the night before, and the reaction was still hitting periodically. I wanted to eat a whole bunch of Mexican food with people I liked and who liked me, drink a beer, then go home. I'd have been happy to swap the talking to Bernie bit for an extra hour of sleep.

Instead, I got to watch Mike give his mother the third degree.

Oh, he waited until we'd eaten. But as soon as we'd all three declared ourselves too full for the pralines Wilda had bought for dessert, he started in. I got up and began to clear the table. I was staying out of this.

"Mom, just what's wrong over at the shelter?"

Wilda frowned. "What do you mean?"

"I mean that something's got the board members all antsy — Jim noticed it, and so did Nell — but Patsy Raymond keeps smiling like mad. What's going on?"

"Nothing, Mike."

"Is the board going to fire Patsy?"

"Heavens, no! Where'd you get that idea?"

"All I can pick up is this vague talk about a reorganization."

"A reorganization is all it is. Not a revolution. Patsy has built that shelter from scratch. She's not leaving."

"In what way are things being reorganized?"

Wilda sighed deeply. "You know. The budget process. The records. Things like that."

"Why?"

"Some changes were needed."

"Why?"

"We want to go for more grants. That requires a different sort of record keeping."

"Why?"

"Good Lord, Mike! I thought I got you out of the 'why' stage by the age of four!"

"Why?"

Wilda threw a tortilla chip at him. "Because!"

"Because why?"

They both laughed. Then Mike patted her shoulder. "Listen, Mom, I don't understand what the board is concerned about, but both Jim and I think it may well be related to people getting killed over there. So, do you want to tell me? Or do you want to tell Jim?"

"It might be easier to tell Jim," Wilda said. She picked up her paper napkin and twisted it into a bow tie. "The truth is, Patsy is a terrific fund-raiser and a marvelous speaker and a very charismatic group leader. But she's not all that efficient."

There was no surprise in that. I kept my mouth shut, got up and looked in Wilda's cabinet for a plastic dish to put the leftover enchiladas in.

"I heard there were no records on that pistol I used."

"Exactly! That's the kind of thing we're concerned about. Oh, Dawn keeps pretty good board minutes, and I think she can handle simple bookkeeping. But there were some problems over the withholding taxes. And some of the donations have not been accounted for properly."

"Are there different accounts? Different budget items? Is there money missing?"

"No, the problem's not with donations of money. It's with things. Stuff. Physical property. People are always giving the shelter things. Towels. Sheets. Toys. Furniture."

"And things disappear?"

"A lot of it doesn't matter." Wilda spoke rapidly. "I mean, children are allowed to take a toy or two when they leave the shelter. Women can take several changes of clothing. Sometimes it's impossible to document."

"But that's not what you meant, is it?"

Wilda shook her head. "No, the fact is, the most valuable items never seem to make it to the storage areas. Or so we're beginning to fear."

"That's a common problem, isn't it? I remember Grandma complaining that she wouldn't give anything to the church thrift shop because the lady who ran it bought everything worth buying. The poor never got a crack at anything good."

Wilda nodded. "It's that sort of thing. I know that some of the volunteers feel that if they pay the shelter for what they take, it's okay. And maybe it is. But that's not what people think they're donating clothing or linens for. They expect the things to help the shelter clients. So we're putting in strict new procedures. Especially since we have better storage space now."

"Where were things stored before?"

"All over! Patsy's garage is full. I've got stuff in the back room at the office. When people began to give good furniture for the bedrooms, we had to rent storage. Best Furniture gave us ten sets of mattresses and springs after their summer closeout, for example. We had no place to store them until the renovations were finished."

"It sounds confusing."

Wilda frowned. "Yes. That's been the problem."

"So what's missing?"

The look Wilda gave Mike told me he'd hit a sore spot.

"We're not sure anything is actually missing," she said. "We simply can't locate a few things."

"What can't you locate?"

Wilda took a deep breath, and suddenly her calm gave way to distress.

"Oh, Mike, it's the Victorian parlor!"

Mike frowned and Wilda went on.

"Isabel Bateson — you know, Mrs. Harold Bateson." Wilda turned to me. "Her husband developed about half of Grantham, back in the twenties and thirties." She turned back to Mike. "She was way in her nineties before she gave up the house on Beacon Street. When she finally moved to an apartment two years ago, she gave a beautiful collection of early Victorian furniture to the shelter. Most of it was inherited from her New England relatives, and it was extremely valuable."

I remembered the furniture in Enid Philpott Howard's offices and nodded. Yes, decorators and collectors would pay big bucks for authentic Victorian furniture.

"It was beautiful, too," Wilda said. "Not

the gimcrack stuff that late Victorian became. Patsy suggested that it be placed in a
special parlor in the new building. I talked
the Eleanor October Gallery into donating
some suitable draperies to go with it."

"And now you can't find the furniture."

"Mike, we're frantic! Mrs. Bateson's children were furious when she gave the shelter
that furniture. If we didn't even take care of
it — "

"It will be embarrassing."

"Beyond embarrassing."

"It sounds as if it's been stolen."

"Stolen! Oh, surely not!"

"Why not?"

"Well, Patsy's records are such a mess — "

I couldn't keep quiet any longer. "How
about Dawn? I thought she was supposed to
be the administrator. Aren't the records her
responsibility?"

"She's only been doing that about six
months. After she didn't work out as a counselor, Patsy moved her to that. She wasn't in
charge of the records when the furniture
came in."

"Surely Patsy had an idea of where it was
stored," Mike said.

"She swears she rented a climate-
controlled storage unit for it. But there are
no records of such a unit ever being rented.

We never got a bill, for example. Patsy has no contract."

"It sounds to me as if it's been stolen," Mike said.

Wilda frowned. "But how could anyone sell it?"

"We're not talking about a houseful, are we?"

"No, a sofa, a love seat, four chairs, three tables. The sofa and one of the tables were fairly large."

"It sounds as if it would all fit in my pickup. If I wanted to steal it, I'd load it up and take it to a Dallas antique dealer. Or just to the Saturday Flea Market at Panorama Point."

"You wouldn't get nearly its value."

"Stolen goods are always sold for cents on the dollar."

"But who would have done such a thing?"

"Patsy? One of the board members? Someone on the staff? It couldn't have been an outsider, Mom."

"There has to be a special place in hell for people who would steal from people who need help as much as the women at that shelter do. But surely it wasn't stolen. Surely Patsy's crazy records just — "

Before she could finish her sentence, the phone rang. Wilda looked around wildly.

She has a cordless phone in the kitchen, and it tends to get lost.

"Where is the darn thing?" she said.

I identified a lump under a cup towel as the phone and handed it to her. Her "Hello" was a bit snappy, as was her "Yes, this is Wilda Svenson." She hadn't wanted to be interrupted.

Then her eyes grew wide. "Oh, no! Have you called 911?"

She listened, then put her hand over the phone and spoke to Mike. "Dawn went over to the shelter to do some extra work, and she found a broken window! And Patsy's missing!"

CHAPTER 21

Mike snapped out a command. "Tell her to get everybody into the lounge! Has she called 911?"

Wilda nodded.

"And tell her we're on the way," Mike said.

Wilda obeyed his instructions, and we headed out. I started to get into Mike's truck, then realized that would mean coming back to Wilda's for my car, so each of us drove.

If you take the interstate's downtown loop, it's usually a twenty-minute drive from Wilda's to the shelter. I made it in fifteen, but Mike was there before me, and Wilda was right on my rear bumper.

Two GPD patrol cars were parked in front of the shelter, lights flashing, and the neighbors were standing in the yard. One of them stepped forward and stopped me as I jumped out.

"What's happened?"

"Nothing, we hope!" I brushed past him and ran for the door. Mike had disappeared — I assumed inside — and Wilda was already pushing the doorbell. We both turned to face the surveillance camera to our left. After Wilda spoke to the intercom, a staff member pushed the buttons to let us inside.

Mike and the two patrolmen stood in the entrance hall. They looked at us, but none of them challenged our presence.

It was about this time I realized I really had no function there. Covering the shelter for the *Gazette* didn't give me the authority to act like part of the inner circle of board members. But I didn't want to miss anything, so I kept quiet and stayed.

Around thirty frightened women and a dozen or more children were gathered in the lounge. Dawn was standing near the door, her hands clutched together prayerfully.

"Is this everyone?" Wilda said.

"We went over the roster, and it's everyone but Patsy. I just can't understand where she could be."

Wilda looked around the lounge. "How about playing a videotape? Something to entertain the kids."

Dawn nodded. She went to a cupboard,

pulled out a box and took a tape of *Mary Poppins*, then inserted it in the VCR. Mike popped his head in the door, told us the patrolmen had already searched the building and asked Wilda to keep everyone in the lounge. He ignored Dawn, who should have been in charge.

Wilda walked around the lounge, acting like a board member and assuring everyone that the shelter staff and police were simply being cautious. A broken window had been found, and Patsy was temporarily missing, she said, but there was no real indication that anything was wrong. Meanwhile, the blinds failed to hide the fact that the number of flashing lights outside was growing; more police were on the scene.

I stood in the corner with Dawn, who was still shaking and wringing her hands. The doorbell rang, and the staffer on the front desk admitted Joe Bob, who said the Lord was looking after Patsy, and that he'd board up the broken window as soon as the police said he could. A sense of excitement began to replace the atmosphere of fear in the lounge.

Everything seemed to be under control except Patsy.

The doorbell rang again, and Boone Thompson came in. He conferred with

Mike and the two patrolmen. Then he summoned Dawn into the office. She was shaking all over and gripped my arm, so I went along. Dawn didn't seem to want Joe Bob, and Mike asked him to stay in the lounge.

It seemed strange to be in the office again. Just a few days earlier I'd been painting it, and Mike had installed the dead bolt on the weapons closet. Later Mike, Patsy and I had sat there in our bloody clothes while the detectives and technicians probed the scene of Paul Howard's death, in the kitchen across the back hall.

"Dawn, what were you doing here this evening?" Boone asked.

"I came in to work on a report for the United Way. It's due tomorrow."

"Where was Patsy when you came in?"

"Nowhere! I mean, I didn't see her. It was later, after the alarm rang, that Germaine told me she was in the building."

"Germaine?"

"The girl on the door. She's got house duty tonight."

"Right. So you had been working in the office?"

Dawn nodded. She pointed to her desk, which was covered with papers. "When the alarm rang, Germaine got on the intercom and asked all the clients to come to the lounge. That's our procedure when the burglar alarm goes off. I mean — we knew it wasn't the fire alarm.

"As soon as we got everybody in there, and Germaine had counted them, she said, 'Where's Patsy?' And that was the first I'd known that Patsy had been in the building. I ran down the back hall and looked in Patsy's private office, but there was no sign of her."

"Is that where she'd been?"

"Germaine said she'd been going back and forth from her private office, down the back hall next to the group counseling room, to this office. This is the main center for accounting and records."

Boone turned to the two patrolmen. "How detailed a search did you make?"

"We looked under all the beds and in the closets," one of them answered, "but we were looking for an intruder, not somebody who knows the building well. We could have missed a lot of hidey-holes."

Right then I became aware that Mike was moving around. He was behind Dawn and me, and I heard the rustle of papers. When I turned around, he was apparently sorting the records Dawn had left on her desk.

Dawn must have heard him, too, because she also turned, and I heard her gasp. And we both saw Mike pull out a yellow tag from the middle of the mishmash on her desk. A string attached the tag to a gold-colored key.

It didn't mean anything to me, but Dawn gave a squawk. "How did that get there?"

Mike held up the key by its string. "I don't know how it got there," he said. "But since it's out, maybe we'd better use it."

"What is it?" Boone said.

"It's the key to the secure closet, the one they use for weapons," Mike said.

He went to the closet and tried to open the door. It was locked. He didn't offer to use the key, but continued to hold it by its string.

"I put that yellow tag on this key myself," Mike said. "It should be locked away somewhere. If it's out, someone may have used it."

"Great!" Boone said angrily. "More missing weapons. Just what we need."

"I think there's another key in Patsy's desk," Mike said. "Let's bag this one, just in case our culprit left a fingerprint."

Boone nodded. Dawn and one of the patrolmen were sent to Patsy's back office to find the second key while Mike and Boone got an evidence bag for the one that had been buried among the papers.

Then Mike pointed to the closet door and motioned for Dawn to open it. She tried, but her hands were shaking too badly. She couldn't get the key in. I felt sorry for her. She was such a hopeless case. I stepped over beside her and put my arm around her shoulder. Then I took the key from her.

"Here, Mike," I said. "You open it."

I led Dawn away and got her to sit down in her desk chair. She put her elbows on the desk and covered her face. I turned back just as Mike swung the closet door open.

The first thing I saw was a shoe. Then a pants leg.

Mike knelt down, and Boone crowded into the closet beside him. Neither of them spoke, but Dawn began to wail.

"Oh, she's dead!" she said. "Patsy's dead! This time — "

Then Wilda ran in the office door, and Mike turned and waved at her.

"Call 911 for an ambulance," he said. "And tell Dawn to shut up. Patsy's not dead yet."

Oddly enough, Dawn did shut up, even before Wilda told her to. In fact, the whole office got rather quiet. One of the patrolmen turned out to be the best first-aider, and he took charge, ordering Mike and Boone to get away from the closet.

"Give her some air," he said. "It's a miracle she didn't suffocate in that closet.

She's got a head wound, too."

Mike hustled me, Wilda and Dawn out of the office, leaving the scene to Boone and the two patrolmen.

"What was she hit with?" I asked.

"There was a leather blackjack on the floor," Mike said. "There isn't any blood. If it wasn't the blackjack, it was something like it. You and Mom keep Dawn out of there, okay?"

We took Dawn into the crowded lounge and found her a chair in a corner, far away from *Mary Poppins*. Joe Bob sat on the arm of the chair and put his arm around her. "Now, now, little lady," he murmured.

Dawn had stopped crying, but she still seemed stunned. I stayed with her while Wilda made the rounds in the lounge, quietly telling the clients that Patsy had been found injured and that an ambulance was on the way. And, no, they couldn't return to their rooms yet.

I sat beside Dawn and Joe Bob and thought. Would Patsy survive? Two other people had been killed. I had escaped an attack similar to the one on Patsy by a "miracle." If Patsy lived, she'd be one lucky woman.

If she lived, however, I was willing to bet she wouldn't be able to remember who attacked her. I didn't know a lot about head injuries, but I knew they caused blank spots in the memory. When I was twelve, I went on a Sunday-school bike hike. One of the boys had hit a rock, somersaulted off his bike and knocked himself out. At our tenth high-school reunion he'd told me he had never remembered the accident. He only remembered riding along the narrow road, then waking up in the hospital with two hours of his life erased. And his had not been a serious injury. Chances were, Patsy would never remember who hit her.

If she lived.

The doorbell rang, and Germaine — still faithfully keeping track of the shelter's comings and goings — admitted Lacy Balke. Mike shooed her away from the office door, and she came into the lounge. Her eyes were big, and her blond hair disheveled.

"What happened?" she said. "Dawn called . . ."

Dawn still seemed to be struck mute, so I filled her in.

Lacy shook her head. "I can't believe all this is happening. The shelter's supposed to be a safe place."

I heard a siren then, followed by a buzzer of a different sort.

Dawn jumped to her feet. "They're at the

kitchen door," she said. She started that way, but Mike ran through the hall, waving at her to stay in place.

"I'll let 'em in," Joe Bob said. He followed Mike.

"It must be the ambulance," I said. Which was news to no one.

Lacy was looking at her watch. "Nearly ten o'clock," she said. "I've got to call Bob and tell him where I am." She walked over to Germaine's phone.

Her comment raised an echo in my mind. Ten o'clock. Ten o'clock? Was I supposed to be someplace at ten o'clock?

Bernie's phone call. Ten o'clock was the time Bernie Fitzgerald had said she'd call me. But at the old shelter, not the new one.

I gasped. "Oh, my God!" I said. "I've got to get out of here."

"I don't think the police want us to leave," Dawn said timidly.

"I'm not a witness," I said. "And I've got to be elsewhere at ten o'clock."

I jumped up and went into the hall, looking for Mike. I didn't want to leave without telling him why and where I was going. But he was nowhere in sight.

I went back toward the kitchen. No sign of him there. I looked at my watch nervously. I had just fifteen minutes to get to the old shelter and be ready to take that call.

One of the patrolmen walked by. "Where did Mike go?" I asked. He ignored me.

I had to leave.

I whirled around, went back into the lounge, and picked up my purse from under the couch next to the chair in which Dawn and Joe Bob had been sitting.

"Listen," I told Dawn. "I have to go over to the old shelter."

Dawn gaped. "What for?"

"A phone call from the elusive Bernie," I said. I quickly filled Dawn in on the way Mary had arranged for me to talk to Bernie. I whipped my notebook open and wrote a quick note to Mike, telling him where I had gone. I ripped the note out, folded it in half and handed it to Dawn.

"Give this to Mike," I said. "I'll be back as soon as I can."

"But . . ." Dawn made a feeble objection, but I ignored her. I slung my purse on my shoulder, took my car keys out of the side pocket and ran to the front door. Germaine punched the buttons to release me, first from the shelter's interior, then from the "lock," the space between the interior and the outside door.

The outside of the shelter was a hubbub of activity. Bright lights, police cars, news crews — a lot had happened in the half-hour I'd been inside.

Television lights and a strobe hit me as soon as I reached the end of the sidewalk. Several people called out questions, but I ignored them and pushed past, headed for my car.

Then someone touched my arm. "Nell! What's going on?" I recognized Judy Connors' voice.

I couldn't ignore Judy. "Patsy Raymond's been attacked," I said. "The ambulance is out in the back."

"But what happened?"

"I don't know. Boone Thompson is in there. I imagine Jim Hammond is on his way. Someone ought to have a statement pretty quick."

I started walking rapidly down the sidewalk.

"Listen, Nell!" Judy said frantically. "I've got to know more."

"I have to get to the old shelter within ten minutes so I can do a phone interview, Judy. I'll call the office as soon as I can. It should be before eleven. If you're not there, I'll tell the desk as much as I can. I'll call from the shelter!"

I pulled away from her, fumbled with the lock to my car — finally figuring out that I'd left it unlocked — and drove off, stirring up dust in the gutter.

Joe Bob would have credited the Lord with more intervention that evening. I did not wreck the little Dodge on the way to the old shelter. And that was definitely a miracle.

Not only did I speed every block of the two miles that separated the two structures — two miles of city traffic — but I also didn't give a thought to my driving. I was frantically trying to think of questions to ask Bernie.

The dumbest thing a reporter can do is go into an interview without preparing questions. That turns control of the interview over to the interviewee. I didn't really expect Bernie to answer a lot of my questions, but I wanted to have some ready.

The first thing I decided was what not to ask. I wasn't going to bring up the pistol that Mike had used to shoot Paul Howard — the one that Washington County sheriff's records showed had been issued to Bernie's husband. That was a problem for her husband and his boss, not me.

I wasn't reckless enough to write in my notebook as I was speeding through Grantham traffic, so I ticked the questions off on my fingers, hoping the memory trick would work.

Forefinger. Did Cherilyn confide in you during the time you were roommates at the shelter?

Middle finger. How did she feel about the shelter? Did she think it was a necessary evil? Or did she think it offered a kind, compassionate service?

Ring finger. Did she have specific complaints about the shelter?

Little finger. Had she had specific comments about the shelter's personnel?

Thumb.

A light turned yellow ahead of me. I forgot about the thumb question and gunned the motor. I made it through the intersection, just missing being broadsided by a pizza delivery car, then turned at the next corner. Only two more blocks to the old shelter.

I skidded to the curb in front of the ramshackle houses, jumped out and ran for the main door. I punched the bell, then banged on the door, as if noise would make it open faster.

The outside door did open quickly, and when I stepped inside I saw that the inside door was already standing open. The foyer was murky, not brightly lit as usual. All the doors off the foyer were open — the doors to the office and to what had been the dining room and to the hallway that led to the bed-rooms. But all those rooms were dark.

I could see Mary Baker in the only pool of light in the foyer, sitting at the rickety desk that had served as a reception area and switchboard.

"Goodness, Nell! You're cutting it close," she said. "It's after ten."

"Has Bernie called?"

"No, but it's just five after. I'm sure she will. Here, take this chair. You can talk on the phone here."

I didn't argue, but I apologized as I took her seat. "Sorry. I got involved at all that mess over at the new shelter — "

"What mess?" Mary's voice was sharp.

I realized that Mary hadn't heard any-thing about the attack on Patsy. I quickly filled her in while I dug out my notebook, a ballpoint and two pencils.

"Goodness!" she said. "I ought to go over there."

"I don't know if they'd let you in."

"Actually, I can't go now." Mary's eyes sparkled mischievously. "I have a pickup to make. Super Grandma to the rescue!" She walked toward the front door. "Punch the green button, please."

I looked at the floor behind the desk, hunting for the buttons releasing the doors.

"The buttons are under the rim of the desk," Mary said.

I ducked my head almost between my knees and found the buttons. A red one and a green one. I pressed the green.

Mary was already inside the "lock." She pushed the outer door open. "When you leave, just open the inner door and prop it with that," she said, pointing at a door stop in the shape of an iron cat. "Then push the red button for the outer door. They both lock automatically when you close them behind you." She waved. The inner door fell shut, and she was gone.

And I was alone.

I was alone in three crazy buildings linked together by odd corridors, porches and closets that had been turned into hallways. I was alone in a dimly lit foyer, with blackness behind me in the room that had once been an office and blackness across the hall in the room that had once been the dining room and blackness to the left of me through a door that had once led to a bedroom area.

All the doors, kept closed when the shelter had been occupied, now stood open. But only the foyer was lit. The rest was dark and spooky.

I took two deep breaths. Well, I could

333

handle dark and spooky. But all the same, I'd turn on some lights.

I pushed my chair back and stood up.

And the telephone rang.

CHAPTER 22

I hesitated, looking longingly at the doorway to the dining room and thinking of the light switch I was sure was just inside. But I didn't have the nerve to run across the foyer while that phone was ringing. Bernie was already nervous, judging from what Mary had said. She might not let the phone ring twice.

I snatched the receiver up. "Hello."

"I'm calling for Miss Matthews. Nell Matthews." The connection wasn't very good.

"This is she. I can barely hear you. Is this Bernie?"

"It used to be. I can't tell you who I am now." The voice was low and throaty. I hadn't been prepared for that. I'd been expecting a weak little voice, I realized, the voice of someone who'd be easy to push around. This one was almost a growl.

"I'm on a portable phone," Bernie said. "I imagine that's why the line is bad. But I can't tell you where I am."

"I understand. I just wanted to ask you some questions about Cherilyn Howard."

"I barely knew her, you know. We only shared a room there at the shelter for three days."

"I know. But you must have talked, shared your problems with each other."

"Some."

"At least you seem to have been the last person to talk to her privately."

"Maybe. But I don't know what I could tell you."

I hadn't had time to write down the questions I'd thought of in the car. Now I tried to remember what each finger had stood for. I looked at my forefinger, and the memory trick worked. The question came back to me. Had Bernie and Cherilyn exchanged confidences? Maybe I should expand on that.

"Did you and Cherilyn have much in common?" I picked up my pen. "Did you have much to talk about?"

Bernie laughed bitterly. "You mean, besides our lousy taste in men? I guess we had a little in common. Grantham's my home town, and back when I was pretty, I did a couple of pageants. We'd both been in the Miss Grantham pageant."

"Had you known each other then?"

"No, she was a couple of years after me. But we knew some of the same people — thc choreographer, the director, like that." She gave the bitter laugh again. "We talked about the best makeup to use to hide bruises."

I scribbled that down and decided to go to the second question, the middle finger. "How did Cherilyn feel about the shelter? Did she regard it as a refuge? Or a necessary evil?"

"Well, neither of us was happy about being there."

"I understand that. But did she like the people who worked there? Did she feel they were — oh, nice? Nice to the clients?"

"Mostly. Of course, you always warm up to some people easier than others."

"Did she have complaints about the shelter?"

Bitter laugh again. "We both said that if we ever got rich, we were going to give them a bundle of money to improve the food."

"The food was no good?"

"All starches and fat. Not the kind of food a TV personality needs to keep her figure. And I want to get back into shape, too. We'd have liked something healthier. But I know they haven't got a lot of money."

"Was that Cherilyn's only complaint?"

"She didn't like the counseling sessions."

"The counseling? Or the counselors?"

"Oh, the new counselors are okay. They were mostly nice people who were trying to talk some sense into the heads of these women who keep going back for more. But Cherilyn and I were way past that stage. I'd given up entirely on my husband."

"Had Cherilyn given up on Paul? Did she think he'd never change?"

"She knew he'd never change, but she felt sorry for him."

"Sorry for him? Why?"

"I never understood it. Well, maybe . . ." Bernie paused, then spoke firmly. "No. I didn't understand why she felt sorry for him. He had problems — we all do. But I thought he brought his problems on himself."

"What kind of problems did Paul Howard have?"

Another long pause. "I don't think I can go into that."

I wrote "Paul's problems?" in my notebook as a reminder to go back to that question. Rocky's theory about Paul's latent homosexuality flitted through my mind.

Then I went on to the little finger question. "You've said that Cherilyn got along with most of the staff. Did she have specific comments about them?"

"Like who?"

"Let's start with Patsy Raymond. What did Cherilyn think of her?"

Bernie laughed. "She got a kick out of her. She admired her, but she thought she was funny at the same time."

"Funny in what way?"

"Well, you obviously know Patsy. She missed a great career as a stand-up comic. But she's really driven, driven to get women out of bad relationships. I think Cherilyn found that interesting. She said something about she was ambitious herself, but she couldn't focus her ambition the way Patsy did."

"How about the volunteers?"

"They were okay."

"Cherilyn was really well known in Grantham. I wondered if Cherilyn ran into any volunteers she'd known outside the shelter."

"She didn't mention it if she did. The only volunteer I got to know very well was Mary Baker. She's a nice person. And she doesn't know where I'm calling from!"

"I understand. How about the other staff members?"

"They're okay."

"What did Cherilyn think of them?"

Long pause. Then, "She tried to get along with everybody."

"Was there someone she had a problem with?"

Bernie's low voice grew cautious. "Look, I don't want to get anybody in trouble."

"The shelter's already in a heap of trouble, Bernie. First there were all those phone calls made to Paul Howard. Then Paul attacks Patsy. Paul Howard is shot dead. Then Cherilyn was killed. Somebody tried to kill me last night — God knows why. And tonight someone hit Patsy Raymond in the head and stuffed her in a closet. If you know anything — anything — that could show that someone had a motive for all this, you've simply got to tell what it is."

"But — I couldn't come back to testify!"

"I see your problem. But if you could give the police an idea about where to look . . ."

Silence took over the phone line. Then Bernie gave an sort of snort. "Damn! This makes me so angry!" she said. "That god-damned jerk I married. I haven't done anything wrong! He's the one! He's the one who put me in the hospital, stood over me and made me lie — tell the doctors I fell downstairs. He's the one who threatened to kill me!

340

"So why am I the one on the run? And now I'm the one who had to quit my job and never see my family and my friends again. He's still got his comfortable life and his stupid pension!"

"He hasn't got his pistol."

I spoke without thinking. I hadn't planned to bring up the pistol. I guess it was such a sore subject with me that it simply popped out.

Bernie was silent again. Then she chuckled. It wasn't a nice sound. It made me look over my shoulder, into the murky interior of the office.

"No, he hasn't got his pistol," she said. "Maybe that'll give him some heartburn. Okay, what did you want to know?"

"I asked you if Cherilyn had any run-ins with staff members. And you said you didn't want to get anybody in trouble. Which sounds like a 'yes' to me. So, what happened?"

She paused another moment, but then she spoke. "You know that mealymouthed little wimp who works in the office?"

"Dawn?"

"You know she used to be a counselor?"

"Yeah, I knew that."

"When Cherilyn first came in the shelter — months ago — she had an interview with that Dawn. She thought everything was confidential."

"It should have been."

"Well, it wasn't! The last time Paul Howard talked to Cherilyn, he called her at the station, and he told her about those crazy phone calls, which he claimed came from Patsy. But the thing that he was really mad about was this secret thing that Cherilyn had told in a counseling session. And she hadn't told it to Patsy. She had told it to Dawn!"

"Dawn could have told Patsy. Or it could have been in Cherilyn's records."

"It wasn't supposed to be that way. We were told that anything we told the counselors would be strictly private. And that even Patsy wouldn't see it."

"I guess Dawn could have told anybody!"

"Right! She could have. But she wasn't supposed to! She's a sneaky, creepy little liar! Listen, Miss Matthews, the lady whose phone I'm using — I gotta go."

"Wait! What if I need to talk to you again?"

"Tough."

"Bernie!"

The line went dead, and I was left sitting there with a receiver to my ear and no one to talk to.

And in the silence, I heard a click.

Someone had hung up a phone. And I knew it wasn't Bernie. It was someone else. It was someone on an extension phone. Someone else who was in the old shelter with me.

I hung up and reached for my purse and notebook.

Oh, the click could have been my imagination. Or it could be someone who was there for a perfectly innocent reason. Mary Baker had said Dawn was doing some work over there — it could be Dawn.

But the thought of Dawn was not reassuring. After what Bernie had said, Dawn became a frightening figure. She was a sneaky, creepy little liar, according to Bernie.

It was only too likely that she was the killer.

And she might be in the building with me.

I was going to get out of that shelter, fast. I tried to scoop up my pens and pencils, and one went flying into the door of the office. I whirled, ready to leave it lying there, but the sight of it froze me in my tracks.

It had rolled against a plain, neat and conservative black pump.

Only the shoe was visible. I couldn't see who was wearing it. But I knew it had to be Dawn's shoe.

My heart nearly stopped. But I gripped my nerve and decided I had to play innocent.

"Hello?" I said. "Who's there?"

I backed up against the desk and felt under the rim for the buttons. The magic buttons that would let me out of the shelter.

Slowly the person wearing the pumps knelt. An arm wearing a white sleeve stretched out and picked up the pencil.

"Who is it?" I said. And my fingers found the buttons.

I poked them both, then whirled around the desk and ran for the front door. I turned the handle and yanked. And I yanked again.

It wouldn't open. I was trapped.

There were footsteps behind me. Slow steps growing closer. I turned.

I'd been right. Dawn was emerging from the office. "You have to open the inner door before you hit the button for the outer one," she said casually.

"Oh," I said. I scrambled for the nerve to continue the innocent act, to pretend I hadn't figured out how likely it was that Dawn was Cherilyn Howard's killer and was the person who had attacked me.

"Dawn, you frightened me," I said. "It's pretty spooky in here in the dark."

Dawn's face was drawn, but she was not

shaking, as she had been when Mike found Patsy. She kept one hand behind her, and with the other, she held up a piece of paper. "I forgot to give Mike your note," she said.

"It doesn't matter. But I imagine I'd better get back over to the new shelter."

Dawn shook her head slowly. "You had to talk to Bernie," she said.

"Well, she didn't know anything."

"Nothing?"

"Not really. No proof of anything."

"But like you told her, what she knew might give the police a new place to look. Then they might find something."

"It doesn't seem likely. Dawn, I do need to leave. Please push the buttons and let me out."

"I can't, Nell. Not after you talked to Bernie." She sighed deeply and shook her head. "It all started out so simply, you know. It was only a way to show the board how unprofessional Patsy was, what a poor job she was doing with the shelter. She was breaking every rule in the book."

"Then you could have turned her in to the state, Dawn."

"Oh, I don't mean she broke the stupid state rules! I mean she ignored professional standards — everything had to be done her way, regardless of how the social work profession would have handled it. But the board didn't get it! They couldn't even see that her negligence had allowed the theft of the Victorian furniture.

"So when a member of the Howard family came into the shelter — I thought the board couldn't ignore unprofessional behavior toward the Howards. Those phone calls. I thought either Paul or Mrs. Howard would complain to the board. But it didn't work out the way I wanted."

I stood there with my back to the door and deduced. Dawn had apparently made the phone calls to Paul Howard, mimicking Patsy's raspy voice. She'd thought Paul would complain to the board. Instead, Paul Howard decided to kill Patsy Raymond. And was himself killed by Mike.

"Nothing worked out the way I wanted," Dawn said petulantly. "Then you kept poking around, trying to figure out what was going on with Bernie. I didn't want to hurt you, Nell. But now I've got to."

She pulled her right arm out from behind her. In it was a striped kitchen towel, which she was holding by the corners. She reached in the pocket of her skirt and pulled out something shiny and gold.

I realized it was the brass rabbit from her desk, the one she used as a paperweight. It wasn't large, but it was heavy. She carefully wrapped it in the striped towel, then gathered the four corners of the towel in one hand. She raised her hand and began to swing the towel around her head.

I realized she had created a very effective weapon.

I also realized that if Dawn hadn't given my note to Mike, then nobody knew where I was. I had to get out of this myself.

CHAPTER 23

I attacked Dawn with a pencil.

It was all I had. I held the pencil in front of me the way Jim Bowie probably held his big knife, ducked my head and ran in under the whirling sling, stabbing at her ribs.

Dawn squealed like a pig and grabbed me. Her oddball weapon swung into my arm, and the two of us went down. I was grunting like a pig, and we rolled around like pigs, too. Unfortunately, instead of soft mud, we were rolling on a splintered wooden floor. It was not fun.

Then Dawn slithered away, and I realized she still had her deadly kitchen towel. I was on the floor behind the desk by then, and I punched at the buttons under its rim, the wonderful buttons that would open the front door. Then I realized that they wouldn't be any help. If you had to punch one, open the inner door, then punch the other one —

well, I wasn't getting out of there that way.

Dawn had scrambled to her feet, and she was swinging her lethal weapon at me again. I ducked under the desk, and the heavy object crashed into the wood above me. She swung the weight back for another try.

I knew I couldn't stay under that desk. Nobody was coming to help me. Eventually she would hit me. I had to go on the attack.

The flimsy wooden chair I'd been sitting in while I talked on the phone was a few feet away. I reached out and grabbed it, pulling it closer to the desk. I upended the chair, tipping its back over my head to use as a shield as I came out from under the desk and scrambled to my feet.

Dawn kept hitting at me with the sling. I kept trying to push her back with the chair.

She kept squealing, and I kept grunting, and the chair and her weapon kept clunking together. But eventually another noise began to be heard.

Someone was banging on the front door. And I heard a voice. It was Jim Hammond's. "Open up! Open up!"

Thank God! I was saved. I nearly dropped the chair.

Dawn didn't seem to hear Jim's voice. She kept whirling that damn sling around her head like a helicopter rotor. She didn't seem to be aiming it at me any more, but I couldn't get away from her.

There was more yelling, and now something heavy was banging into the door. I realized that Jim had pals along, and they were trying to break in. But they were attacking a heavy steel door designed to keep out abusive husbands armed with shotguns and rifles. It was not going to be an easy chore to knock it down.

Then the sound of Jim's voice was drowned out by the roar of a motor. Even Dawn seemed to hear that. Something loud was outside, and it was coming at us.

An enormous crash sounded from the next room, the dining room. Dawn turned toward the noise, and I saw my chance. I used the chair legs to push her against the wall, as if I were a lion tamer and she was a recalcitrant lion. I managed to pin her right arm with one of the chair legs.

And she finally dropped the sling.

I leaned all my weight on that chair, and I yelled, "I can't let you in!"

"It's okay. I'm already in."

Mike's voice was close. I turned toward it and saw him standing in the dining room door.

"How did you get in the dining room?" I said.

"I came in through the window." Mike took hold of the chair.

"The window? That dining room only has one window. That big one. It doesn't open."

"It's open now. Let Jim in. I haven't got any handcuffs."

Mike used the chair to hold Dawn, who had burst into tears, while I punched the buttons in the proper order and let Jim and two patrolmen in the door.

Jim handed Mike a set of handcuffs and scowled at him. "Are you nuts? You could have killed yourself!"

"I wanted in," Mike said.

"How did you get in?" I said again.

Jim and Mike didn't answer, so I looked through the dining room door. The big picture window was a shambles of glass and wood. Just outside was the camper on Mike's black pickup. He had backed in through the big window.

"Jim's right," I said. "You could have been killed!"

"My girl was in trouble inside," Mike said. "I had to get in."

I began to babble then, telling Mike and Jim about the call from Bernie and about what Cherilyn had told her — the implication that Dawn had made the phone calls to Paul Howard.

Jim shrugged. "Once Mike got on Dawn's tail, we were going to get her, even without that testimony," he said. "But I guess hearing Bernie say that scared Dawn."

Mike helped put Dawn into a patrol car, and Judy Connors showed up, just ahead of three television news teams. Jim and I both talked to Judy, and Jim talked to the TV teams. Mike disappeared.

When a wrecker came for Mike's truck, Jim found him in the front passenger seat of my little Dodge, tipped all the way back. Sound asleep.

Jim and I looked at him. "Jim," I said, "I don't think he's slept since — since everything went to hell Saturday night."

"Maybe he can sleep now. Do you want me to help you get him home?"

I pulled out my car keys. "If I can't wake him up to walk in the house, I'll call you."

I managed to get Mike into his bed. His first nightmare hit at two a.m. When I woke up, he was sitting on the edge of the bed, shaking violently.

We both went in the living room, and I started a tape of *The Gods Must Be Crazy*. I put my arms around Mike, and he sat on the couch and shook for half the movie. Finally his teeth stopped chattering, and he gradually stopped shivering. And in a few minutes he kissed me. He tweaked the belt of the robe I wore.

"I'm glad you're here," he said.

An hour later we were snuggled together in the king-sized bed, and I thought Mike was drifting off again.

"Listen," I said to his neck. "I've got one question I'd like answered before you go back to sleep."

"Shoot."

"When you headed out to rescue me, how did you know where to go? Dawn was the only one I told I was going to the shelter."

"No. You told Judy Connors, too."

"I'd forgotten that!"

"When you and Dawn disappeared at the same time — "

"She must have run out the back as soon as I ran out the front."

"Jim and I were afraid she'd gone after you. For once, that gang of reporters outside was some use. When we went outside, I grabbed Judy, and — luckily — she'd seen both of you leave. In separate vehicles, but headed in the same direction. And you had told Judy you'd call the office as soon as you took a phone call. You said you were expecting a call at the old shelter."

"Talk about a lucky break!" I said. "If I hadn't just happened to run into Judy I could have been . . ." I couldn't bring myself to say the word "killed." I shuddered. Then I went on. "But why did you and Jim think that Dawn was after me?"

"I'd suspected her all along," Mike said.

"Why?"

"First off, because of that fit she threw after Paul Howard was killed, yelling, 'Patsy's dead.'"

"I thought she was just upset."

"That was a possibility, true. But I observed that when Dawn is upset, she gets real quiet. That was the way she reacted when Patsy walked out, alive. She shrank down on the porch like a burst balloon. Besides, why had she assumed that Patsy had been the person who was killed?"

"Patsy had been the focus of threats in the past."

"That's true. But Dawn's whole performance seemed odd. It made me notice her. Then, after Mrs. Howard made all those accusations about the phone calls to her son — well, who was in a better position to make calls from the shelter office than Dawn was? And I checked with Grantham State Alumni Association. Dawn was the same age as Cherilyn, and she went to Grantham Central. She probably has one of those yearbooks that had the picture of Cherilyn and

354

me in it. So she had the means to commit the crimes. And she had the opportunity. What was missing was motive. I didn't see why Dawn would want to cause trouble for the shelter."

"When she confronted me," I said, "after I'd talked to Bernie — she said something about trying to get the board to see what a poor job Patsy was doing with the shelter. She said it was Patsy's fault that the Victorian furniture was stolen."

"She's probably right there."

"You can't think that Patsy stole the furniture!"

Mike shook his head. "No, but I think Dawn was right in seeing that there was a lot of mismanagement at the shelter. Patsy's run it as a one-women show, and she's been real vague about details. I'll bet a lot of valuable things that were donated to the shelter wound up in the flea market booth that Dawn's mother runs."

"Dawn's mother runs a flea market booth!"

"Actually a little secondhand business. Baumgarner's Treasures."

"Now I remember that she answered the phone that way — the night I called trying to find Dawn. So you think Dawn was the thief?"

"Why not? With a little help from her mom. They could always use the money, and it fit right in with Dawn's plan to show that Patsy was doing a poor job of running the shelter. But the board members weren't about to fire Patsy over the missing items. In spite of her faults, Patsy is too valuable to the shelter."

"Besides, even if they did fire Patsy, the board would never hire Dawn to run the place," I said. "Dawn is just as inefficient as Patsy. Her whole crime spree proves that. If Lacy Balke had decided to kill someone, she'd get away with it. If Mary Baker had been after me, I'd be dead now. But Dawn just confused things, panicked and generally messed up her try at a life of crime."

Mike laughed. "You're right there. Dawn's initial scheme, stealing donated items, failed miserably. Then Cherilyn Carnahan Howard became a shelter client, and Dawn came up with a new plan. By manipulating Paul Howard, making him believe that Patsy was making crazy phone calls, she'd get Enid Philpott Howard to oppose Patsy."

"And Enid Philpott Howard can sink anybody in Grantham."

"Yep. Of course, that didn't work for Dawn, either. Once Mrs. Howard met Patsy — "

"Patsy won her over!"

Mike chuckled. "Even those of us who see Patsy's faults put up with her because she gets things done, and because she really cares about the shelter and its clients. Mrs. Howard caught on to Patsy's modus operandi right away, but Dawn hadn't expected that. Earlier, of course, Joe Bob Zimmerman had appeared in Dawn's life and complicated things even further. Though I could never see what Joe Bob saw in Dawn."

I thought back to the testimony Joe Bob had pressed on me when we were stuck in the entry hall at the new shelter. "Joe Bob is really rather sweet about his feelings for Dawn," I said. "Apparently he'd done a lot of running around before he got religion, and he felt that his worldly ways had destroyed his first marriage. He wanted to find a wholesome, pure woman — and outwardly Dawn filled the bill. She was modest in her actions and dress, she took care of her mother and helped her with her business. And Dawn was even in an altruistic profession. Joe Bob assured me Dawn had devoted her life to helping others. He regarded her as the answer to his prayers. And he sure must have looked like the answer to her prayers to Dawn."

"Why?"

"Look at Dawn's life! She was Miss Mouse! No personality, no looks, no opinions — and apparently no friends. Maybe her mother had kept her completely under her thumb. Or maybe she's just a social misfit. She's smart, but she can't deal with people — the shelter hired her as a counselor, for example, but moved her to the office because the clients wouldn't talk to her. Joe Bob would have been a Godsend to Dawn!"

Mike laughed. "I wouldn't have pictured Joe Bob as a dream lover."

"There's nothing wrong with Joe Bob," I said defensively. "Believe me, there are lots of women who would settle for a guy who treats them right, who earns a good living, and whose worst flaw is he wants to go to church all the time. I feel sorry for Joe Bob! Dawn fooled him completely. But it's easy to be taken in by someone who speaks religious jargon fluently. Look at these TV evangelists who got caught in all sorts of naughtiness. Millions believed they were devout because they talked holy."

"Do you think Joe Bob might have deterred Dawn from her life of crime?"

"If he'd showed up a little earlier, he might have," I said. "Maybe Dawn would have seen marriage to a contractor with his own business as a way out of her dead-end job at the shelter. But by the time Joe Bob appeared in her life, she must have been committed to this crazy scheme to discredit Patsy."

"A scheme that didn't have a chance of working."

"If Paul Howard just hadn't attacked Patsy . . ." I quit talking.

Mike finished my sentence. "And if I hadn't killed Paul Howard, Dawn might have brought the scheme to a halt. But after Paul cracked and attacked Patsy, Cherilyn became a problem for Dawn. As soon as she'd recovered from the first shock of Paul's death, Cherilyn would be sure to tell someone what Paul had said about the phone calls. And about the fact that the caller knew some private bit of information she'd told only to Dawn."

"Cherilyn called the shelter late the night Paul was killed," I said, "trying to reach Patsy. Dawn must have called the answering machine to check the messages — which she could do from her home — after she got back from her dance lesson with Joe Bob. So when Cherilyn went to her parents' home alone, she played right into Dawn's hands. Dawn followed her there."

Mike nodded. "Cherilyn wouldn't have

been afraid of Dawn, so she let her in the house. Probably told her she was going to tell the board that she'd been making harassing phone calls to Paul. So Dawn attacked her with a trophy."

"I guess Dawn was also the one who came after me in the backyard," I said. "But why?"

"I expect she didn't want you to talk to Bernie."

"But I didn't really want to talk to Bernie! I only did it because Patsy insisted."

"Did Dawn know they were trying to find Bernie for you?"

"She could have — yes, she was in the office and Patsy and I were just outside when Patsy told me she'd try to get Bernie to call me. Of course, Patsy wanted Bernie to tell me about that pistol, the one Bernie stole from her husband and left in the shelter. But Dawn probably didn't know why Patsy wanted me to talk to her."

"I'm just glad Dawn didn't make you her third victim," Mike said.

"And I'm sorry about your truck. But I've really been worried about your sanity."

"Was I that bad?"

"You've been talking crazy. Once you told me, *'Cui bono?'* or 'Follow the money.' As if the two phrases meant the same thing. And the night Cherilyn was killed, you said something about you were sure somebody was keeping an eye on her. But you didn't seem to know why anybody should have been."

Mike's arm tightened around me. "I feel really bad about that. I guess my subconscious was trying to tell me that Cherilyn might have talked to Paul and might have information that would put her at risk. But I was so sunk in self-pity that I couldn't explain it. The same with the 'cui bono' and 'follow the money' comments. I don't know what I meant."

"And Jim complained that you were asking questions about Patsy's ex-husband and about who worked with Paul Howard at the bank."

"That was a little more obvious. I may have strongly suspected Dawn, but we couldn't rule out some other motive for the crime. Patsy's ex might have been mixed up in it — actually, we found out that he apparently straightened himself out and now lives in Seattle. And somebody at the bank might have been wanting to get Paul Howard out of the way. They wouldn't necessarily have wanted him dead, but they might have wanted him to crack up and get out of the bank. Neither of these possibilities seemed likely, but they needed to be checked out."

We stopped talking then, and we were both asleep when the phone rang at eleven a.m.

It was Wilda. After she'd checked with Mike, she asked to speak to me.

"The board held a special meeting this morning," she said.

"Hell's bells! I should have covered it."

"I'll let you listen to the tape. Patsy staggered out of the hospital in time to attend. She tendered her resignation."

"You're kidding!"

"Of course, we didn't accept it. But we got her to agree to the reorganization plan. Lacy's going to take over as administrator until we can hire somebody. Which we'll have to do pretty fast, since Lacy has to go to Russia next month."

The board president, Mrs. Doubletree, had flown back from California because of the crisis, Wilda said. I arranged to meet the two of them at Wilda's office at two o'clock to get the story.

I jumped into my clothes, but Mike stopped me before I could leave.

"Listen," he said. "I may not be here tonight."

My heart gave a little leap. "Oh? Where are you going?"

"Sometime — Sunday, I guess — Mickey

called and suggested he and I go fishing."

Relief flooded over me. Mickey O'Sullivan had a big role in Mike's life. He had been Mike's dad's best friend. He was now Wilda Svenson's boyfriend. He was a good friend to Mike.

And, fifteen years before, Mickey had left the Grantham Police Department under a cloud. The department had faced a scandal after Mickey O'Sullivan — then a division chief — had shot and killed an unarmed man.

Mike went on. "So if Sergeant Beznosky says I can leave town — maybe that would be a good idea. Mickey and I might go down to the lake for a few days."

"Mike, I think that's a wonderful idea."

Yes, Mike could talk easily with Mickey, and Mickey had faced the same demon that Mike was facing now, the knowledge that he'd killed someone. Mickey was more likely to be able to help Mike than forty psychologists were.

"I think that a few days with Mickey and some time out in a boat is just what you need," I said. "Just give me a ring when you feel like it. Okay?"

"I feel like giving you a ring now," he said, "but apparently you don't want one." Mike sat on the edge of his bed, pulled out the drawer of his bedside table and produced a page torn from a magazine. It was a jewelry ad.

And I realized that he'd been talking about a different kind of ring. A finger ring, not a telephone ring.

This was no time to continue our engagement ring argument. "Mike," I said, "I'll wear a ring in my nose if you want, but maybe this isn't the time to talk about it."

But Mike pushed the page toward me. "If you don't want an engagement ring, will you settle for this?"

I looked at the picture. It was a wide, gold wedding band topped with a diamond solitaire in a Tiffany setting.

"My dad left me his mother's diamond, and I wanted you to have it," Mike said.

I couldn't answer.

"Of course you may not get it anytime soon." Mike ran his hands through his hair. "Nell, I've got to get my head on straight. I don't want you to marry a nutcase!"

I sat in his lap, and we put our arms around each other. "I wouldn't mind marrying a nutcase if he had red hair," I said.

"When I make all those promises, I want to be sure I'm mentally competent. But about the diamond — I showed it to the jeweler. It's half a carat. He said it would look nice set like this. If you want it."

"I want it," I said. "Whenever you're ready to give it to me."

The employees of Thorndike Press hope you have enjoyed this Large Print book. All our Large Print titles are designed for easy reading, and all our books are made to last. Other Thorndike Press Large Print books are available at your library, through selected bookstores, or directly from us.

For information about titles, please call:

(800) 223-1244

To share your comments, please write:

Publisher
Thorndike Press
P.O. Box 159
Thorndike, Maine 04986